Praise for *Fiddl*

"Readers will love Thompson's comical, wisecracking protagonist (think Donald Westlake's Dortmunder). The narrative is full of action, the dialogue snappy, and the conclusion startling and satisfying. *Fiddle Game* is a romp of a read; a little gritty, a little sexy, and a whole lot of fun."

—Jackie Houchin, *Mystery Scene*

"The game, which has been so long afoot, finally tracks back to St. Paul, where the complex plot plays itself out in a surprising and satisfying way. At the very end, in a reflection that might as well be a voice-over from a Humphrey Bogart movie, Herman sums things up in a wistfully noir and philosophical way. He looks out into the morning fog and thinks 'about appearances and disappearances and names and labels and illusions and scams and how very muddled they all get at times. I thought about the violin case under Wilkie's arm and wondered what was really inside it. Evil? Salvation? Or just an old fiddle? I hadn't looked inside the case, and I didn't intend to.' Deliciously ripe. Anyone who makes it to the end of this hometown caper will hope that Herman will show up again to walk the mean streets of St. Paul."

—Robert Brusic,
Minnesota Independent Scholars Forum Practical Thinking

"Jackson is a nice guy, the sort who'd be called a gumshoe in earlier fiction. He's surrounded by likeable secondary characters, including his no-nonsense secretary, Agnes; Wide Track Wilkie, his big enforcer; and a loopy-but-maybe-smart street guy called the Prophet. St. Paul readers will enjoy this book's sense of place. Here's Jackson musing about his city: 'The trendy shops come and go. Here in St. Paul, Minnesota, the capital of Midwest niceness, the only really solid growth industries we have are government and crime."

—Mary Ann Grossmann, *St. Paul Pioneer Press*

Praise for *Frag Box*

"A gritty thriller that will hold you captive until the last page . . . Tough truths emerge in this superb suspensor."

—Mystery Lovers Bookshop

"A dark and in some ways, sad and vicious novel of demons and their aftermaths . . . This novel is well conceived and executed. It grabs you early on and maintains a relentless pace, even in its flashbacks, something not easy to do . . . A simple story line has developed tentacles and layers of intrigue and darkness . . . The darkness that stalks this story is leavened by the cynical, wise-cracking voice of Mr. Jackson. His attitudes are well founded. He's seen and experienced enough of the venality of society's representatives, whether they reside on the side of the dark angels or of the haloed ones. Kudos to Mr. Thompson. Here's an author definitely worth paying attention to."

—Carl Brookins, for Agora2

"The writing style resembles an old-fashioned detective novel. The action is non-stop. The intrigue is dazzling. This is the type of story that you never tire of reading. I'm looking forward to the next book and reading *Fiddle Game*."

—Reviews by Teri

"Even better than the first! . . . I really, really loved this book. In an era when it seems that every murder mystery has to have a cute gimmick, it is refreshing to find a straightforward story full of compelling characters doing interesting things, with a surprising yet convincing ending. I'd say 'they don't write them like that anymore,' but thanks to Richard A. Thompson, they do."

—Margaret Yang

". . . A dash of romance, plenty of action and an appealing, wisecracking hero enhance this detective story with an old-fashioned noir flavor . . . The story is well constructed, the characters compelling, the murder mystery itself satisfyingly complex. It's a solid follow-up to the first mystery in this series, *Fiddle Game*. But where *Fiddle Game* is more thrilling, *Frag Box* is more thoughtful, an interesting contrast in this series of just two books (to date) that illustrates the range of this author's talent."

—*Publishers' Weekly*

Praise for *Lowertown*

"An involving and smoothly written mystery (with a) perfect sense of place."

—Mary Ann Grossmann, *St. Paul Pioneer Press*

"*Lowertown,* Richard A. Thompson's third novel about a bail bondsman who makes a bad choice and lives (barely) to regret it, has smart characters, riveting action and an authentic noir-ish tone that would fit in nicely with the work of Black Mask writers like Hammett, Chandler, Gardner, Daly, and Cain."

—David Housewright

"The world is ready for a hard-boiled hero named Herman. Especially this one. He's a bondsman in a shady part of St. Paul—the Lowertown of the title—and he's witty, urbane, and good-natured."

—Don Crinklaw, *Booklist*

"Herman Jackson is not the sort of citizen you'd like to see dating your daughter. On the other hand, if she was somehow tangled up with some really evil people, he might just be who you would be looking for to help her out. *Lowertown* is a solid punch of novel that delivers a load of suspense, some serious thrills and a clever plot with enough twists to satisfy the most rabid of crime novel aficionados."

—Carl Brookins, for *Vine Voice*

Praise for *Big Wheat*

Winner, 2012 Minnesota Book Award

"*Big Wheat* is Thompson's first stand-alone historical mystery, and it is deeper and richer than the more jaunty Jackson books. *Big Wheat* will keep you reading. It offers a plot that picks up speed as it goes along; it foreshadows the coming of the Great Depression and gives an authentic sense of rural life in the early 20th century. It profiles one very bad man . . . and several good men that give this story a rich sense of human decency."

—Mary Ann Grossman, *St. Paul Pioneer Press*

"Seldom have I read a mystery novel more in the moment than Richard Thompson's *Big Wheat*. It's the summer of 1919, and heartbroken by lover Mabel, who has cast him off, twenty-three-year-old North Dakota farm hand Charlie Kreuger pins his abusive father to the kitchen table with a carving knife and hits the road to seek his fortune. Unfortunately, Mabel has become one of the long string of victims left behind by the Windmill Man, one of the creepier villains of recent crime fiction, and Charlie's disappearance in conjunction with Mabel's has led local law enforcement to believe Charlie killed her and ran away. The sheriff is after him and so is the Windmill Man, who is afraid Charlie will recognize him, but Charlie makes plenty of friends along the way, including George Ravenwing, a chance-met Lakota Indian who may or may not be corporeal; Avery, the paterfamilias of the Ark (just read it) who gives Charlie his heart's desire, a job on a steam engine; and Emily, the feisty Brit who becomes his new love.

"Here's one of my favorite passages, when avaricious banker Emil Puckett, thwarted from stealing Joe Wick's farm out from under him, mulls over the deplorable decline of the western world:

> Probably all due to the war, he thought. People went over to France, picked up its loose morals, and brought them back home. Pretty soon the whole country was full of upstarts and Bohemians. There was a rumor just that month that a professional baseball team had taken some gamblers' money to deliberately lose the upcoming World Series, if you could believe such a shocking thing . . . a formerly sensible President of the United States was advocating fixing up the nation's sovereignty to that wobbly-commie League of Nations. Worst of all, it looked as though women were about to get the vote . . ."

"Talk about setting a scene. This is not what we in the business call an expository lump, a gigantic dump of information left for the narrative to stub its toe on. No, this is a master hand coloring a character in all the way to the edges, while at the same time firmly fixing his novel in place and time, with the reader hardly noticing.

"That, folks, is craftsmanship. Solid plot, a villain who gets more out of control and more terrifying with every turn of the page, good dialogue, wonderful description of land and weather, and great characters combine to make this a really good read."

—Dana Stabinow

Also By Richard A. Thompson

Fiddle Game

Frag Box

Lowertown

Big Wheat

DEMON IN THE HOLE

A Thriller

Richard A. Thompson

Conquill Press

DEMON IN THE HOLE

Cover Design: Rebecca Treadway

Photograph of Pilatus plane on front cover by JDrewes, slight edit by Alvesgaspar.

Library of Congress Control Number: 2016941879

Thompson, Richard

Demon in the Hole: a thriller/ by Richard A. Thompson – 1st edition

ISBN: 978-0-9908461-4-7

Conquill Press/November 2016

Printed in the United States of America

10 9 8 7 6 5 4 3 2 1

In Memory of Gary Shulze

Chapter One

Badlands

Summer 2010, somewhere in North Dakota

The sun beat brutally down on the orange and pink rock formations and the brown dirt that filled the hollows between them. It pulsed and hammered as if God, impatient with trying to melt the rock, had decided simply to flatten it. But the hobo didn't mind. He liked the Badlands when they were hot, because he knew he would have them all to himself. That could be a problem if he were short on supplies, but on this particular day he had a can of corned beef, two cans of sweet peaches, one of tomato soup, and some taco-flavored corn chips in his pack, plus plenty of water in his canteens and some packets of Tang to mix with it. He also had some salt for the evening meal, when he would cook the rattlesnake he had killed that morning. Life was good.

He didn't know why he had come to this exact place. But then, he was never quite sure why he went anyplace else, either. There was the solitude, of course, which he cherished. But there was also the vague feeling that he was about to find something. Something wonderful that nobody else would ever find, because nobody else ever came here. He only got the feeling when he was going someplace he had never been. As a result, he went to quite a lot of new places.

For two days he had been following a strange stripe. Not that there was any shortage of bizarre, odd-colored natural stripes and bands from the primordial formation of the rock all around him. But this was different. It ran across the desert floor, not across the vertical face of any butte or mesa. It was about a foot wide and perfectly straight, and it went for miles into the distance. Sometimes it would disappear for a mile or more, but if he followed the original direction of the thing, he always found it again. It almost looked as if somebody had gone to the unbelievable work of digging a trench in the hard rock and then filling it back in with packed dirt. Very packed. He had no idea why anybody would do that, but he wanted to see where it ended, all the same. It made him feel like an explorer of ancient ruins. It was good, having a goal.

In the middle of the third day, he came across a crumbling farm tractor. It looked like some model of International Harvester Farmall, at least sixty years old. If so, the rust had long ago taken over the original red paint and decals. And what the rust missed, the sun had bleached out to an anonymous ashy gray. Still, it looked like an IH, rather than a John Deere or a Case. He knew about these things, having grown up on a farm, longer ago than he could easily remember. The big, heavily cleated tires were crazed and cracked and flat, and the machine sat totally alone in the middle of a shallow baked clay depression that he guessed to be at least a hundred acres. From a distance, it looked as if it had a man sitting at the wheel, perhaps a dead man. But on closer inspection, it proved to be a scarecrow, made mostly out of coveralls stuffed with straw. It was tied to the steering wheel and the seat with twine that was almost rotted through. It had no hands or feet, but there was a head made up of a basketball with a broad-brimmed straw hat on top of it. The basketball was now deflated, but it and the hat were held up by some kind of wire armature.

"Mr. Spalding, I presume?" He touched the brim of his own battered hat. "I'd say you need some wrinkle cream, about worse than any man I ever seen." He paused as if expecting the dummy to reply. When it didn't, he said, "Well, the same to you, too, sport."

Then he noticed the camera.

The exhaust pipe for the tractor engine came straight up through the hood, as one would expect. But at the end of it, instead of a rain flapper, there was what could only be a video camera, pointed back toward the scarecrow. It was obviously much newer than the machine it sat on.

The hobo walked around the tractor and watched the camera carefully. It looked dead. It did not turn to follow his movement, and it did not have any little lights turned on, at least that he could see. He climbed up on the hood and put his ear against the enameled metal box. It did not make any noise. He tried to pull it off the pipe, and it came easily. The wires that were attached to its bottom snapped off, and some of their insulation crumbled. He dropped the camera rather than throwing it, so it might look as if it had fallen off on its own. Then he set up his camp for the night under the tractor, built a fire close by, roasted the snake, and waited.

By the next morning, nobody had come to check on the dropped camera, and he decided it was safe to assume nobody would. After a breakfast of leftover snake meat and instant orange juice, he made a more thorough inspection of the tractor. He found a small toolbox attached to the back of the seat, but it had nothing in it except an empty one-quart Mason jar, an unopened can of thirty-weight motor oil, a couple of rusty wrenches, and a small crowbar. He couldn't tell if there was any gas in the tank above the engine, because he couldn't get the cap off. He pushed the scarecrow aside and sat down in the driver's seat on the rotting remnants of a plastic-covered cushion.

"New driver, Spalding. Nothing personal, but you just ain't been making enough progress."

There was a key in the ignition. It seemed absurd that the engine might actually start, but he decided to try it anyway.

He pushed down what looked like the clutch pedal and moved the gearshift, with great effort, into what he assumed to be neutral. Then he turned the key. To his amazement, the ancient instrument panel flickered to life, showing that he had half a tank of gas, a slight battery drain, and no oil pressure. Well, he wouldn't, would he? He chuckled. To the right of the switch was a smooth, chrome-plated button with remnants of the word START still legible on the panel under it. He pushed it.

The engine did not turn over, but he heard and felt a deep rumbling, like something impossibly heavy being dragged across a rough floor. He held the button down. Twenty yards away from the tractor, a crack opened up in the desert floor, and dust began to pour into it. He continued to push on the button, and the crack opened up more, defining a square perhaps fifty feet on a side, with an extra crack running right down the middle of it, dividing it in two. Then the center crack got really big, as two enormous trap doors, at least three feet thick, swung up and open. Below them was a surface that looked like the deck of a battleship, gleaming in new-looking white paint, riddled with rivet heads, and containing two manhole covers. One was huge, maybe as much as thirty feet in diameter. The other was a more ordinary size. It looked like an entry.

"Holy shit," was all he could think of to say.

He jumped off the tractor, then down into the hole from the big doors, and had a better look. The white deck was as solid as the ledge rock around it, and he walked across it without fear. Both manholes had been welded shut, though not too thoroughly. The weld beads were only a few inches long, with large gaps between them. And unlike the metal around them, the weld joints had not been painted. Now they were so rusty, they powdered to the touch. The hobo went back to the tractor and got the old crowbar. It took him just over two hours to get the smaller manhole open. It was, he now saw, bigger than a manhole that one might find in some ordinary street. And it was at least a foot thick and tapered, like a huge cork. It was mounted on a pair of big, spring-loaded hinges that still worked, and it opened upward and stayed open. Inside the hole, a steep metal stairway spiraled down into darkness.

He went back to his campsite and fashioned some crude fagots out of sticks and rags, soaking the cloth with some oil from the can in the tractor's toolbox.

"You know, Spalding, I can think of about a thousand reasons why I shouldn't be doing this." The deflated basketball made no reply, and he left it and returned to the open hatch.

"Make that two thousand," he said, looking down into the void.

He took a very deep breath, lit his first torch, and descended.

Chapter Two

Demon in the Well

The stairway was enclosed in a continuous wire mesh cage, and he had a hard time telling how big the actual shaft around him was. He decided that it changed size from time to time but was mostly much bigger than it needed to be. The stair and its cage seemed to be floating in blackest outer space. At one point, he tried to tell the depth of the shaft by dropping a lit match down it. The match burned out before it hit any bottom. He kept going. After what seemed like a thousand steps, with the entry hatch now just a tiny pinpoint of light above him, he came to a landing that gave access to a big, round-cornered door with a wheel on it, like a hatch on a ship. The stairs continued down from there, but ten or twenty feet below him, he could now see that the shaft was filled with water. Or some very black liquid, anyway. He made a mental note not to drop any more matches.

Turning to the door, he saw that it was plastered with warning notices in large block letters.

ABSOLUTELY NO UNAUTHORIZED ENTRY
BEYOND THIS POINT

NO SOLO ENTRY

HAVE YOUR ESCORT WITH YOU
AND YOUR PASSWORD READY

TRESSPASSERS WILL BE SHOT AND/OR GASSED

There was also a black and yellow radiation hazard symbol.

"Jesus, some people have no sense of humor whatsoever."

The wheel was stiff, but it moved. He cranked it counter-clockwise as far as it would go, took another deep breath, and swung the heavy door toward himself. Beyond the door was a chamber no bigger than a single-car garage, empty and featureless except for another door at the far end of it, this one with a small porthole in it. He guessed this was where they held you while they looked you over through the porthole and decided whether you should be gassed or shot or both.

He made his way to the second door, his torch reflecting off the gleaming white walls. The second door had a similar wheel on its face, but it also had a keypad of some kind next to it. He decided his expedition was just about over. But when he pushed on the new door, it slowly swung away from him, without even needing the wheel turned. Maybe there really was somebody back there, just dying to shoot him. He went through the door anyway. On the wall just inside the door was a large electrical switch box. With a shrug and an "Oh, what the hell?" or two, he threw the big lever to the ON position. And to his astonishment, the whole place lit up. So the stripe on the desert floor had been a trench, at that. It had been dug for an electric line. He threw his torch down on the painted concrete floor and stomped on it until it went out.

The illuminated chamber he now stared into was cavernous, with walls and ceiling flowing seamlessly into one another in a single vaulted arch with countless perforated ribs supporting it. The phrase "belly of the whale" came to mind. He half expected the place to start moving, to crush him or chew him up. He found himself being careful not to make any noise. But he pressed on.

* * *

He lost track of time, exploring the complex. But he did not lose his sense of impending doom, and he seriously wondered what he thought he was doing there. And still he pressed on, just marginally more curious than afraid.

The first big chamber turned out to be nothing more than a junction point for half a dozen smaller tunnels and vaults going off in all directions. Some led to spaces full of incomprehensible machinery or control panels with gauges and switches ripped out and left on the floor. Some were living quarters, including a large communal kitchen with empty refrigerators but cupboards with more canned food than he could ever hope to carry. He decided he would have a quick look at the rest of the place, then pack up as much as he could handle and get the hell out of there.

Nowhere did he see any of the usual signs of a long-abandoned building. The place smelled slightly damp, but there was neither mold nor dust on the floors. And there were no spider webs. He had thought it was impossible to build a structure totally free of spiders, and yet there was no sign of them, nor any other life form, however small. He thought about the radiation sign on the first door, and he wondered if being stationed here had actually been a death sentence. He imagined a memo being circulated at some federal prison. *Persons serving life sentences wanted for underground housing experiment. May earn pardons.*

He was also surprised at the lack of any signs of personalization in the living quarters. No pinups on the walls, no graffiti in the restrooms, no snapshots over the bar, no homemade signs saying, "I hate this place!" Kilroy was not here, apparently. Or if he was, somebody had erased his mark.

The hobo did not explore every tunnel. The last one he went down led to what at first looked like a dead-end wall, all covered in wide black and yellow diagonal stripes. But when he got closer, he could see that it was really another door, a huge one, like something for a bank vault. Having denied himself no sights anywhere else, he cranked open the big wheel locks and pulled the twin door leafs inward. And gasped. For there, propped up by a complicated array of struts and braces and adorned with catwalks, hoses, and cables, towering above him in its silo, was absolutely, undoubtedly, an intercontinental ballistic missile. And to his unpracticed eye, it appeared to have a warhead on it.

"Sweet suffering Jesus," he said half under his breath. "Those stupid, *stupid* shmucks have left a nuke out where even somebody like me can find it. How the *hell* could they do that?" As he stared at the missile in horror and astonishment, it seemed to him that it was making some kind of sounds, dim but distinct, as if the beast had its own life and its own mind and was clucking its tongue as it contemplated just when and where to blow humanity straight to hell.

He ran. He did not pause to collect any canned goods or blankets. Twice he had to catch his breath on the long spiral stairs, but he never stopped for long. At his campsite, he tried to pack up anything that might be tied to him. It occurred to him that he should have wiped down the missile complex for fingerprints, too, but no way he was going back there. The place was evil, and it housed pure death. And even if you survived it, you could probably go to prison for about a thousand years just for being there. He set off across the desert at as fast a pace as he thought he could maintain.

Two days later, he was back at the fringes of the Badlands, where scraggly pines and other scrub brush began to take over from the completely barren lands. Near dusk, he encountered a man sitting on his backpack and looking into a campfire. When the man first saw him, he picked up the rifle that was on the ground next to him. But as he got closer, the man relaxed, put the rifle down again, and stood up.

"I'm Ben," the man said. "I didn't expect to see anybody this far out in the boonies."

The hobo made no reply.

"I said, 'I'm Ben.' Are you—"

"Oh, sorry. I don't talk to people for a while, I sort of forget how. My name's Jack, but they call me Solo Jack. Pleased to meet you, Ben."

"I just made some coffee. You want a cup?"

"Now that would be just purely paradise, yes, indeed."

"A lot of people don't like coffee in hot places." The man called Ben took a tin cup out of his pack.

"A lot of people are stupid." He dropped his own pack on the ground and sat down. Ben poured him a cup of coffee, and he took it with both hands.

"Oh, that's fine, it is." He took a sip. Then he looked at the gun again, wondering if Ben was going to pick it up. "That's a mighty impressive-looking piece of artillery you got there."

"Remington thirty-ought-six semi-auto with a twenty-four power scope."

"What are you hunting, tanks?"

"White-tailed deer. They're skittish and fast. They never let you get closer than a thousand yards, and they never give you a second shot unless you knock them down with the first one. You need something with a lot of range and a lot of shocking power."

"Well, you've sure as hell got that, all right. But I thought deer season was always in the fall."

"That's the legal season. Where I come from, the rest of the year we call it 'government beef.' You got a problem with that?"

"Not me. And you ain't going to find a whole lot of government enforcers out this way, either."

"Why do you say that?"

"Well, I just come from a place ought to be crawling with them, and it was completely abandoned."

Ben looked up sharply. "What kind of place?"

"You won't believe me."

"Try me."

"Goddamn nuke-you-lure missile silo, is what. And with the missile still in it."

"You're sure about that?"

"Swear to God. I was inside it. Scariest damn place I've ever been."

"And there were no people guarding it?"

"No people, period. Damn place is completely deserted."

"But there's a missile there?"

"That's what I said. And that's what there is."

"Well, doesn't that just beat all?"

"Don't it, though?"

"More coffee?"

"Much obliged."

"And just exactly *where* was this place, again, Solo Jack?"

"Well, there's this stripe on the desert floor, see, and . . ."

The next day the deer hunter rose at first light and rekindled his fire. He breakfasted on coffee, fried bread, corned beef, and canned peaches. Afterwards, he rolled up his sleeping bag, cleaned his utensils in the sand, put out the fire, and broke camp. He buried most of the signs that anyone had ever been there. But he didn't bother to bury Solo Jack. He was in a hurry. He threw the hobo's body into a ravine and tossed some tumbleweeds on top of it. Then he shouldered his pack and rifle and set off at a steady, determined pace. North by northeast, toward the mysterious stripe on the desert floor.

Chapter Three

The Launch Pad

Long Beach, California
Present day

The bar dated to the early '80s, the heyday of the aerospace industry. Back then it had been shiny, new, and filled with loud music and happy chatter. Now it was worn, quiet, and dimly lit. It smelled of stale beer and failed dreams.

"Ready for another one, ace?"

Douglas Wright looked down with some surprise to see that his glass had nothing left in it but the melted water from the ice cubes.

"Sure," he said, and he pushed his highball glass over toward the bartender. She was a forty-something redhead with short, brittle hair and a rather hard set to her jaw and eyes, but he supposed most of the customers didn't notice that, since she worked topless. She had a really nice set of breasts, he thought, even though they weren't huge. She also had the beginnings of a pair of love handles bulging out above the waistband of her miniskirt, but instead of making her look sloppy, they made her somehow more *real.* They made him want her all the more. *Jesus,* he thought, *how long has it been, anyway?* Too long, obviously.

She went to a different part of the bar, did a few things below the bar top, and came back with a fresh glass and napkin. He tried to watch every one of her bounces and sways without seeming to stare. When she got closer, he made a point of looking into her eyes instead, which turned out to be green.

"On your tab?"

"No." He dug into his hip pocket. "If I run a tab, it's too easy for me to get carried away."

She nodded and gave him a wry smile as she took his money.

"You're one of the guys they canned over at TechnoDyne, aren't you?"

"How would you know that?"

"I remember when you used to come in places like the Launch Pad or the Dee-Brief Room down the street. I also worked there for a while. It was Fridays, usually, with a lot of other guys with pockets full of fancy pencils and stupid frat boy grins, trying to outdo each other at throwing money around. You drank single-malt Scotch back then, and you always went home by eight o'clock. Now you come in alone almost every night with a rumpled shirt and nothing sticking out of your pocket. You don't smile, and you stay late and see how long you can nurse your gin and tonic. Yup, I'd say you're an out-of-work rocket engineer."

"Wow. You're smart as well as being a dish."

"Yeah, right. And you're stupid as well as being a mess, if you think you can get in my pants with a line like that."

"I'm sorry. I meant it as a compliment."

"Sure you did." She looked at the white stripe on his bare ring finger. "Does your wife know?"

"What, that I compliment bartenders?"

"No, that you got the axe."

"I told her."

"A lot of the guys don't, you know. They're afraid they'll get dumped if their wives know they're not rich anymore."

"Yeah, well, I told my wife. And it took her exactly two weeks to throw me out and file for divorce. She says I betrayed her by losing my job, but I think she's had something else going on behind my back for a long time."

"Oh, shit. I'm sorry I asked."

"That's all right. I always figured she married me just because I was a rising star in a rich industry. If all you care about is status and money, I was quite a catch, once. I thought maybe she would pick up some character after a while, anyway, but I guess some women never do."

"Some people, you mean."

"Yes. I do mean that. And now I've insulted you again. I apologize."

"What about you?"

"I give up, what about me?"

"Did you pick up any character?"

"Oh. Um. I guess I don't know."

She looked at him for a long moment. "Not the worst answer in the world. Your apology is accepted. And being insulted goes with the territory, I'm sorry to say. I'm Brenda, by the way." She offered her hand.

"Doug," he said, taking it.

"I'll be right back." She left him to go take care of some customers at the other end of the bar. He liked watching her go, because he could stare at her swinging hips without her knowing it. Well, without her being *sure,* anyway.

She was quite different from his ex-wife. Not as stylishly beautiful and certainly not as educated, but probably a lot smarter, and in her own way, honest and wholesome. Definitely not one of the shallow, "smart" set. She made him think of everything he had lost. Or had he thrown it away? Whichever it was, it had happened twice.

When he was young, he had never wanted anything out of life except to be an engineer. In his college years he had eschewed the party crowd and even the girls and had thrown himself into the intense study of exotic topics like thermodynamics, fluid mechanics, and deformable-body physics. He had a near-straight A average, and he had no doubt that someday there would be some very fine inventions with his name on them.

Not so many years later, he realized with something of a shock that he had traded that dream for a different one. It was often called "The American Dream," but it wasn't his. His employer, a major defense contractor, had dangled large sums of money and an important-sounding job description in front of him, and soon he was doing jobs that involved less and less real engineering, until he reached a point where he wasn't even sure if he still knew how to do any. He had a big car and a big house and a fancy title. He also had an empty marriage and a career that really didn't matter. But he considered it a contract, all the same. His father had made a similar contract, albeit in a totally different world. He had worked for decades at a dreary factory job in return for a good wage, paid up medical care, and the promise of a good retirement. It wasn't a great bargain, but it was a bargain, in every way that mattered. And his father always kept his word. So did Doug. It was sacred. Doug had sold out, but he had done so in good faith, and he would not back away from it. But then his employer and his wife both broke their word to him. He had sold out for an unworthy dream and an unfulfilled life, and now he didn't even have that. And he had absolutely no idea what to do about it.

The other customers in the bar looked like farmers or cowboys, not the usual clientele for a bar in the heart of aerospace country. They had overly long, uncombed hair poking out from under dirty baseball caps and overdeveloped upper arms straining against the rolled-up sleeves of their flannel or twill work shirts. They were drinking beer in long-necked bottles, and they seemed to be looking at him.

When Brenda came back, she brought him another gin and tonic. "Compliments of the Brothers Hayseed over there." She jerked a thumb over her shoulder, which made one breast jiggle in a delicious way.

"Really? Why?" He raised his new glass to the two figures and nodded to them.

"They want to know how pissed off you are at life in general and at your old employer in particular."

"What do they care?"

"They're looking to buy an engineer, they said."

"Buy one? What does that mean?"

"I don't know, exactly, but I think they want you to do something illegal. Anti-establishment, anyway. For money. They seem to have a lot of that, even if they do look like hicks. Shall I tell them you're interested?"

"Well, I damn sure don't owe TechnoDyne anything. But no, I think I'll pass. Sorry."

"Hey, it's no skin off my ass."

"Well, I'm certainly glad of that."

"You just don't quit, do you?"

"Sorry. It's been a bad month. I'm usually more of a gentleman."

"Yeah? Huh. Where are you living, Doogie-the-gent, now that Mrs. Gotrocks threw you out?"

"Motels, sometimes. Sometimes in my car."

"Jesus. You really have been dealt a shitty hand, haven't you?"

"You know what I really hate about it? She got to keep the dog. The house, I don't care about so much. I always thought it was a little pretentious anyway. But I liked that dog, and she knew it. Look on the bright side, though: the car's paid for."

She smiled at that but didn't laugh. "Tell you what: I get off at twelve-thirty. If you can keep from getting shitfaced by then, you can take me home."

"You seriously mean—"

"We'll see. Deal?"

He pushed both his glasses toward her. "Give me a straight tonic, okay?" It was the first time in months that he had felt positive about anything, and he did not want to run any chance of screwing it up.

At 12:35, he was leaning against his Lincoln Navigator in the back parking lot when Brenda let herself out the door, wearing a light blue raincoat and matching heels. She locked the door behind her, turned and spotted him, and waved. As he moved to meet her, he was dimly aware of footsteps crunching on the gravel behind his back.

Suddenly his feet were knocked out from under him, and when he hit the pavement, one set of hands grabbed his arms while another put some kind of cloth bag over his head. He had never smelled ether before, but from descriptions he had read, he figured that must be what was in the bag, in addition to his head. He had a very short moment in which to be amazed at how fast it worked.

Chapter Four

Abandon Hope

When he came to, he found himself in a small, damp basement lit by a single naked bulb with a pull chain attached to it. It was one of the new, energy-efficient, twisted fluorescent jobs. So he had "green" abductors, apparently. How nice.

As his head cleared, he became aware of being naked. His clothes were nowhere in sight, and even his watch was gone. He was sitting up against a rough concrete wall, and his wrists were chained to brackets on it. On the opposite wall, some sixteen or twenty feet away, he could dimly make out some lettering, spray-painted in white: KNOW THAT YOU DO NOT FALL INTO OUR HANDS FOR A FEW HOURS OR DAYS OR EVEN MONTHS, BUT FROM NOW UNTIL THE MOMENT OF YOUR DEATH, WHICH WE SHALL CHOOSE.

There was absolutely nothing else to look at, and he found it terrifying. Who the hell would want to choose the time of his death? And who would bother with trying to intimidate him? He hadn't had either money or secrets for ages now. Somebody had made a huge mistake, and he desperately needed to tell him so. But there was nobody to tell, and after what could have been hours or days, he fell asleep.

He was awakened by a bucket of cold water thrown in his face. The man who threw it was standing in deep shadow, but he could see the bucket itself. It was green plastic. *Amazing, the amount of utterly useless detail I'm picking up here.*

Standing in front of him, in better light, was a tall man in a dark expensive-looking suit. He was a big man, but not quite fat, though his suit was so perfectly tailored, it was hard to tell. He had a round, soft-looking, almost baby-like face, with no eyebrows at all and no hair on top of his head, either, though he did have a pencil moustache that was an odd shade of blond. He also had a long, angry welt of a scar across the top of his pate. When he spoke, his voice was soft and low, and Doug had to strain to hear him clearly.

"Hello, Mr. Wright. I trust you—"

"Look, I don't know who you guys are or what—"

The bucket hit him on the side of the head, so hard he would have gone flying across the room if he hadn't been chained to the wall. The big man leaned over closer.

"I am Mr. Black, but you will not call me that. You will not call me anything at all. You are about to begin a very painful learning process, Mr. Wright. Call it obedience training. And the first thing you will learn is to keep your mouth shut unless I tell you to open it."

"Okay, whatever you—" He looked to his side in time to see the green bucket again swinging at his head.

"Wait!" The man in the suit held up a restraining hand, and the bucket froze in mid-swing. "Stay away from the head. I don't want that damaged. And switch to the rubber now. I want deep bruising and deep pain, but nothing that will show, at least for very long."

The bucket clattered off into a dark corner, and he was hit instead on the shoulder with some kind of rubber bludgeon. It hurt more than the bucket had.

"You will not say 'okay' or 'yes' or even 'yes sir.' Because I say so, you will keep totally silent and listen."

Doug was reeling from the blow, and he had a sharp pain that ran from his shoulder all the way down his arm. He gulped air through his mouth, but he managed to hold his tongue and stare at the man.

"When you do speak, you will have only one chance to do so. If you hesitate, you will not get another, for a long and painful time. Nod if you understand me."

He nodded.

"Good. Much better. The point, you see, is that we now own you. We can do absolutely anything we want with you or to you, and there's nothing you can do about it, now or ever. At this point, you can't even ask why. Brenda?"

A door opened in the wall above and behind him, and he turned his head to see the pale blue heels coming down a creaky set of wooden steps. Soon he could see the rest of the bartender as well, still in the blue raincoat. She walked over to the big man and stood beside him, facing Doug. The big man undid the belt of her coat and pulled it roughly open. He pulled it down behind her shoulders, pinning her arms behind her and showing that she was still as topless as she had been in the bar.

"We own her, too, you see. Don't we, my dear?"

"Yes, sir."

"Very good. Now show him what that means."

She managed to shrug the rest of the way out of her coat and then proceeded to strip off her skirt, hose, and panties, slowly and sensually. Doug found himself with an erection. He was sure that was a very bad idea, and he couldn't believe his body was that stupid.

"Brenda, if I told you to go over to that man and perform oral sex on him, would you do it?"

"Yes, sir. Of course."

The erection got harder.

"Or regular sex?"

"Yes."

The erection got very hard, and there was absolutely nothing he could do about it. Had there been a little something in that last tonic? Tonic water would hide the taste of almost anything. Suddenly the man from the shadows smashed his erection with the rubber truncheon. He screamed in agony and pulled his knees up to try to protect himself. The man smashed him on the shins, one at a time, and then on the kneecaps. He screamed again.

"Sorry, my friend, but I did tell you to keep silent, didn't I? I did not promise you it would be easy. You're probably thinking 'dirty pool,' because you didn't scream until after we hit you. But that doesn't matter, you see. You have to play strictly by the rules, but there are no rules for us. None at all. You'll have to have some extensive training now. Do try to remember it this time." To the bartender, he said, "That will be all for now, my dear."

She picked up her clothes and left the way she had come. The big man went over to the man with the instrument of pain and showed him the face of his wristwatch, pointing to a place on it that Doug couldn't see. "Until then."

The other man nodded.

"Don't break anything yet."

He nodded again.

The big man climbed the stairs, and the other man proceeded to beat Doug savagely over his entire body. After what seemed like hours, he finally managed to pass out.

He was beaten twice more, just as savagely but not as long, before the baby-faced Mr. Black returned. After the second time, he hurt everywhere except in his arms. He couldn't feel his arms anymore. And he was dying for a drink of water.

"Name, rank, and serial number," said Black.

He tried to speak, but no sound came out. He tensed, expecting to be hit again. But instead, somebody put a paper cup with water in it in front of him, and somebody else unlocked his manacles. His arms flopped uselessly to his sides. Nobody made any move to help him. Twice he knocked over the cup trying to pick it up, and it was replaced by another one. Finally, he shook his arms to get the circulation going and managed to pick up the cup using both hands, which trembled badly. He drank it all.

"Name, rank, and serial number."

"Huh?"

"Name. Rank. Serial number."

"Um, Douglas Wright. But I've never been in the military. I don't have a rank or serial number."

"Good. You are whispering, Mr. Wright. Do you have to do that?"

"Yes, I think so. Please don't hit me again for it."

"No. Not for that. There are many things we want you to learn, but oratory is not one of them. Very well, then, in whatever voice you can muster, you may speak to me now, but you had better not waste my time."

"Please listen to me. There has been a terrible mistake here."

"No, there has not."

"But I'm not a criminal."

"And who said you were?"

"No, I mean I'm not a spy or a terrorist, either. I'm just—"

"We know exactly who and what you are. Shall I tell you? Can you bear to hear it? You are a washed-up, phony engineer. You have spent years riding the public gravy train, but the ride is over now and you are stranded."

"That's not true. I'm a good engineer. Before the economy went to hell, I was an important person. I was promoted to—"

"No, Mr. Wright. You may have had the makings of a good engineer when you got out of college, but you took a job where you never did an iota of real engineering. You were promoted several times, just so you could generate a lot of expensive time for which your company could bill the government. Every time you got promoted you became less of an engineer and more of a nominal slot on a billing sheet. Everybody else knew that, even if you did not. And they also knew when the game was over. Totally. You have nowhere to go now, except to us."

"But I still know how to—*what did you say?*"

"We brought you here to recruit you. And you would be foolish to refuse. In a word, you want what I am selling, Mr. Wright."

"And what is that? Pain?"

"Resurrection."

Chapter Five

Marching Orders

The brutality of Doug Wright's "recruitment" had two purposes, he was told. The first was, obviously, to make sure he never entertained the slightest thought of crossing his new employers. The second was so that he could see he was working for people who were totally above any law. "The power that we wield over you, you will also have over your subjects, once you start your duties. You may find that very pleasant, even intoxicating."

"My duties? What possible duties could you have for me?"

"Think of yourself as a cross between a Judas goat and an avenging angel, Mr. Wright. It's a good job. It involves travel, adventure, and a lot of unofficial perks, and it even pays well. First, however, you need some training in other things besides obedience. When it's over, you can ask questions. Not before."

He did not go back to the Launch Pad, and the vehicle he had been living in was taken away somewhere. He was shunted around several dormitory-like dwellings that always seemed to be empty except for him and his trainers. The intimidation sessions were replaced by personal tutoring by an assortment of strange individuals in a variety of settings. Most of the sites, he couldn't place. But some, like the YMCA where he worked free weights four days a week and the firing range where he practiced shooting every day, were quite public. He also had "field exercises" and survival training in downtown areas and out in open country. Mr. Black, always with his impeccably tailored dark suit, was often at his sessions, but usually just to observe. Or quite possibly, he was there just to remind Doug that whatever he was allowed to do, he was always on a short leash. There was a lot of emphasis on physical and psychological intimidation. "The job of a spy is spying," said one of his instructors, "but his craft is the give and take of pain. When necessary, it is the give and take of death."

He dutifully wrote "give and take of death" in his trainee's notebook. In his mind he wrote *Bullshit. Are these guys completely nuts?*

But in some ways, they weren't crazy at all. He recognized their strategy easily enough. He had never been in the military, but he knew boot camp when he saw it. And boot camp has probably been essentially the same for as long as there have been armies. It begins with the total destruction of the identity and confidence of the recruit and the induction of a constant state of terror. The subject is utterly dependent on the approval of his new masters, and he can't even tell what that approval requires. None of his old skills or qualities will help him at all. His identity is gone, and nothing works. Eventually he will be allowed to "discover" a new identity, quite different from the one he started with. And if everything works right, he will not only embrace it, he will revel in it. The sequence is *No matter what you do, you're in deep shit,* followed by *Learn what you're supposed to and maybe they will leave you alone,* finally culminating in *Get good at your job and you will be hailed as a hero.* Doug wondered what kind of hero they were going to make him into.

He learned armed and unarmed combat, how to tail somebody, and how to spot and lose a tail, in a vehicle or on foot. He learned how to use or disarm a variety of explosives, how to steal cars, how to pick simple locks, and how to run an assortment of short con games. He became qualified on ten different kinds of handguns and eight rifles and machine guns. He learned six ways of killing a man with his bare hands and four more with a knife. He also studied codes and ciphers and standard letter-drop techniques that the "enemy," whoever that was, might use. He strongly suspected that most of the code material was hopelessly out of date. He would be tested on it later, of course. But would the test be to see if he could handle antique code breaking, or merely if he was eagerly trying to assimilate whatever they told him?

When he did poorly, he was beaten or deprived of food. When he did well he was rewarded with high-protein food like steak and eggs or lobster, and he even occasionally had a bottle of wine with them. Mostly he did well. The beatings became less and less frequent and then stopped altogether. He had never thought of himself as very athletic and had never been interested in guns or martial arts, so he was surprised to find that he was good at it all, including the combat training.

But his individual combat trainer was not impressed.

"If you ask me, we're wasting our time with you," he said. "I can take one look in your eyes and see that you're not a killer and never could be."

"I probably can't become an assassin," said Doug. "And to be honest, I don't want to be, either. But if it comes down to kill or be killed, I'll do what has to be done."

"No, you won't. You'll take too long deciding, and the opportunity will be lost. When you get yourself in that situation, remember I said that."

He turned away from Doug, apparently to walk off the practice mat. Doug relaxed, and suddenly the instructor whirled around and kicked him solidly in the jaw. He poked gingerly at his teeth to see if any had been knocked loose.

"Remember that, too, trainee. Be ready for anybody to attack you, any time, any place. Know what you're going to do about it before it happens."

Doug looked him squarely in the eyes and when he was sure he had the instructor's full attention, he kicked him in the groin. "Got it," he said.

"Maybe you do, at that." The instructor hunched over a bit but showed no other signs of pain, though he must have had plenty of it. "That was your best move so far." They sparred for another ten minutes, and Doug was solidly out-fought. But he was getting better. And he had just learned another lesson. *Never pass up a chance to land a sucker punch.* Even as he thought it, he was dismayed. He was learning how to be successful by being underhanded, and it went against all his instincts.

Instincts? They were not so easy to define anymore. He not only no longer knew what he wanted, he no longer knew what he *should* want. He began to fully realize what should have dawned on him a long time ago, back when he had first started living in his car and hanging out aimlessly in bars: that his old life, imperfect as it was, was gone and was never coming back. Not in any way, shape, or form. He needed a totally new life, and he had no blueprint with which to build one.

He gained weight, most of it muscle. And with it, he gained confidence. He began to be intrigued. Could this really be a US government agency? Even after 9/11, how could anything that out of control, that blatantly illegal, exist? But if not that, what were they, really? And more to the point, why did they want him? Was somebody seriously expecting him to play James Bond? If so, where were all the sexy women? Hell, where was his Aston-Martin? But even without them, the idea of a second career of catching bad people and possibly atoning for all his years of amoral work had a definite appeal. Was it possible?

"You are preparing to catch terrorists and *potential* terrorists," said Mr. Black, though he still had never said what agency he or Doug was working for. "People who hate their country. People who are traitors in every way, whether they have committed any overt acts or not. We are fishing for one very big one in particular, and you are the perfect person to use as bait."

That made a little more sense to him. But he decided he wasn't really being groomed to be an *employee*. Employees for any real agency were recruited by slick talent scouts in conservative suits at college placement offices. They were given tests and interviewed in comfortable, air-conditioned spaces, and they were investigated, or "vetted," after they were hired, not before. No, this was something else. "Bait" was probably closer, at that. What the intelligence community called an "asset." Something that can be used. And assets were nothing if not expendable. It was still all quite vague, and it had a feeling of utter unreality to it. He wondered if they really would pay him a salary.

As the terror of personal intimidation subsided, it began to be augmented by anger, then hate. He had thought he hated his former employer for using up his prime years and then dumping him. But now he realized that before Mr. Black came along, he hadn't known hate from a hole in the ground. Now he did, and he felt it growing inside him every day.

Not knowing the names of his employers made them harder to hate, but he managed it. In his mind, he called them Spooks R-Us, and he saw them as just as self-aggrandizing and smug as they were vicious. He began to wonder if his training would be good enough to let him escape from them. To where or what, he didn't know. That was a question he wasn't ready to answer yet. But escape was the only really palpable goal he had.

Then they took that from him as well. It was as if they could read his mind. One day he successfully eluded a six-man surveillance team in a downtown field exercise called a "foxes and geese" operation. He quickly went to a parking ramp and looked for a car he knew how to hot-wire. But his newly issued cell phone immediately began to vibrate in his pocket. He hadn't even thought it was turned on. He pulled it out with a shaking hand and found that he was suddenly short of breath.

Don't even think about it, said the voice at the other end of the connection. *Punishment for trying to escape is worse than anything you can imagine.*

He left the phone on and put it gently down on the concrete floor of the ramp. Then he got into an unlocked Chevrolet Impala, started it up, buckled his seat belt, and put the gas pedal to the floor. At the ramp exit, he didn't slow down for the yellow-and-black barrier arm. He sent it flying off to parts unknown and peeled off into the city street, not looking at traffic at all. A block later, he was hit from the side by a big SUV coming out of an alley. An assortment of emergency vehicles was on the scene before he could even get his seat belt undone, and the next thing he knew, he was strapped to a gurney in the back of an ambulance that quickly left the scene.

It took him straight back to the dingy basement with the lettering on the wall, where his ordeal had first begun. They left him strapped to the gurney while they pumped him full of unknown drugs. Then they threw him on the floor, and several men took turns beating him, often in places he'd never been hit before, like the soles of his feet and his armpits. Sometimes they stabbed him with long needles that penetrated all the way to bone, where they made rasping, scraping noises.

For a long time, he was amazed that he could hurt that much without passing out. Then he seriously wondered how he could hurt that much without dying. Later still, he wished that he could die. Dying had more appeal than anything else he could imagine. But of course, it was not his to choose. The writing on the wall said as much.

He lost track of time completely. After several eternities, the beatings must have stopped, because he woke up with his face on the concrete floor and realized that his pains were all residual, not new. At least, that's how it seemed, though some of the pain was so sharp, it was hard to be sure. He crawled over to a small water puddle on the floor and greedily lapped it up, not bothering to check to see if he was being watched. When the puddle was dry, he went to sleep, his chin still on the damp spot on the floor.

He spent a long time in rehab after that. Real rehab, in some kind of real medical facility somewhere. Through all the exercises and routines and drugs, no mention was ever made of his escape attempt. The physical lesson spoke loudly enough, it seemed.

In the deeper corridors of his mind, a new dream was slowly taking shape. He called it "escape-plus." *Okay, so I can't have my old life back, or even anything vaguely like it. But if I stay with this organization, I can't have any life, period. This is not an outfit that gives honorable discharges. So it's not enough just to escape. Somehow, some of them have to die. Maybe a lot of them. Enough so the rest lose interest in pursuing me.* And at the top of the list, of course, was Mr. Black.

It was a scary vision, and one with a low probability of success. But it was all he had. He thought of a saying he had heard once from a coworker who was an Army veteran. "I ain't afraid of dying; I just hope it doesn't hurt too much." His death would hurt a lot. So it behooved him to make somebody pay for that in advance.

* * *

Eventually, he was back in training as if nothing unusual had happened at all, other than his acquiring a slight limp and a crazy look in his eye.

"You need to learn to live off the net and under the radar," said Black one day. "Your story is that you are an unemployed engineer with no other skills, and you are beginning to get desperate. There must be no record and no action that contradicts that."

He wondered whom he was hiding from. Other agencies, maybe? Did Black carefully hide his "assets" from all the ordinary, legitimate government agencies?

Black gave him three credit cards in his own name.

"If you need general backup, use the Visa for anything at all, and up to six agents will be available to you within 24 hours. If you need immediate help, use the Mastercard, and you'll have armed assistance within an hour. Otherwise, don't use them at all. Use only cash for your expenses. You'll have plenty of it, though you can't show it off."

"What about the Macy's card?"

"It only looks like a Macy's card. Use it with the number on the Visa card, and you can get cash out of any ATM in the country. Forget about your old credit cards. Don't bother to pay them off, either. A string of bad debts is exactly what you should have, in case anybody checks. And don't flash your new cell phone around. It's permanently locked on silent ringing mode, so it won't draw any attention. Any time you turn it on, we will know where you are."

"And I can call you on it?"

"No, nor anybody else. But we can and will call you." He still didn't mention the incident in the parking ramp, and neither did Doug.

Doug was also given a crash course in the more popular anti-establishment theories of the day—the Christian Identity movement, the Posse Comitatus, the believers in the Zionist

Occupied Government, or just ZOG, and the whole business of secret armies and black helicopters.

"Are you telling me sane, rational adults actually buy that bullshit?"

"I didn't call them anything of the sort, Mr. Wright. These are people who are angry. Very, very angry. And when they have been angry enough for long enough, they look for a nice, easy-to-understand bogeyman. They don't care if it sounds irrational. The world they see around them looks irrational, too. Why else would it be out to destroy them?"

"Do they call themselves Zoggies?"

"I'd be very careful with that kind of talk if I were you. These people have no sense of humor whatsoever. It's one of the things that makes them easy to spot."

"Them?"

"Anarchists, Mr. Wright. Homegrown, spontaneous, agrarian anarchists. People who want to destroy anything they can, any way they can. They have no sense of humor and no pity for anybody else, and they look, um—"

"Pissed."

"Yes, exactly. They look pissed, all the time. But it's not looking-for-a-fight pissed; it's more like a 'you stole my crayons' pissed. It's intense and sullen, but it's impotent, too. These people have convinced themselves they are beaten at the starting gate. You can spot most of them from across the street."

"Then why do you need me? You don't seem to have any reservations about snatching anybody you want. Why don't you just pick up everybody who looks pissed?"

"Because we don't just want them. We also want them to lead us—you—to their toys. They won't do that merely because we catch some of them and hurt them. We know; we've already tried."

"Their toys?"

"Yes. We are looking for somebody who has a very big, very nasty toy, in particular."

"A lethal virus?"

"Worse."

"Poison gas?"

"Worse yet."

"You can't mean some kind of nuke?"

"The worst kind. The kind that has a rather large missile attached to it."

"How the hell can that be? I mean, an ICBM is not the sort of thing you throw in the back of your pickup and make a run for the border."

"No. You find a launch site and take it over."

"So go attack the site and waste them. Flood the damn place with nerve gas. What the hell do you need me for?"

"Stop trying to get out of your job. It's not that simple. There are some sites that are—how can I put this? There are some sites that are lost."

"*What*? How do you *lose* a whole ICBM site?"

"It's complicated."

"Oh, I'm sure of that."

"Let me tell you a little story, Mr. Wright. Once upon a time, early in the cold war, we had a Secretary of Defense who was a man of great strength and vision, which he thought the President sorely lacked. In a word, he didn't believe the President had the will to ever use the nuclear arsenal. So he decided there should be a second arsenal, secret to almost everyone, including the President, and controlled solely by himself. It was the most secret project since the making of the first atomic bomb, maybe even more secret, and it also created a secret quasi-military agency to staff and guard the completed sites."

"Is that your agency?"

"No, Mr. Wright, it is not. It hasn't existed for a long time now. If any of its members are still alive, their whereabouts are quite unknown."

"How could he get the project funded?"

"Is that a serious question? This was the height of the Cold War. The Department of Defense had more money than it knew what to do with, a lot of it with no oversight whatsoever. The sites were built, crews were recruited, and fewer than a dozen people in the world knew about it."

"Just the crew of one silo would be way more than that."

"True. But they never knew where they were. They were flown into the sites in planes with blacked-out windows. They stayed strictly on station for three months, then were flown back and given three months' leave. It was considered choice duty."

"Didn't anybody notice that the secretary had acquired a Secret Service bodyguard with a briefcase full of launch codes?"

"These missiles were special, Mr. Wright. They had no launch codes. A single secure phone call from the secretary was sufficient to send them on their ways."

"That's insane."

"It was an insane time. Quite possibly, it's always an insane time. Don't interrupt again, please.

"Things were unchanged for a long time, and the secret arsenal was handed down from one Secretary of Defense to the next. But then the mood of the world changed. In the sixties we got the first arms limitation treaty, SALT I, and in 1991 we got START, and we and the Soviets actually set about dismantling some nuclear sites. We filled some of our missile silos with concrete and let the Russians watch, and they did the same for us. And at some point, somebody decided it was time to deal with the super-secret sites. But they couldn't be dismantled, at least openly, because to do so, we would have to admit that they existed in the first place. And that would be very embarrassing indeed. So the crews were ordered to ship all their computers and software to the archives at Los Alamos, turn out the lights, weld the doors shut, and just walk away. Which they did. In ten or fifteen years, it became practically impossible to find anybody who knew anything about them."

"Are you telling me that now we think that one of these anarchist groups has found one? How do we know, if we don't know where it is?"

"We don't know. We only suspect. That's where you come in."

"Christ on a crutch. So I'm going down, down the rabbit hole, because *if* one of these groups actually exists and *if* they have a site, they *might* believe that they need somebody like me to show them how to make it work."

"Well put."

"What if I don't know how?"

"It doesn't matter. All you have to do is sound like you know how. You know how to do that, I'm sure."

"And am I also supposed to pretend I buy into all this ZOG crap? I don't think I can do that. It's just too—"

"No. They wouldn't believe you if you tried. You've been establishment for too long to be an overnight convert to the gospels of the haters. All they have to know is that you have been out of work for a long time, and you're fed up and desperate. Also, of course, completely professionally amoral, which is something else you should have no trouble with. So, when they offer you a large sum of cash to do a job for them, you accept. Simple."

"Do they actually have a large sum of cash?"

"Maybe, maybe not. But if not, they will promise it anyway."

"And I will buy the promise and go with them."

"Just that simple."

"What if they really do have a big bunch of money? Do I get to keep it?" He thought that was too much to hope for, but it couldn't hurt to ask.

"We are not a for-profit organization, Mr. Wright. As long as we find out where the site is, we don't care what happens to the money."

His mind began to spin. What if, just *what if* he managed to get through one undercover operation and emerge as a wealthy man? He couldn't go back to his old life, for sure, but maybe he could do a respectable job of running away. Of course, if the operation wound up taking years and years, that could be quite another matter. He could grow old planning on a future that never came. He decided to ask the question he really didn't want to know the answer to.

"How many of these lost sites are there, by the way? Do we know?"

"We think sixteen."

"Jesus H. fucking Ch—"

"I foresee a long career for you, Mr. Wright."

Thirteen weeks after his abduction, Wright was finally pronounced fit for duty.

"Your apprenticeship is over, Mr. Wright. Your probation is about to begin. Work hard at it; not many people like you get a second chance."

And in a strange rush of *déjà vu,* he found himself back at the Launch Pad, nursing a gin and tonic. It was late, and he had let himself get half in the bag when Brenda again put a free drink in front of him and pointed over to a couple of burly blue-collar types at the other end of the bar.

They were different from the men he had gotten a drink from the last time he was there, though obviously cut from the same cloth. One was slightly built and had a thin face with dark, unkempt hair falling over heavily lidded eyes. He had a half smirk on his face and an arrogant posture, as if he were constantly thinking, "I told you so!"

The other one looked more thoughtful, though his eyes had the same deep fire in them as the smaller man's. He had strong, blocky, Nordic-looking features, a wide brow, and blond hair that didn't quite reach his collar. Doug raised his drink and nodded his thanks to them. The blond man nodded back and gave him a tight-lipped smile. Doug drained an inch off the top of the drink and walked over to them. *Oh, my God,* he thought. *It's really happening. Is there a patron saint of spies? I need to talk to him.*

Chapter Six

The King's Shilling

"I'm Doug Wright." He extended his hand, and the big man took it. "Do I know you?"

"No, but we think you ought to. I'm Ben. My sour-faced friend here is Max. He won't shake your hand, but don't take it personally. He generally acts like an asshole towards everybody."

"No I don't, just towards people who are establishment," said Max. "And he is. I told you that before."

"He used to be, Max. But he's been through a lot since then, haven't you, Doug? Have a seat. We have things to talk about."

"Thanks. But just how would you know what I've been through?" He slid onto the stool next to Ben.

"Cause we ain't stupid, fella," said Max. "You come here in your vee-hickle that was expensive as hell a couple years ago but now ain't been washed in months and looks like somebody's living in it. You wear a rumpled shirt, drink the cheapest thing you can order, and bounce between looking pissed off and just down-and-out beat. Only way you get like that nowadays is if you been fucked over by the fat cats. Don't matter which ones; they're all the same, all a part of ZOG. And being shit on by them would make you one of us, except that before they turned on you, you used to be part of the system, too. So I don't see how—"

"Easy, Max."

"He looks like a screw."

"Excuse me?" said Doug. "A what?"

"Max did some time in a federal pen. Everybody in the square world looks like a screw to him."

"Really? I've never known an ex-con before. What were you in for, Max?"

"For exercising my constitutional rights."

"Income tax evasion," said Ben. "He decided to be a church, and he quit paying his taxes."

"Oh. What kind of church?"

"The Church of Max Almighty! What the hell is wrong with that? You can't be a church without a goddamned pope? You got to put a steeple on your garage? The Constitution says—"

"Max tried blessing the judge, but it didn't seem to help."

"Goddamned slimy Jew bastard." He stared into his beer and got a faraway look in his eyes. "Gave me two to five, for nothing. Nothing! I damn sure let him know what I thought about it, too."

"I bet that helped a bunch."

"It couldn't make things any worse. And now we're talking to you? You're just some damn guy we don't even know who's probably another—"

"I told you to put a lid on that kind of talk tonight, Max," said Ben.

"Yeah, you told me. But I got a right to say what—"

"*Not* if you're with me, you don't. And you *are* with me, yes?" He gave the smaller man a look that would wilt most people.

Doug decided it was a good time to underplay his role a bit. "Look," he said, "I don't want to be starting a fight among friends. Why don't I just leave you two alone? If you don't mind, I'll keep the drink, though."

"Please stay, Doug. I promise, it'll be worth your while. And Max was just about to apologize, weren't you, Max?"

Max made some kind of grunt.

"I can't hear you." He stared intently into Max's eyes, and the look there gradually changed from anger to something else.

"Yeah, okay. Sorry if I was out of line, Mr. Wright."

"Hey, no problem."

"So," said Ben, "what did you do back when you had a job, Mr. Wright?"

"I was a design engineer for TechnoDyne Systems."

"Would that be what most people call a 'rocket scientist'?"

"Yeah, you could say that, I guess."

"You used to build things that kill people?"

"Well, things that *could* kill people."

"And that didn't bother you?"

"Hey, somebody's going to do it. And it paid good money. It's not like—"

"It's an easier line to step over than most people think," said Ben, "that killing line. Sometimes you don't even see it."

"Yeah," said Max, nodding solemnly. "You know, one time, back home, me and Ben took this banker, and—"

"Max, wait outside."

"I'm just telling him—"

"Go. Now. Don't make me tell you twice." Again, the big man skewered Max with his stare. Max hesitated for a moment, then got off his stool, kicked it, and strode out the back door, saying nothing.

"I really didn't mean to be causing you any trouble," said Doug.

Ben shook his head and smiled slightly. "Forget about it. Max is a true believer. He can't see things in any other light. But he eventually does what he's told. He doesn't act crazy, he just thinks that way."

"And you?"

"What about me?"

"You're not a true believer?"

"Not in that. Do you know the story of Don Quixote, Doug?"

"I saw *Man of La Mancha*; that was enough."

"You didn't like it? Why not?"

"For my money, Quixote was an idiot and a loser. At some point, he deliberately chose to be delusional, and we're supposed to like him and even admire him for it. That's bullshit."

"Believe it or not, you and I agree. But did you ever think about why he chose a windmill to take for a dragon?"

"Because he couldn't find an elephant?"

"No, because he couldn't defeat it. As heroic as he thought he was being, a big part of his fantasy required that he could never win. He *wanted* his dream to be impossible."

"The point being?"

"There are a lot of Don Quixotes around. Max is one. He likes to believe in huge conspiracies because they are big enough and evil enough to explain all his frustrations. They're a lot of fun to hate. But he also likes them because he can't ever beat them. They scare him, just enough. And you can't hate something you don't also fear."

Three months earlier, Doug would have had no idea what Ben was talking about. Now he just nodded.

"Finish your drink, Doug." He motioned to Brenda to bring them two more. The night wore on, and the two turned into several. Now and then, Max would come in from the back parking lot, whisper something in Ben's ear, and leave again. Ben did not seem to be concerned. Doug began to worry that they were never going to get around to talking any serious business. He was also worried by the fact that he was starting to like this man.

"So what do you believe in, Ben?"

"I believe in big G, without the Z or O in front of it."

"And what is that?"

"Greed, Doug. Big Greed. We have become a nation of greedy, immoral people who all think they are so goddamned smart. They all think they invented wanting more than their fair share of everything and not worrying about how they get it. And they all think they are acting separately. But nobody really acts alone. And collectively, they do terrible things. They break people, drive them to kill, and ruin everything that was ever fine in this country. And there's no end to it. It's a loaded freight train, running down a mountain."

"So you, too, are saying you can't win."

"Oh no, I'm not." He turned and gave Doug a strange, satisfied smile. "Do you want a job?"

"More than you can imagine."

"You said it didn't bother you, designing things that could kill people."

"That's right, though keep in mind, I'd just as soon not go to jail for it. What have you got in mind?"

"I'm going to blow up the goddamn tracks. I'm going to drop the freight train in a gully so deep, it can't ever be pulled back out."

"I see." He took a long pull on his drink. "And where do I fit in?"

"You're going to show me how."

"Got it. But since I'm probably one of those greedy, immoral people you were just talking about, that's going to cost you."

"How much?"

"How far do I have to run afterwards?"

"Far. You'll probably have to disappear forever."

"Two million."

"One."

"Have you got a million?"

"No, but I can get it."

"In cash?"

"All cash, totally clean."

"We have a deal. When you get it, we'll talk again."

"Yes we will, but not here. Meet me in two weeks in Albuquerque, in the Old Town market. Noon, when it's good and crowded. Just wander around like a tourist, and I'll find you. Don't be followed. Here's some traveling money to tide you over." He stuffed a folded-over wad of bills in Doug's shirt pocket. "What's that bulge in your front pants pocket, by the way?"

"Huh?' Doug looked down. "Oh, that? That's just my cell phone."

"Let's see it." He reached out his hand, and Doug gave him the phone. "Brenda? Give me about two thirds of a mug of beer."

He looked over the small black device, shook it, and held it up to his ear. Then he dropped it into the mug of beer that Brenda had just brought.

"You won't be needing that anymore."

Chapter Seven

Down, Down the Rabbit Hole

While Doug stared stupidly at the mug of beer with his cell phone in it, Ben left quietly by the rear door.

"They're not going to be happy about that, you know," said Brenda, nodding at the mug.

"Well, what the hell was I supposed to do?"

"You shouldn't have let him see it in the first place."

"It was inside my pocket, for chrissakes. How was I supposed to—"

"I'm just telling you how they think, that's all."

"It's not fair."

"It never is."

"I did what I was supposed to."

"Almost." She dumped the beer out into the bar sink, wiped the phone off with a rag, and gave it back to him. He tried the power button a few times, to no effect. "I guess it's not a Timex," she said.

"Maybe the tracker will still work, anyway."

"They gave you an antique, Dougie. That baby is tanked. I've heard you can dry it out by sealing it in a bag with some uncooked rice. It takes a couple days, though."

"God damn it, it's not my fault. You've got to tell them—"

The back door slammed, and Ben came back in, suddenly looking totally sober and in an obvious hurry.

"Are you looking for Max?" said Doug. "He didn't come back in here."

"Max is gone."

"Maybe he got tired of waiting. It was kind of a long—"

"No, Doug, he did not get tired of waiting. I told you, he only thinks crazy. Somebody has either snatched him or is trying to. They'll try me next, then you." He pulled a large semiautomatic pistol out of an inside coat pocket and pulled the slide back to check the chamber.

"Me? I haven't done anything but drink and talk."

"Sometimes that's enough. Wait a few minutes after I leave. Then get out, any way you can, anywhere you can. I wouldn't take my own car if I were you. Everything that's in that parking lot will be flagged by now, some way or another."

"But it's got all my stuff in it."

"You can buy more stuff. You can't buy your way out of a cell at Gitmo."

"Yeah, but—"

"You don't see it yet, do you? You've committed the overt act now. You're fair game. And sometimes all the game can do is run. See you in two weeks. Don't forget the money."

"Huh?"

But Ben was already gone, the glass front door hissing quietly as it closed behind him. Doug looked at Brenda and found nothing helpful in her expression. "I don't get it," he said. "Why would he tell me not to forget the money? Shouldn't I be the one telling him?"

"Beats me. Did he set up another meeting?"

"You didn't hear it?"

"I don't hear everything that's said at the bar, you know. I actually have some real customers now and then."

"You're a big help, you know that? Yes, we set up another meeting. In Albuquerque, in two weeks. So what do I do right now?"

"If you were as square as you're supposed to be, you wouldn't believe him about the car or the cell at Gitmo.

You'd just take your car and go off to make the next meeting, that's all. If you want to look a little nervous about it, that would be okay, but you seem to have that part down, anyway."

"It must be a big burden, being so smart."

He went to the back door, cracked it open an inch, and took a quick look. The parking lot looked deserted. He swung the door wider, had a better look, and then ventured out, his footsteps crunching on the gravel. At one edge of the lot, between two parked cars, he saw a figure lying facedown in what could have been a pool of blood. He looked quickly away and increased his pace. Could Spooks R-Us actually have killed Max? What the hell for? Despite the rising panic in his gut, he went back for a better look.

The man was half a head taller than Max, and he had shorter hair and a lot better clothes. Could Max have offed one of Black's agents? The body didn't look like any of them Doug had seen. But whoever it was, the parking lot had become a bad place to hang around. He broke into a brisk trot toward his wheels.

Ten yards away from the Navigator, he punched the remote "unlock" button on his key fob, and the vehicle instantly exploded in a ball of flame.

He stopped and stared, dumbfounded. After half a minute of frozen inactivity, he spun on his heel and ran back inside the bar.

"Did you hear it? Somebody blew up my car!"

"I heard. Why would anybody do that?"

"That's what I'd like to know. And with my phone drowned, I can't report back in and ask. Do you have a number you can call on your landline? You must have."

"I can try. There was no operation planned for tonight, but maybe there will be somebody there anyway."

"Try it. Tell them I made a deal with an anarchist. They'll believe you. Ask them what the hell happened in the parking lot."

She produced a phone from under the bar and turned her back to him while she dialed. Soon she was in a very animated conversation on the device, and when she turned back toward him, he saw that her face was growing more pale and still by the second.

"Let me talk to them."

She shook her head, putting a finger to her lips as she listened. Finally, she said, "Yes, sir," and hung up.

"They don't believe me," she said.

"About what?"

"About anything. But especially about what just happened. They say they have no agents here tonight."

"Well, somebody sure as hell does."

"They say all they know for sure is that you somehow disabled your cell phone, and you're in deep shit for it."

"But you saw what happened. Why didn't you tell them?"

"I did. They think you screwed up and I'm lying to protect you. They're going to come and have a look."

"Well, what am I supposed to do? I'm not going to hang around and wait for somebody to put a bag over my head again."

"No, you shouldn't. I have to wait for them. But if I were you, I would do exactly what your new farmer friend said: get out, any way you can. I'll tell them you left before I finished the phone call."

"They're not going to be all that kind to you, either. Come with me."

"I can't. They want me here. Go now, while you still have a chance. Go produce something for them, and maybe you can get back in their good graces. But go, no matter what."

He was surprised to find that he was really sorry she couldn't go with him.

If there were agents in the parking lot, they were doing a good job of staying out of sight. He moved out hesitantly at first and then, after he got around the body and the blood, at a dead run. Ten blocks later, he found what he was looking for: a battered blue Ford Taurus on a desolate-looking side street. He remembered reading in *Time* once that Ford had made seven and a half million of that particular model. That made it the perfect vehicle to disappear in. The door was unlocked, and the ignition was easy prey for his special new Swiss army knife. Soon he was accelerating up the on-ramp for California Trunk Highway 22. Then he saw the face in his rearview mirror. He stood on the brake pedal and pulled off onto the shoulder.

"*Who the hell are you*?" he screamed.

"Hey, man, who you think sleeps in a junker car like this?"

"The owner?"

"I thought that was you."

"Me? I stole it."

"You stole this piece of shit? Oh, man, you got to be—"

"Well, you picked it to sleep in. What are you bitching at me for?"

"I got to bitch at somebody. I ain't had my sleep. What time is it, anyway?"

"Now he wants the time."

"Sure, man. You got a watch."

"It's a little after eleven. Who are you?"

"I'm a guy who sleeps in shitty cars, what's it look like? Who are you?"

"A guy who steals cars that nobody will miss, okay?"

"And nobody will buy them, either. What are you, some kind of fugitive?"

"That's one way of looking at it, I guess. Are you a wetback?"

"A what?"

"You know what," said Doug. "An illegal."

"Why would you say that, man?"

"Are you or aren't you?"

"What if I was?"

"That would be good. It would mean you're not likely to blow the whistle on me."

"You got that part right. I ain't got a whistle and never did have and wouldn't know how to blow it if I did. But you better not have one, either."

Chapter Eight

Road Buddies

The maybe-wetback's name turned out to be Sancho Reyes, and when Doug pulled the Taurus onto the highway and back off again and finally came to a stop by a dark parking lot, the man made no move to get out.

"So where we goin', man?"

"Who's this 'we' you're talking about? You got a gerbil in your pocket?"

"What's that? Is that some kind of middle class white thing? I don't know no gerbil."

"Just get out, okay? Go steal your own car."

"It's time I got out of this town. And I'm thinking you need my help, man. I can tell you don't know nothin' about this fugitive stuff."

"I didn't exactly say I'm a fugitive."

"Come on, *amigo*. I'm homeless; I'm not *estupido*."

"I'm not your *amigo*."

"You're not Jennifer Lopez, either, but I can make allowances. Where we tryin' a get to?"

Doug sighed and flopped his forearms on the wheel. "I've got to be in Albuquerque in two weeks."

"That's an okay place, but you ain't gonna make it."

"Why don't you let me worry about that?"

"Hey, I'm a worrying kind of guy. And I never been to Alba-kwer-kwee. I'll help you, maybe teach you some things on the way."

"What are you going to do to help me?"

"Listen, *amigo*; I been, um, *on the run*—"

"You mean illegal."

"I mean on the run, okay? For nine years now. What's that tell you? I know how to be invisible. You'd like to do that, right?"

"As a matter of fact, I've been trained to do exactly that."

"Oh, yeah? You been trained to be invisible from everybody but the people who train you, I bet."

"Um, well—"

"That's what I thought. You wanna be more invisible yet, you need me. Cruise around some. I'm gonna show you something."

Two miles of side streets later, Reyes pointed to a row of parked cars in front of a seedy-looking apartment building. In the middle of the row was another dark-colored Taurus.

"Pull around the corner and park, *amigo*."

Doug did, and Reyes pulled something out of a ragged backpack and then opened his door.

"Don't go nowhere with my pack, man."

"Okay, but whatever you're going to do, hurry it up, will you? This is not a neighborhood I want to get to know."

"You watch. You ain't never seen fast before, but here it comes."

He got out and quickly removed both their license plates, the front one first. He tucked them inside his jacket and walked briskly back the way they had come and around the corner toward the Taurus they had passed. Two minutes later he was back, still with the bulge under his jacket. He pulled out two license plates and bolted them on the Taurus. Then he got back in, this time sitting in front.

"See, if somebody wakes up tomorrow morning and reports this pile of shit stolen, then you don't get stopped by the cops, 'cause—"

"I get it, okay? What if somebody wakes up and reports these plates stolen? Then what happens?"

"I didn't leave the other car with *no* plates; I just left it with different ones. Who looks at their own plates, man? Do you?"

"Well—"

"Pretty good, huh? I got more."

"It'll do."

"So le's go to Alba-kwer-kwee."

"And why do you want to go? Somehow I missed that part."

"I need a job, okay? And teaching you how to run is as good an offer as I got right now."

"You haven't got an offer. Do I look like I can afford to pay somebody else a salary?"

"Hey, until you fall into the good times, I work for three squares and a rusty roof. How can you go wrong?"

He thought it over for a minute, then started the engine and headed back toward the highway. "So, what's next, Paco?"

"Sancho."

"Whatever."

"Next, I think, we got to get you a gun."

"Why do I want a gun?"

"To shoot people?"

"Of course. Everybody needs to do that."

"You do, man. You got it written all over you. You got bad people coming after you."

"Besides being illegal, you're crazy, you know that?" But at some level, he rather liked the idea of adding a little firepower to his meager assortment of assets.

On a different highway, Ben Savitch checked his rearview mirrors, as he systematically did every fifteen seconds. The entire view to the rear was black, empty. Ahead of him, the road was straight as far as he could see. He touched an often-used control and dimmed his dash lights as low as they could go and still be on at all. He waited until his eyes adjusted, then a bit longer. He activated the cruise control at exactly two miles an hour below the speed limit and then killed the dash lights completely. After another minute, he killed all his lights. There were a few moments of visual disorientation, during which he concentrated on not moving the steering wheel even slightly. Then he found his night vision, and the ribbon of two-lane highway ahead came into view, first the staccato of white centerlines, then the brown-gray shoulders, and finally the blacktop itself. He began to mentally count. *One, one thousand, two, one thousand, three . . .*

If he was being followed by a loose tail, hanging far back and using their own lights seldom, they would now conclude that they had lost him and would speed up to reestablish contact.

Seventy, one thousand, seventy-one…

All his mirrors remained black. At a hundred and twenty seconds, he turned off the cruise control, not using his brakes to do so, and let the speed bleed off.

Still dark. At five hundred and twenty-one seconds, he saw the tiny pinpoints of bluish-white halogen headlights far ahead of him in the oncoming lane. He turned his own headlights back on but kept the speed down. As the approaching vehicle closed, he shifted his sight to the right shoulder but stayed alert to his peripheral vision. Soon the interloper flashed past, easily breaking the speed limit by twenty or more miles an hour. Mid-size, European-style sedan, probably a BMW or Audi. This was good. Not an agent or a cop, and at that speed, it would be a magnet for any stray highway patrols who happened to be prowling the area. He watched as the taillights shrank and finally vanished in his mirrors. No brake lights, no sudden maneuvers. He put the dash lights on again and brought the machine back up to cruise speed. He began to feel both excited and content. Things were shaping up. He could *feel* himself vanishing into the night. *It's just like that night back on the prairie, after we did the first banker*. He smiled at the memory.

Chapter Nine

The Road to the Dark Side

It was 1986, and the banker's name was Calvin Hobart, Junior, or Little Cal to his friends, which many people claimed to be. He lived in the town of Dickinson, North Dakota, and he bought everything that it had to offer and held loans on most everything else. He drove a Cadillac Seville, which he paid one of the town boys to wash and polish twice a week. He wore wool and silk blend suits that the Dickinson Mercantile ordered specially for him, and he had them custom tailored for him by a part-time seamstress named Roberta Jane Sunday. He was not above pressing Ms. Sunday into other services as well, though he was respectably married and had three children. It was easy to do, since he also held the often-overdue mortgage on her small dry goods and crafts store. He lived, of course, in the biggest house in town. But he bought his groceries at the local IGA. And while his cart had a rather high number of T-bone and porterhouse steaks in it, he somehow managed to kid himself into thinking that gave him the right to call himself "just folks." After all, he didn't vacation in Europe, did he?

Banker Hobart had foreclosed on the Savitch farm, along with many others. As with all of them, he had done it slowly, raising the interest rate on the Savitches' last machinery loan a half point at a time over several years. At first, Ben's father had been able to make the payments. Then he had only been able to make them with the help of the extra income Ben earned working at the Cenex grain elevator. But when the rate got up to twelve percent, all they could do was pay the interest, with nothing left to apply to the principal. When it went to thirteen, Ben's father threatened the banker with his shotgun. He was arrested and spent ninety days in jail. While he was there, the rate went to thirteen and a half percent. After he got out it rose to fifteen, and he killed himself.

Having gotten as much cash as possible out of the Savitch loan, Hobart promptly foreclosed on the family farm. He had the papers drawn up and processed in time for the funeral.

Ben waited almost a year before he decided to kill the banker. And even after he made the decision, he took his time, doing it carefully, getting it right.

First he went to a gun show in Tulsa, where he bought a nice .38 revolver with rosewood grips and a tooled shoulder holster. Saying that he didn't want to take it on the flight back home, he had the vendor ship it to him. Or rather, he had the vendor ship it to Calvin Hobart at Dickinson, North Dakota. The vendor did not ask for any ID, and he guaranteed an arrival date.

When the gun arrived, the FedEx man politely explained that no, there had not been a mistake. He also implied that since the gun had been legally purchased in Hobart's name, it might not be very smart to let it fall into somebody else's hands, like whoever decided he wanted it back at the FedEx office. So a bewildered Calvin signed for the package and put it away somewhere.

Two days later, Ben and his closest childhood friend, Max, wearing ski masks and bulky clothes, mugged the banker. The bank had also displaced Max's family, and he had needed little persuading. They jumped Hobart as he was leaving the bank early and by the back door, as usual. They tied a bag over his head, bound his hands behind him with electrical ties, took his wallet and keys, and beat the living crap out of him. They saved the cash but threw the wallet and keys, including credit cards, in a county drainage ditch.

Ten days later, they did it again as he was leaving Roberta Sunday's house by the back door. This time, as well as beating and robbing him, they made a point of tearing his fancy suit.

After another week, when the county sheriff was utterly unable to produce any viable suspects, the banker started to carry his unordered gun. It made a visible bulge in his suit coats, and he did not have them re-tailored to hide it. He wanted the world to see that he was ready.

For the final assault, Ben and Max didn't bother with the ski masks. With guns of their own, they were waiting for the banker inside his garage when he keyed the remote door opener and drove in. They got in the Cadillac beside him, one on each side, and pushed him to the center, guns poking in his ribs. All they said was, "Shut up if you want to live," and he did. Max took the .38 from the fancy tooled holster.

They reopened the big door, and Ben drove the car out and quickly away. Half a mile later, they stopped near Ben's pickup. Ben got out. "You drive now," said Max, giving Hobart an extra poke with his gun. "Follow him."

Pickup and sedan headed out of town to the west, taking secondary roads to the yard of a long-abandoned farm. They pulled to a stop behind a rotting barn, and Ben rejoined the other two in the Cadillac, sandwiching the banker between him and Max. He was wearing latex surgical gloves, and he had a clipboard with a piece of paper on it.

"Sign this." He shoved a pen in the banker's hand.

"It won't have any legal standing, you know. A coerced—"

"Then you don't need to worry about it, do you? Sign it."

The paper had a very short typewritten note on it. It said, simply, "I am so very sorry for all the lives I have ruined."

Hobart looked at it, and his face went pale, the first time that he had shown any fear.

"Um. The FBI, you know, can, um, tell what typewriter that was written on, you know. They can—"

"Sign." In point of fact, the note had been typed on one of the courtesy typewriters at the bank, and on bank letterhead.

"If I sign this, you will kill me."

"We will anyway. But sign it, and we promise not to kill your wife and your spoiled kids."

"And his dog," said Max.

"Oh yeah, I forgot about the damn dog. Him, too."

The banker cried quietly. "Have you no mercy? Please, I never—"

"We have more mercy than you ever did. At least you'll die quickly."

"I can pay you. I can—"

"Now, you slimy sack of shit."

He signed. Ben laid the note on the dash, took the keys out of the ignition, and got out of the vehicle, closing the door behind him. He went around to the passenger side, opened the door, and traded places with Max, who handed him the banker's gun.

"I'll do it, if you want."

"No, Max. This asshole is all mine." He pressed the gun tightly against the banker's head, just ahead of the ear, and pulled the trigger. The driver's window was splattered with blood and brain matter, but the glass didn't break. Ben replaced the keys in the ignition and squeezed them with the banker's thumb and forefinger. Then he produced an unfired .38 shell from his other jacket pocket. He pressed it against the banker's left index finger and thumb, swung out the cylinder on the gun, and used the new cartridge to replace the spent one. He didn't know which hand the banker used to push the bullets into the cylinder, so he pressed the man's left thumbprint onto each of the six cartridge bases. Then he closed the cylinder, wiped down the gun with a rag from his back pocket, and put it in the dead man's right hand, changing the exact grip several times, to leave multiple prints. He started the car, cranked down the power window on the passenger side, and, holding the banker's hand in his own, fired another shot outside, away from the old barn. He ran the window back up, shut off the motor, and replaced the hand with the gun on the banker's lap. As he got out of the car, he heard a soft warning chime and a recorded female voice that said, "Keys in ignition, keys in ignition."

"Call a cop, why don't you?" he said and got out and slammed the door. He wiped down all the door handles except the one on the driver's door, on which he merely smeared all the fingerprints.

Finally, they got in Ben's pickup and left. Ben made a wide U-turn and straightened out with his tires carefully placed in the tracks from the Cadillac. Then he stopped, and he and Max got out and used straw brooms to obliterate their tracks from the big turn. They went back to town, driving away from the setting sun, into delicious blackness. Then they waited.

It took a week and a day for the sheriff's troops to find the missing banker's body. Random searches and checks with the highway patrol produced nothing. Finally, they started checking at farms that were abandoned because the bank had foreclosed on them, but there were a lot of them, and it took some time to even put together a list.

Ben's father's suicide had not made front-page headlines, nor had any of the others that had contributed to making suicide the leading cause of death in rural areas, far eclipsing the old standard of death by machinery accident. But the "suicide" of the banker made the front page of several papers. That made Ben smile, and he realized with some surprise that it was the first time he had smiled in years. He hadn't known what to expect he would feel after killing somebody. He vaguely thought there might be some kind of bad emotional repercussion, but he had resolutely pushed himself into the act anyway. And now he found that far from feeling guilty, he felt liberated. He had destroyed a tiny part of the evil machine, had robbed it of its power over him. And that made him feel just fine.

Max, who had not actually pulled the trigger, nevertheless had problems with both guilt and fear, and for a while, Ben seriously worried that he might lose his nerve and give them both away. So he took Max down to Oklahoma, where they picked another predatory banker and gunned him down on a country road. This time, Max was fully blooded, and Ben could only hope the experience would be good for him. He was never quite sure, though, especially when Max started getting more and more involved with groups that Ben regarded as self-deluding lunatics. But whatever his ideology, Max remained fiercely loyal to Ben and would follow him anywhere and do anything he said. That was enough.

They killed the Oklahoma banker with deer rifles they had bought at another gun show under totally bogus names. After the killings, they wiped them down and threw them in a ditch, making no effort to conceal them. The retribution business was starting to get expensive. So now and then, instead of merely killing a banker, they would also rob his bank. But not often. Not often enough to establish a pattern or to justify a task force to hunt them. Ben knew that bank robbery was a high-risk operation at best, and he became even more careful and methodical than before. Gradually, he recruited a small cadre of men he trusted to follow his orders and keep their heads under pressure. Over the next ten years, they assassinated twelve bankers but only robbed three banks. All but two of the bankers' deaths were successfully made to look like suicide.

None of the robbers quit his day job, and they lived simply, not drawing attention to themselves.

Then one fall, while hunting out-of-season deer in the North Dakota Badlands, Ben ran into a hobo with a strange story and a scared look. And following the fellow's directions, he found it: the demon in the silo, the touchstone of Armageddon, the most feared of all weapons. After that, the whole game changed. Slowly, carefully, and very quietly, he began to assemble the people and materials he would need to make the demon his own and unleash it. The time of Big G was coming to an end.

Chapter Ten

Strange Highways

Doug stopped the Taurus a quarter mile from a 24-hour gas station and C-store that was too far off the freeway to have much business. He and Sancho doctored their license plates with some black electrician's tape, making an L into an E, a D into a crude B, and a 3 into an 8.

"You really think that's going to fool anybody?"

"Not up close, but it's good enough for a video camera, man."

"I hope you're right."

They waited until the last customer left, and then Doug drove to the station, leaving Sancho by the side of the dark road. He pulled up to one of the gas pumps and took his time filling the tank. Then he went inside and picked out some candy bars and a bag of chips.

"Not much traffic tonight," he said, pulling out his wallet at the checkout counter.

"Never much, this time of night. Don't know why we bother staying open." He was middle-aged and pot bellied, and he had "I hate this place" written all over his sagging face. He took Doug's fifty with a scowl and shambled over to a padlocked box in a back corner. As he was sorting through his ring of keys, Sancho came in the front door, made a beeline for the back of the store, and immediately stuffed something in his jacket pocket.

"What do you think you're doing back there, you damn punk?" He put Doug's fifty in his shirt pocket, moved back to the counter, and produced a nightstick from some shelf under it. Sancho tipped over a display rack of bagged snacks, and the clerk moved out from behind the counter and advanced on him.

Doug moved quickly behind the counter and, exactly as Sancho had predicted, found a semiautomatic pistol on the same shelf that had held the club. He stuck it in his waistband under his coat and went back to where he had been, while Sancho let the red-faced clerk chase him twice around the store. Then Sancho ran out the main door and off into the night, escaping easily. The clerk shouted at him through the door, but he did not chase him any farther.

"God damn kids today, I don't know. He look like a Mex to you?"

"I couldn't tell," said Doug.

"Damn right he was. Damn Mex come up here to rob decent folks."

"It's all the fault of those northern liberals, I say." Doug made no move to leave. *Rule number one of the short con: if you haven't been fingered, don't run.*

"Sure as hell is! You can't tell nobody that, though. People just keep voting for—"

"Um, about my change?"

"Yeah, all right. You got seventeen thirty-two coming, as I recall."

"Look, I probably distracted you when the kid came in. How about if you give me a ten, and we'll call it square?" *Rule number two: always let the pigeon think he's getting something he didn't earn.*

"Say, that's mighty decent of you, mister." Rather than going back to the register, he pulled a wad of bills out of his pocket, peeled off a ten, and gave it to him. Then he shook Doug's hand.

"It's nice to meet an honest white man, for a change."

"See you around," said Doug, gathering up his purchases.

"You drive careful, now."

He had all he could do to keep from laughing out loud as he walked back to the Taurus. He waved at the clerk and drove away at a sedate pace. A short way down the road, he found Sancho waiting for him. They pulled the tape off the license plates and went on their way.

"What'd I tell you, man?"

"When you're right, you're right, Paco. We just got ourselves a gun for seven dollars and thirty-two cents."

"Have a beer."

"You got beer, too?"

"Man, it wouldn't have been right if I didn't steal something."

"I guess not. Okay, then, give me one."

"Watch out when you open it. It's all shook up."

"How fearsomely apt."

"Huh?"

"Never mind. That's probably another middle-class white thing."

Ben pulled over and stopped on the shoulder next to a jumble of pipes that was a pumping station for a cross-country gas pipeline. One of the pipes had a white rag tied on it. He killed his lights and waited. After a few minutes, Max emerged from the dark field behind the apparatus and got in the pickup. Ben put his lights back on, and they drove away.

"You all right, Max?"

"Yeah."

"Who's the dead guy back at the Launch Pad's parking lot?"

"I don't know. He looked like a screw."

Ben smiled. "So you killed him?"

"Not me. He was reaching for something in his jacket, could have been either an ID or a gun, when somebody took him out from behind with a silenced sniper rifle. I beat it into the shadows and worked my way back to where I thought the shooter might be, but I didn't find anybody. Two blocks away, though, there was a van with more damned antennas stuck on it than a bug-eyed space alien. I kept going."

"Good move. What about the bomb?"

"No problem. I set that way before Mr. Clean showed up and got himself killed. I tripped it from a hiding spot in the bushes, just like we pllanned."

"That's good. I want our reluctant engineer to have no illusions about being able to go back to his old life. What did you call the dead guy?"

"Mr. Clean. He had short hair and no beard, and he wore a coat and tie, like he was going to the prom or something."

"That's about right. I thought he looked like FBI."

"That doesn't make any sense, Ben."

"No, it doesn't. Not the same people that have been dogging us lately at all. And even if they were, who goes around killing G-men? Unless . . ."

"I'm listening."

"Unless we have two different agencies looking for us, and they don't get along with each other."

"Don't get along? That's a hell of a lot of 'don't get along,' if you ask me. What do you mean?"

"I mean they're at war."

"How can they be at war? Aren't they all the same?"

"To us. But maybe it's a lot different to them. That's what it looks like, anyway. And if that isn't just funnier than a rubber crutch, I don't know what is. But we need to find out for sure. I think we need to plan a little something special for Albuquerque."

"Is that where we're headed?"

"No. First, we're going someplace that points straight away from Albuquerque. We need some money to pay our new engineer. It's time to rob another bank, Max."

"I like doing banks."

"I've noticed."

Doug drove through most of the night, then stopped for a long nap in a small grove on an abandoned-looking farm. The grove had several junked cars and some rusting appliances in it, and the Taurus did not stand out.

Late the next morning they set out again, staying on secondary roads and not speeding. At the next town where they bought gas, they got burgers and fries at a McDonald's, some cheap camping gear at a United Surplus store, and a bottle of gin and some more beer at a liquor store. Outside the store, they were approached by a ragged, shapeless bag lady with a thin tale of woe and an even thinner hand stretched out. Doug told her to fuck off, but Sancho gave her two dollars and a can of beer.

Back in the car, he said to Doug, "What'd you tell her that for, man? You got money."

"She's a loser."

"So?"

"You reach down to losers, you become a loser. It's like a contagious disease."

"That's bullshit, man. That's what they teach you in success school, I bet. You act like that, all you do is get people pissed at you."

"Maybe I don't care."

"Sure you do. Someday, you're gonna be the one on the ground with a boot in your face, and then you'll need all the help you can get."

"All the help? You think *she's* going to help me?"

"It's not like that. It's not like she's the one who's gonna help. It's more like you got to store up credits, see? Like racking up points to get into heaven."

"I don't believe in heaven."

"You didn't used to, but now you do, 'cause now you're little people. And little .people got to believe in helping each other and in the hope of getting paid back."

"Sounds to me like you're saying little people have to be stupid."

"No, man. Little people got to be good. Big people, it don't matter. T-Bone Fuckins, he can be just as big an asshole as he wants and it don't matter, 'cause if you got that kind of money, it's like having bad blue jeans, and—"

"Bad *what*?"

"You know, those little things in your blood that make you—"

"Oh, genes, you mean."

"What I said. You got big shot's jeans, there ain't no hope for you. But little people got to be good, because then they can overcome being little people, see?"

"And get rich like T-Bone Pickins?"

"No! Jesus, you are so stupid! I just about can't talk to you, sometimes."

Doug thought about the bag lady and rich people and poor ones. Did he really have all the attitudes he had just spouted, or was he just mimicking all the yuppies he had worked with for years? He wasn't that far from being a street person himself at the moment. And if it could happen to him, it could happen to anybody.

"Maybe you're right, Sancho."

"Hey, yeah? You getting religion now?"

"Something like that."

* * *

They stopped for the night by a secondary county road, well off the paved surface, on some kind of dirt access trail that led back through a field of burned-looking bean plants to a scraggly grove of aspens. They planned to sleep in the car, but they pitched a tent alongside it anyway. Sancho was back to talking.

"See, if you just sack out in the car, with no tent, then some cop driving by thinks you maybe had a heart attack or you're sleeping off some drunk driving, and he stops to have a look. Or best of all, to him, he thinks maybe you're screwing your girlfriend, and he comes over to watch. Whatever his reason is, talking to a cop is never any good. But if you got a tent, then he figures you're just some cheap bastard trying to get out of paying for a motel on your way to the promised land, and he don't bother you."

"The promised land?"

"California, usually. Maybe Texas. And for all he knows, you got a mean woman and some screaming little kids along, too. He won't waste his time with you, unless he's INS, but they mostly don't get out to places like this."

"Why not?"

"It's low payback, man. It's not on the way to anyplace that uses a lot of illegals."

"That's all pretty convoluted. Why didn't we just go to a cheap motel?"

"A middle-class white guy and a young Latino checking in together? *That* is guaranteed to bring somebody with a badge."

"Oh."

"Have some gin and another beer, man. You'll still be just as confused, but you won't think you are."

It got chilly after dark. They built a small fire, drank some more, and talked about how to kill the next several days until Doug needed to be in Albuquerque. After a while they saw a figure approaching across the fields. He carried a huge backpack on his stooped shoulders, and he wore a torn Army fatigue jacket over mechanic's coveralls. When he got into the light of the campfire, Doug thought he had the most weathered face he had ever seen.

"Hey," said the raggedy man.

"Hey, yourself," said Doug. "Want a drink?" He surprised himself, saying that. Not very long ago, he wouldn't have talked to this tramp at all. Maybe Sancho's rant had gotten to him at that.

"Thanks, but I give up on the hard stuff some years back. Guts couldn't take it no more."

"Just have a beer, then," said Sancho. "You look like God's wrath, two houses, and a woodshed fell on you. I'd say you need something."

"Yeah, sometimes I feel about like that, too. Okay, then, a beer. Much obliged." He dropped the pack on the ground behind him and sat heavily on it, facing the fire. Sancho went into the trunk of the Taurus and produced a cold beer and a partially depleted bag of potato chips, which he brought to the man.

"Oh, now that's the good stuff. You get a special place in heaven for that."

"What did you say?" said Doug, looking up sharply.

But the man's expression conveyed nothing, and he acted as if he hadn't heard the question. He stuffed a handful of chips into his mouth and crunched loudly. "I'm Burt," he said with his mouth full. "Burt Pollack."

"I'm Frank," said Doug, before Sancho could say anything, "and that's Paco. We're headed for Colorado."

"I didn't ask where you were headed. You want somebody to believe a lie, wait until they ask."

"Oh. Yeah, okay." So in his new role of going to ground, he had done one thing right by remembering to use an alias, but one thing wrong. That was not a good average.

"You don't use the roads?" said Sancho.

"No, I don't. To tell the truth, I don't have much use for roads or cars, either one. It's like I decided a long time ago to walk back to the nineteenth century."

"Oh, yeah? How's that working for you?"

"Not bad. I think I almost found it a couple times. It's got to be around here somewhere. And I keep running into people who say when I do find it, I should come back and tell them where it is."

"And will you?" said Doug.

"You crazy? I find that, I ain't *never* coming back."

When the gin ran out, they let the fire burn out as well. They offered to let Burt sleep in the tent, but nobody stayed awake to see if he did or not.

The next morning, he was gone. On the bare ground, in more or less the place he had been sitting, there was a cell phone that looked exactly like the one Doug had last seen on a bar top, soaked in beer.

As he looked at the device with astonishment and dread, it rang.

"Um, yes?"

Try to keep this one dry, said a metallic voice.

"Oh. Okay." He felt a chill leap into his stomach and spread outward. "Um. I'm on my way to—"

We know where you are on your way to.

"Good. Then you know I'm on the job."

There was no response. After a long pause, he added, "Who died back at the Launch Pad, by the way?"

Nobody.

"There was a body in the parking lot."

No, Mr. Wright, there was not.

"But I saw—"

You saw nothing.

The phone went dead. He dropped it down by his side, stared off into space, and said,"Oh shit," quite a few times.

"What's going on?" said Sancho. "Some bum leaves a phone, and then it talks to you? What kind of goofy shit is that?"

"My new employer is reaching out to me."

"That's the people you're trying to get away from?"

"No, I'm not," he said, a bit too loudly. Then he stuffed the phone in Sancho's pack, put it behind him, and whispered into Sancho's ear, "Maybe I am. I haven't decided yet. I'm not even sure if it's possible. I mean, they just found me, didn't they?"

Sancho whispered, too. "I think maybe it's time you told me some shit, man."

"I think maybe it is, at that. But first we have to go on a bug hunt."

So they did.

Chapter Eleven

Bank Shot

Ben decided to do an armored car job instead of a bank. He had files on several of each that were updated from time to time by sympathizers all over the country, and he generally made a choice based on payoff versus risk, plus the talent available to him at the moment. The talent pool of the day included a former Army explosives expert named Jake Wolf.

Wolf had grown up on a wheat farm in northern Kansas. His mother died when he was just starting school, and his father raised Jake and his younger sister, with great sorrow but no complaints. Unlike many of the farmers around him, Jake's father did not go bankrupt, but he could see it coming, as surely as the next bad winter. So one year, after the harvest, he sold out. Jake never knew how much money he got for the farm. Not enough to make up for the loss of his identity and way of life, but enough for him to retire to a modest house on the coast of South Carolina, where he sat in a lawn chair, stared at the ocean, and drank a quart of vodka every day. He never talked to his children again, possibly because he didn't feel he could face them anymore and possibly just because they were linked in his mind with all the other things he had lost.

With no marketable skills except farming and no land of his own, Jake joined the Army. After five years of unmemorable duty stations and assorted advanced training, he became a tech sergeant. He was sent to Iraq, where he spent two years dismantling homemade bombs, or IEDs, and the makeshift factories where they were made. He got to be quite good at it, which he attributed to the fact that he didn't care all that much if he got killed. He thought that getting blown to bits was infinitely preferable to merely getting crippled. So he had a positive work attitude and a lot of poise under pressure.

The one source of joy in his life was the email that he exchanged with his little sister, who worked as a waitress in a Kansas City diner and often told her customers about her big brother, the one-man bomb squad. She told a lot of customers, and one day when she found an especially interested and attractive one, she also told him about the decline and fall of her father.

A few days later, during a break at a forward operations base, Jake got an email from somebody calling himself Doc Savage. *How would you like to get back at the people who ruined your father and stuck you in the shittiest place on earth?* it said.

How? he replied.

Be all that you can be, Jake.

He considered several replies, including, "What the hell does that mean?" and "Are you completely crazy?" Instead, he simply wrote, *YES.*

Email me when you get back to the states. We'll find a place to talk.

Three months later, he mustered out and embarked on a new career.

The place Ben picked for the job was Cedar Rapids, Iowa. It had become famous in the spring of 2009 for enduring "the thousand-year flood," and it was exactly for this reason that he liked it. The hilly river city had a lot of underpasses and short tunnels, where radio transmission would be poor to nonexistent. It also had plenty of places where one could barricade off a street with a sign that said CLOSED DUE TO FLOODING and not have anybody question it.

Ben's plans tended to be highly detailed and totally rigid. He did not trust anyone, including himself, to improvise in the middle of the operation. If any tiniest thing did not fit the plan, he would abort the job and scatter the team without a moment's hesitation. In Cedar Rapids, everything fit.

The armored car was carrying cash from a regional office of Wells Fargo to several branch offices around town. It also carried a driver and two guards. After it turned a corner in an industrial area by the Red Cedar River, two men quickly pulled a pair of sawhorse barricades across the street behind it. One of them spoke quickly into a radio handset, and six blocks ahead, two more men did the same thing with another set of sawhorses. Then all four of them took up concealed sniper positions a hundred yards to either side. They used .50 caliber rifles with armor-piercing ammunition.

Three blocks past the first barricade, the vehicle went into a shadowy underpass below a railroad line. In the middle of the tunnel, it was slammed into by two of what the Army called EFPs, or explosively formed penetrators. They were the simplest of all anti-armor weapons to build, consisting of just a block of high explosive, usually C4, and a soft copper plate against one face of it. A hiker's backpack could hide one very nicely. When the explosive blew, the malleable copper assumed the shape of the shock wave itself, becoming a semi-molten projectile of terrible velocity. It wasn't accurate, but it was used at a range where it didn't have to be. The armor on an Army Humvee couldn't stop one and neither could the armor on a Wells Fargo bank truck. The two slugs blew through the side of the vehicle as if it were made of wet tissue, spraying the interior with blobs of hot copper that killed everybody inside.

A "stop stick," a chain of wickedly sharp spikes, across the street blew the front tires on the truck and made sure it came to a complete halt. But even before it stopped rolling, three men with ear protection and gas masks ran up to the disabled vehicle and sprayed machine-gun fire through the holes in its side, making sure everybody inside was dead. They also shot off the radio antenna. Their weapons were Russian-made AK-47s. Ben liked them. He usually made a point of buying American-made hardware, but he liked the idea that some simple-minded law enforcement people might need nothing more than a few spent shells to assume they were dealing with Arab terrorists.

The job required one more bomb blast, on the hinges, to get the back door open. Jake Wolf applied putty-like charges strung on a wire like Christmas lights. He detonated them with a motorcycle battery. It was now less than thirty seconds since the setting of the first barricades.

The beauty of the EFPs was that none of them set fire to any of the contents of the truck. Anything that didn't have molten copper on it was fine. Ben, Max, and Jake spent another thirty seconds unloading the obvious cash bags from the back. Then Ben checked in with his lookout-snipers on the radio. Hearing that there was no approaching traffic in either direction, he had his people take the rest of the cargo as well—courier pouches whose contents were mysteries. They threw it all into a small delivery van with a souped-up engine, radioed an all clear to the lookouts, and left on a street perpendicular to the one the truck had been taking. Half a mile later, they transferred everything to a different vehicle, an aging SUV, set fire to the van, and continued on their way.

The lookouts all left their posts in separate cars. They took their rifles, but not the sawhorse barricades. They kept their radios turned on, and they were prepared to use their cars as *kamikaze* vehicles to run interference for the SUV, if necessary. But they didn't have to. None of the robbers ever saw a policeman. They made their leisurely separate ways 120 miles west to a rest stop on Interstate 35, where they met in groups of two and three. Jake Wolf and the four lookouts got new instructions and went off in three different compass directions. Ben and Max, with the loot in a false bottom in the bed of Ben's pickup, headed south toward Las Vegas. They left the SUV at the rest stop.

Chapter Twelve

Feds

Agent Abby Webb had worked her way through college, and she had a bachelor's degree in economics and a master's in law enforcement. From mid-2008 onwards, she had spent her days chasing bank robbers from the Kansas City office of the FBI. For reasons nobody had ever explained, Kansas had a lot of bank robbers. Not that she was sent there because anybody thought she would be good at catching them. The job was her "reward" for two and a half years of hard work at the New York FBI office. She had built solid criminal cases against several very big, important bankers who had personally brought the country to the brink of bankruptcy and made themselves filthy rich in the process. She had the naïve notion that they had broken both federal and moral law and ought to go to prison.

Her supervisor was more politically sensitive. While he never mentioned the White House directly, he let it be known that her efforts were not appreciated in some very powerful quarters.

"There's a saying, Agent Webb: if you want to run with the big dogs, you better learn how to piss in high places."

"I probably don't care about running with the big dogs, sir."

"Oh, really? But you've definitely been pissing in high places, haven't you?"

"Maybe. I go where the case takes me, okay?"

"Not okay. You're pissing off the wrong people, and your conscience is not worth my job. Turn in all your files. Today. You're going to purgatory."

"And where is that, sir?"

"Kansas City."

"Kansas City, Kansas, or Kansas City, Missouri?"

"Kansas."

"Wow, somebody really is pissed, aren't they?"

"More than you can ever know."

"So what happens to my cases?"

"What cases?"

And for this, she thought, *I left a perfectly good career as a cocktail waitress.*

The other agents in the Kansas City office knew perfectly well that Agent Webb was an exile, and probably a toxic one at that. Nevertheless, they did not ostracize her. She was assigned to a partner named Frank Connelly. The two of them regularly practiced at the target range, ran laps at a gym, and stood ready to spring into action the moment John Dillinger blew into town. As if.

"You'll like this detail," he told her.

"Because of the nonstop action, right?"

"No. Because bank robbers are so stupid. They're really fun to catch."

"Except that there aren't any."

"Patience, ye of little faith. The times get bad, people rob banks. And the times are damn bad and getting worse."

But the first case she got involved robbers who were anything but stupid.

The job was done at night, when the bank was closed. It featured two diversions, both far away from the real target.

One was the explosion of an underground gasoline storage tank at a gas station, and the other was the explosion of a tank truck on the interstate, which created a traffic jam of epic proportions. The city's fleet of emergency vehicles and its 911 phone lines were both taxed to capacity.

At the bank, there were two explosions. The one that lit up the night was high up on the wall of the building, and it took out the bank's power and communications terminals completely. That generated an automatic alarm call, but it didn't say the bank was being robbed, merely that the system was down. The FBI wasn't notified right away.

The second explosion was inside the building, at the back wall of a basement vault. It blew a hole in the wall just big enough to walk through. It damaged some of the contents but did not set fire to anything. The robbers took everything that was loose and nothing that was under secondary lock. They were in and out in a very short time. Nobody saw them.

By the time Agents Webb and Connelly arrived on the scene, there was nothing to look at but a couple of smashed glass doors and a vault full of smoking debris.

"How do you suppose they knew where they could blow the hole without destroying the money?" said Webb.

"They could make an informed guess. This is a cookie-cutter building. Back when the chain was Great Plains Federal, they built hundreds of the things to the exact same plan, all over the country. They got better prices on the construction that way."

"So our guys could have looked at the permit plans at the Building Department in some completely different city and found out everything they needed to know."

"That they could, but we should still check here."

Webb looked again at the ragged hole. "Well, it wasn't a truck bomb," she said. "So what the hell was it, an RPG?"

"I don't know, but we'll find out. Explosives are good. They leave lots of fingerprints."

"Oh, really?"

"Sure. Chemical tests will tell us what the explosive was. And things like detonators and triggering devices are all highly controlled and traceable. They get smashed all to hell, but being at the center of the blast, getting pushed from all sides, they don't really go anywhere. The lab loves bombs."

But the lab didn't love these bombs, either from the bank or the gas station (nobody found any pieces of the bomb from the tank truck.) The explosive itself, though chemically very similar to C4, was almost certainly homemade. The detonators were harder to identify at first. The lab technicians were baffled by the glass and ceramic fragments they had found, which were quite unlike anything from any known type of device. Then they saw a fragment of a Bosch logo on one of the ceramic pieces. The detonator was an ordinary automotive spark plug, sealed to a small glass vial of ether fumes. And the triggering device was part of a radio control model airplane kit available from any hobby shop. None of the hardware required any ID to buy or generated any record of sale.

The bank estimated that it had lost a little over two hundred thousand dollars, mostly in bills that were not marked, though their serial numbers were recorded.

The agents waited for the robbers to do another job. They didn't. They checked with the Building Department in Kansas City and learned that construction plans were saved for eight years, but no record was kept of people who asked to look at them. They waited for the flagged bills to show up. Eventually, most of them surfaced at Las Vegas banks that regularly took large deposits from casinos.

The trail was worse than cold; it was totally dead.

As agent Connelly had predicted, there were more bank robberies over the months and years that followed, daylight holdups by people who were laughably easy to catch. But there was no repeat of the job with the homemade C4.

Then there was an armored car robbery in Iowa.

Sometimes the Bureau had to stretch the boundaries of the Hobbs Act a bit to make armored car robberies its purview, but in this case the local police asked for help and the agency was happy to give it. And a lab technician in Quantico recognized the explosive signature—a bomb triggered by a spark plug. Better still, he remembered where he had seen it before, and Agent Webb got a call from a regional supervisor, asking her if she wanted the case.

"That's a trick question, right, sir?"

Chapter Thirteen

Bugs

Doug stripped down to his shorts, and he and Sancho scrutinized every square inch of his body, looking for a scar where some electronic device might have been surgically implanted. Finding none, they turned to his clothes. They worked in silence. *Jesus,* he thought, *is there any point in this at all? The technology they have today, it could be nothing more than a button. And we are not going to cut apart every button I have.*

Then he pulled the stays out of the collar on his favorite Van Heusen semi-dress shirt. One of them was fatter than the other. A lot fatter, as well as less flexible. Was it possible? How on earth would they have known which shirt he would be wearing? Could they have bugged all of them? He tapped Sancho, who was busy inspecting his belt, on the shoulder and pointed to it. Sancho nodded but then made a gesture with his hands, indicating a wide space, which he then squeezed down.

He's right. Something that small would have to be very short range. There must be something bigger that acts as a relay. And they both immediately stared at his shoes. It would fit: a mike in the collar, where it could pick up his voice easily and relay it to a transmitter in the shoe.

He took his Swiss army knife and began to pry the heel off his shoe. When he got the back edge of one heel up about a quarter of an inch, he got a glimpse of a wire, and he immediately jammed it back where it was, giving Sancho a significant nod. Just to be safe, they also checked his wallet and belt, but they found nothing else unusual.

Doug finished dressing and they packed up the pieces of their camp, making empty small talk. Back on Interstate 40, they came to a multi-store outlet mall, not in any actual city.

"You know, Sancho, I've been thinking that when I get to Albuquerque, I ought to make an effort to blend in with the locals, you know?"

"Well, here's a good place to buy some new clothes, man."

"What a good idea." They winked at each other.

Doug bought cowboy boots, a denim jacket, two blue chambray work shirts and two khaki ones, some wrinkle-resistant chinos, and a straw cowboy hat. He changed into them in the dressing room of a Gap store, where he also bought some much-needed underwear and socks. He also bought a nylon backpack to put everything in. As he was stuffing his old clothes and shoes into a plastic shopping bag, he pulled the wad of money Ben Savitch had given him out of his old shirt pocket, looking at it for the first time.

The bankroll was fatter than it should have been because it had something else inside it: a matchbook. The front cover had a photo of a naked woman romping in the surf on some beach. Sancho looked over Doug's shoulder at it and gave it an approving nod. The back cover had a black and white cartoon of a biker with a Nazi helmet and some carnival lettering that said *DIRTY DICK'S BAR; The Shame of Omaha.*

"What you want to do with your old clothes?" said Sancho, loud enough so he was certain to be heard. They didn't know, of course, if they were really being listened to or merely tracked, but for now, they were assuming the worst.

"We'll just throw them in the trunk for now."

They looked around to be sure there was nobody else close to them in the parking lot. Then Doug jimmied open the trunk of a nearby car that was much too old to have a working alarm on it. He threw the bag of clothes inside and slammed the lid loudly. Then he and Sancho went back to the Taurus and drove away.

"Now we talk, man?" said Sancho.

"Now we talk."

"What's with the book of matches? You don't even smoke."

"No. And the guy who gave them to me knows that. I think it's a fallback meeting place."

"Oh, one of *them*. You gonna tell me what kind of weird shit you're into or not?"

"I work for some very bad people, okay? I don't want to work for them, but they'll cut off my thumbs if I try to quit."

"That's not so good."

"That's just a guess. It could be worse. Whatever they do, it'll hurt."

"So what do they want you to do?"

"I spy on a bunch of crazy farmers who want to blow things up. I have to meet them again in Albuquerque."

"You got to kill anybody?"

"No."

"And nobody's trying to kill you?"

"Not yet."

"Does anybody pay you for all this spying stuff?"

"Actually, the bad guys and the nut cases both pay me. Or they will, anyway. The crazy farmers have promised me some very big money."

"That doesn't sound so bad, man. You ought to be able to get through all that in a walk. But you should have thrown your old clothes in a trash can."

"Why?"

"Because then you could pretend you were just dumping them and you didn't know anything about the bug. But you put them in somebody else's trunk, your number one bad guys are gonna figure out you're trying to give them the slip."

"Oh, shit. You're right."

"You maybe can't never go back to them, man."

"No." He thought of the writing on the cellar wall, back when he had first been grabbed, and the phrase about his employers choosing the time of his death. "Jesus Christ, what have I done?"

"Put your neck in a noose, I think. But it ain't tight yet, maybe. You gonna lose the phone, too?"

"I don't think so. I might still want to talk to these people. It's probably time to get rid of this car, though. That phony bum could have put any damn thing in it, and we'd never find it."

"And then what do we do?"

"We go to Albuquerque."

"Still? You crazy loco, man? Why?"

"Because that's where the man with the big, big money will be."

But it wasn't just about the money. It was about pride and professionalism. Somebody actually wanted his skill and knowledge, and that hadn't happened for a long, long time. If he was honest with himself, it hadn't really happened at TechnoDyne at all, ever. And even the otherwise enthusiastic Mr. Black assumed that as an engineer, he was a shallow fake. With some surprise, he found himself thinking about a time, way back in his childhood, when he had built rubber band-powered model airplanes that could stay airborne for five minutes and clockwork tanks that fired bottle rockets in timed sequence. He was just a little kid, but he was a real engineer, in every way that mattered. How had he lost that? How could he have allowed people to take it away? And how wonderful would it be if he could get it back?

Now there was the anarchist farmer with a million dollars. And a project. He suddenly realized that he wanted the project much more than he wanted the money. One last *real* engineering project before he retired forever. And he would retire from the field on his own schedule, not that of some impersonal human resources manager. It would be magic.

The dream of going back to southern California and a life of conspicuous consumption was gone now. Maybe it hadn't really been his dream in the first place, just one that he had somehow been issued. Maybe he had picked it up off the street, as a lot of other people did, a dream with no substance. Whatever the case, it had died when he double-crossed the agency of Mr. Black. Now he had to think in terms of fleeing to some third world country where he could disappear and assume the identity of an American expatriate with a shady past and enough money to buy anonymity. He wondered if he knew how to do that. But first, there would be the project. And that would be enough.

At some point, though, he would have to figure out a way to give Mr. Black the location of the missile silo without actually giving up himself. That could be more than a bit tricky. But after all, it was unthinkable that he could actually let Ben and his friends set off an A-bomb.

Chapter Fourteen

Money Man

Harry Scully lived in a poor neighborhood in Las Vegas. He paid taxes on thirty thousand dollars a year and listed his profession as that of a professional gambler. He lived very simply. He felt that was what he deserved. A typical dinner for him was canned pork and beans on dry toast. Sometimes he would add a scrambled egg. A huge celebratory feast was takeout Chinese. His car was an eighteen-year-old Honda that had not had new tires in forty thousand miles. His good clothes came from J.C. Penney's. He was a dedicated man, and he allowed nothing to distract him.

When he had work to do, he would walk to a casino with an attaché case full of money, usually no more than twenty or thirty thousand dollars. He would convert it all into chips, get himself a beer, and proceed to gamble. Sometimes he bet at the craps tables, but he was never the shooter. He made very conservative side bets and didn't win or lose very much. Sooner or later, he always moved to the blackjack tables, where he made larger bets. He had taught himself to count cards, a practice which all the casinos now banned, without being obvious about it. He had learned it through long, hard drills, which he still did at his home every night. He took his time with the game, never getting greedy, never drawing attention to himself. When he was ahead by a few thousand dollars, he would make a couple of rather big bets and would deliberately lose them. Then he would gulp the rest of his beer in apparent dismay, say something like, "Guess my good luck is all done for today," and leave the table. He would go back to the teller, cash in all his chips, and exit the building with his attaché case now full of money that had been washed as clean as the driven snow.

He would walk back home with the money, and at times when he had a lot of funds to launder, he would immediately repeat the process at another casino. Sometimes he visited six or seven of them a day, working until late at night.

Years earlier, Harry had been an assistant manager at a bank in Sioux Falls, South Dakota. He had been hired there as a teller, straight out of the junior college where he earned an associate degree in business, and he had worked his way up. He had been involved, in one way or another, in many foreclosures on farm and home loans, and the weight of them was a millstone around his heart.

Then he had an epiphany or a nervous breakdown, depending on who was telling the story. He spent most of one week obliterating both paper and electronic records of hundreds of mortgages and sending letters to the debtors. The letters said, "We have had some problems with the records of your loan. Please do not make any more payments until we contact you again." He did not keep copies of the letters. When he was done, he took all of them to the post office, mailed them, and then attempted to kill himself by stepping in front of a speeding semi truck on a main highway.

Fortunately or unfortunately, he was not very athletic or quick, and the freeway traffic kept managing to miss him. But the police didn't. They arrested him and after a short interrogation sent him to the psych ward of a large hospital. A local TV reporter got wind of his story and did a five-minute piece on him on the evening news. It was well done, and it got picked up and aired all over the Midwest and Great Plains.

Ben Savitch came to see him shortly after that. And he gave Harry Scully what the doctors couldn't: a reason to live.

After the Cedar Rapids job, Ben met Scully at a truck stop on the edge of Las Vegas and gave him a large suitcase.

"Three or four of the regulars will be stopping by in the next day or two, looking for some walking around money. Give them five grand apiece."

"No problem. I have more than that in inventory. What about the rest?"

"In a few weeks, a guy you don't know will come looking for one and a half mil."

"How do I recognize him?"

"He'll have a matchbook like this one."

Scully looked at the naked woman and whistled through his teeth. Then he pocketed the matches and walked away with the suitcase.

Chapter Fifteen

Ghosts of IEDs Past

The preliminary FBI report and file on the Cedar Rapids job, handed over to Agents Webb and Connelly, leaned heavily toward the theory of a funding raid by some secret Muslim terrorist group, if only because of the EFP and the empty AK-47 shells.

"I think whoever wrote this report just wanted to suck up to Homeland Security," said Webb, over coffee and pastry at a sidewalk café in the gentrified Power and Light District. She took a bite of her bagel and made a face.

"You don't buy it?" said Connelly.

"This bagel or the report?"

"The report. I already told you, you should have gotten the apple fritter. Even in Kansas, they know how to do them. A bagel? No way."

"No, I don't buy the report."

"You're a troublemaker, you know that?"

"That has been pointed out to me, yes. If you're afraid of the turbulence, bail out."

"Oh, no. I'm going to stick around and watch you crash. So what don't you like?"

"It's too easy, too pat." She reached across the tiny table and helped herself to a piece of his frosted cake doughnut. "It's like our bad guys left a note that says, 'Round up the usual suspects. Shake the palm tree. Arrest a raghead. You'll like it.' And we bought it."

"But who does that?" he said. "Regular bank robbers don't bother to leave false trails, because they don't figure they're ever going to get caught anyway. I told you that. They're stupid."

"Except when they're not, Frank. No, these guys are special. And they only do a job every three years or so."

"That we know of. So?"

"That we know of, yes. But even if there are a few jobs that we haven't seen, we're talking about bank robbers who are not greedy. What kind of an oxymoron is that?" She swallowed the piece of pastry and began reaching for another. "You know what I think?"

"You put your hand on my doughnut again and I promise you, it won't work when you pull it back."

"Speaking of greedy." But she withdrew the hand. "Okay, try this: our robbers are not greedy because they don't want the money for themselves. They want it for some special project or cause."

"Like what?"

"I don't know. Something that would set off even more alarms than a bank robbery."

"That sounds like a major terrorist attack."

"It does, doesn't it? And it also fits with the fact that these guys are totally ruthless. With the bank, there were no people around to get hurt, but the robbers weren't worried about who got wasted in their diversionary explosions. And with the armored car, they intended to kill the crew, right from the get-go. No way the script would have worked with any other strategy. They flatly don't care about having a murder rap on their heads. "

"So we're back to agreeing with the prelim report. Why do you have to complicate everything?"

"Because it dances to their tune. It points to the wrong groups, the groups the robbers want us to target. What we should be looking for is somebody who wants to do a big-time bad act, but in the meantime doesn't even want us to know they exist. And they don't wear turbans or read the Koran."

"And that would be . . . ?"

"How the hell do I know? Homegrown terrorists? Survivalists? Right-wing nutcakes?"

He sighed. "You know, it doesn't seem so very long ago that there weren't any American-born terrorists."

"Yeah, and presidents didn't tell the FBI not to arrest bad guys. It was called the golden age, only we didn't know it at the time. Welcome to the brave new world. The Bureau must have some kind of branch or task force that keeps tabs on these guys, yes?"

"'These guys'? You mean homies who like to kill indiscriminately?"

"Something like that, yeah."

"I assume we do. Maybe several task forces. And if they aren't too solidly under the thumb of the Homeland boys, they might even talk to us."

"See if you can get us a list of 'persons of interest,' okay?"

"That could be a hell of a list."

"Hit it with some sorting categories right off the bat. People with ties to Cedar Rapids, Kansas City, or anyplace in between. Also people who are either active military or ex-military."

"Now you figure the Marines robbed the armored car?"

"No, but I think it could be somebody who learned about homemade bombs from dismantling them in Iraq. I'll contact the Army and Marines and see if I can get a list of people who are knowledgeable about EFPs."

"Gee, Agent Webb, that almost sounds like a plan."

"Don't you just love it? Can I have the rest of your doughnut now?"

"It's not *that* much of a plan."

As far as the Army was concerned, it was considerably less of a plan than Webb and Connelly thought. An enlisted "senior clerk" in the Pentagon not too carefully explained to Webb that he couldn't do a blanket query of personnel files by occupational specialty. Webb suspected that what he really meant was that he just didn't want to go to the trouble.

"Look," she said, "what would you do if you wanted somebody to head up a new bomb squad for a task force in Katmandu, ASAP?"

"We'd probably send around a memo asking for volunteers."

"You've got to be shitting me, Specialist."

"Would I do that to a *real agent* of the big, bad FBI?"

"If I didn't think so before, I do now. Look, if I gave you the name of a soldier, you could look up what kind of training and duty postings he had, couldn't you?"

"Yes, ma'am."

"Even if he was no longer on active duty?"

"Absolutely."

"Okay, then. Just plug in the names of everybody who was active or recently inactive in the last half of 2012 and the first quarter of 2013 and make me a list of everybody who comes up as knowing about explosives."

"Now who's got to be shitting? That could take days."

"Well, there are worse ways to spend one's days, aren't there? Like going on patrol in Afghanistan?"

"You can't make that happen."

"Try me. I'm thinking your replacement is liable to be a lot more helpful."

"Where do you want me to send that list again?"

She gave him a Bureau email address that was not connected to the other office communication network, as a protection against viruses in attachments. She was sure her clerk would attach one if he knew how, though she seriously doubted that he was that smart.

Agent Connelly made out somewhat better. A group working out of the San Francisco office of the FBI, with the impressive title of the Director's Task Force on Domestic Anarchy, had just received increased funding and personnel after one of their agents was murdered in the line of duty in the parking lot of a bar in Long Beach. They were eager to get some payback in the works, and they quickly put together a list of names for Connelly, including people with ties to Iowa, Kansas, and Missouri. It also included persons of no fixed address, plus associates and associates *of* associates. It was, as Connelly had predicted, a hell of a list. But if he and Webb could match anybody on it to something else, the task force was dying to know about it. The agent Connelly talked to was named Basten.

"You get any kind of an operation going from this list, we'd like to be in on it."

"I don't think I have any problem with promising you that, Agent Basten. You appear to have better funding and more resources than we do. It could only help, having you on board for the party. I assume I can expect the same courtesy from you?"

"You have my word. Just remember, though, some of these 'interesting' people are also damn dangerous."

"You think somebody on this list took out your man in Long Beach?"

"Somebody. The most likely candidate is a guy named Ben Savitch. We think he's a real stone killer, but we don't have anything resembling a case yet. Just be careful, okay?"

"Got it."

* * *

Three days later, they got the list of names from the Army, and they immediately set out to do a cross match. An "associate" of the person of interest named Ben Savitch, one Jake Wolf, appeared on both lists, and he had mustered out of the Army a month before the Kansas City bank job with the first spark plug detonator. Unfortunately, neither man had any known, fixed address. But Jake Wolf had a sister who did. Connelly and Webb immediately went to talk to her.

A thousand miles to the south and west, Ben Savitch stopped a Jeep Cherokee next to a crooked tree by a dry arroyo in the middle of the New Mexico desert, twenty-five miles from any road.

"From here, we walk," he said. He, Jake Wolf, and Max got out, and Ben locked the Jeep. They started walking down the creek bed.

"Pace yourself," said Ben. "It'll take a while."

"I'm sure it'll be worth it," said Jake. "God, I wish I could tell my sister about this. I mean, Jesus, a real nuke."

"You see your sister a lot, do you?"

"Every chance I get. She's the only person I really care about anymore."

"What do you tell her you do for a living?"

"Oh, I just kind of avoid that topic. If she really pushes me, I tell her I work for the government, doing something very hush-hush."

"But important?"

"Yeah, I guess I tell her it's important, maybe." He grinned. "I mean, there's nothing wrong with telling her that."

"Not a thing, Jake, not a thing."

"She likes to be proud of me."

"I'm sure she does." He patted Jake on the shoulder with his left hand. With his right one, he pulled a .22 semiautomatic pistol out of his pocket and shot him in the head, twice. Jake still had the smile on his face when he dropped to the ground, from thinking about his sister.

Max said nothing as they walked back to the Jeep. Ben had always had an instinct for potential security risks, and Max had no reason to doubt his judgment now.

Chapter Sixteen

Going to Ground

Doug and Sancho decided that they had enough money to go slightly more legit, as well as disappear. On the advice of a gas station clerk, they left the main highway and went thirty miles off into the arid New Mexico countryside to a place that could have been a failed ranch, a chop shop, a coyote base of operations, a very small village, or all of the above. Several dilapidated buildings were arrayed around a gravel yard that was littered with rusting old cars, chicken feathers, and beer cans, and several young and old men milled about aimlessly. In a far corner of the complex, some children played in a battered single-engine airplane that only had one bent wing and no tail. Doug stopped in the middle of the yard, and he and Sancho got out.

"Leave the doors open and the engine running," said Sancho.

They walked up to a big man with a pockmarked face and a thick moustache, who was sitting on a folding chair and whittling a stick with a knife that looked like it had been made for a much more serious purpose.

"*Buenos días,*" said Doug.

"Yeah." It sounded distinctly like a threat. "*Buenos días,* yourself." He stopped whittling and held the knife up in front of him, as if he were visually measuring it against the size of Doug's throat. "You got some kind of business here, *hombre*?"

Sancho said something to him in Spanish, nodding his head toward Doug, and the man's manner softened somewhat.

"We need a car," said Sancho.

"What do you call that thing you drove up in, a lawn mower?"

"It's not so good, man. You can't take it to church, see?"

"Oh, you want to go to *church*." He pointed to an ancient Chevrolet Suburban with more rust than paint. "That thing runs mostly okay. And you can take it to church and to grandma's afterwards, too."

"What does that mean?" said Doug under his breath.

"It means he's got good plates and papers to go with them. The insurance is probably fake, but at least he's got a card."

"I trade you even up for fifteen hundred, US," said Mr. Moustache.

"*Bandito*!" said Sancho. "That thing ain't got enough rubber on it to make one good tire, the headlights are all sand blasted, and it droops on one corner. We give you three hundred and half a case of beer."

"I think maybe you should get in your not-so-good Ford and get out of here. But you leave the case of beer, anyway."

"Half a case."

"I knew right away I wasn't going to like you."

The conversation shifted back to Spanish, with lots of gesturing, some spitting, and some kicking of dust. Finally, Sancho shook his head and walked away. After half a dozen steps, the man called him back. This time, they talked more slowly, and without the gestures. Finally, they shook hands.

"We just bought a car for seven hundred bucks, man. Pay this guy." Very quietly, he added, "And *don't* show him how much more you got on you."

Doug turned his back for a moment while he peeled off seven hundred-dollar bills from the roll Ben Savitch had given him. He turned back and handed them over to the man, who did not offer to shake his hand. Then they transferred their gear to their new vehicle and got in. It took about thirty seconds for the Chevrolet to start, first making a lot of pathetic noises as its feeble battery barely turned it over.

"Hey," said the seller, looking over the Ford Taurus, "this thing ain't got no keys."

"Somehow, I think you'll figure something out," said Doug, and he threw some gravel with his new, bald tires and headed back toward civilization.

"Now we go to Alba-kwer-kwee and get us some jobs," said Sancho.

"We do what?"

"You want to hide in plain sight until it's time to meet your man, then you want to look like a local. Locals got jobs, man. Gives them a reason to be there."

"I've got to tell you, Sancho, you never say anything predictable."

"I guess that's good, huh?"

"I guess. What kind of jobs?"

"Where do you meet your man?"

"Old Town, at the outdoor market."

"Then that's where we look for work. Probably nobody will trust a stranger to handle money, so selling stuff is out. But there ought to be some cafés around there that need kitchen help. What you got that pained look for?"

"I can't cook."

"I think maybe you just don't like the idea of manual labor. It's okay. It don't hurt."

"I'll admit I've never earned my living that way. Pissed my old man off something fierce. He was a blue-collar snob, worked for fifty years on the assembly line at GM. The only time he ever took a vacation was after his second heart attack."

"His *second* one?"

"Yup. With the first one, he didn't bother. Finished his shift and then drove himself to the hospital."

"I think your old man was one tough *hombre.*"

"He was an asshole, is what he was. Never approved of what I did for a living."

"Okay, he was an asshole. But hard work didn't make him that way. I told you, it don't hurt. It makes you . . . um, sort of generous, like."

"Are you serious?"

"Sure, man. People who work hard and don't have nothing appreciate other people who work hard and got just as much nothing. It makes them kind. It's sort of like the little—"

"You told me about little people already, okay?"

"Maybe I didn't tell you loud enough."

"We'll try things your way, all right? Settle for that."

"Hokay."

Doug would not have believed, a short time earlier, that he would actually wind up missing the Taurus, but the Suburban made him miss it instantly and bitterly. The steering wheel vibrated, the body rattled, the brakes were soft, and the vehicle managed to leave a cloud of dust in its wake, even on hard pavement. He decided that was really just dirty little particles of disintegrating engine being spit out the tailpipe. But at least it had a tailpipe. It also had air conditioning, and sometimes it worked. Sancho thought it was great.

"Man, at seven hundred dollars, we stole this thing, you know?"

"No, Sancho. We stole the Taurus. This thing, we practically traded our first born child for."

"You got to learn to loosen up your standards sometimes. You should have seen the thing I came to this country in."

"It doesn't bear thinking about."

Chapter Seventeen

Persons of Interest

Jake Wolf's sister, Ellen, worked at a small but neat-looking diner on the fringe of downtown Kansas City, and she was as guileless as anybody agents Webb and Connelly had ever encountered. They took a table by a window and ordered sandwiches and coffee. They got a different waitress first, but she wasn't miffed when they asked if they could talk to Ms. Wolf.

"Lots of people ask for her; she's always so nice."

"We just wanted to—"

"That's okay, really. We all share the tips, so it works out the same. I'll tell her."

When Ellen Wolf came with their orders, they let her look at their ID cards, not too obtrusively, and asked if she had a brother named Jake.

"Oh, wow, do you guys work with Jakey? That is just so neat!"

"Are you free to talk about him a bit, Ms. Wolf?" said Agent Webb.

"Oh, sure. Just a second, okay?" She went back to the pass window from the kitchen and called to somebody named Lou that she was going on her break. Then she poured another cup of coffee, brought it back to the table by the window, and sat down. The agents introduced themselves and she eagerly shook both their hands.

"My brother mostly never gets to talk about what he does, so this is really a treat for me."

"Does he tell you he works for the FBI?" Webb again.

"No, he never says just which agency he works for, but I sort of figured it out, you know?" To Webb, she said, "What's it like being a, you know, lady agent? Is that what they call it? Is it a good job? Your folks must really be proud of you."

"It has its days, yes."

"When did you last talk to your brother, Ms. Wolf?"

"You don't have to be going with the 'Ms. Wolf' thing all the time. You can call me Ellen. Or Ellie."

"Your brother, Ellie?"

"Let me think. Three, maybe four weeks ago. He's out of town a lot, you know. He's always going on some big operation."

"That's what he calls it, an operation?"

"I think so. I mean, that's what they're called, aren't they?"

"Sure. Does he ever call you when he's on these operations?"

"No, he can't, usually."

"Email?"

She shook her head. "I don't have email. I used to, but my computer's broke and I can't afford a new one."

The agents looked at each other. Agent Webb produced a business card and handed it to the young woman.

"The next time you see Jake, or the next time he calls you, would you please give me a call? Any time of the day or night."

"Okey dokey. There isn't anything wrong, is there?"

"We think your brother may be being followed by some bad people. We need to find out where he is as soon as we can, so we can deal with them. And we need you not to tell him about us."

"But why would he—"

"He's not so likely to blow his cover if he doesn't know we're helping him out," said Webb. "Can you do that? Can you keep it a secret from him?"

"Well, sure. I mean, I'd do anything to help Jakey." She stood up and picked up her coffee cup.

"You're leaving? We haven't offended you, have we?"

"Oh, no. It's just, my break is only fifteen minutes, and if I want to use the bathroom and go have a smoke, I have to go now. You want some more coffee?"

After she left, Connelly looked over at Webb and said, "What do you think?"

"I'll tell you what I don't think. I don't think she's a terrorist. If that was an act, it was awfully good."

"Best I've ever seen," he said, nodding. "And we are awfully screwed."

"That, too."

Later that day, their luck changed. Connelly called Agent Frank Basten in San Francisco to tell him about the link they had made with Jake Wolf's name. "The bad news," he said, "is that he's not in town and we have no clue where to look for him. He has a sister here. We're hoping that sooner or later, he's going to come back to see her. We really don't have the manpower to put a watch on her, though. And even under the new proactive assessment rules, we probably can't get a phone tap."

"Your timing is uncanny, you know that?"

"How so?"

"I had an anonymous phone call earlier today telling me that Jake Wolf is going to be in Albuquerque a week from next Wednesday to meet with some guy named Douglas Wright, which is a new name for us."

"And you were just about to tell me, right?" He flipped out his pocket notebook and began to write.

"Hey, I didn't know yet that you'd made a hit on Wolf's name, okay? I don't tell you about *every* call I get."

"Fair enough, I guess. How did this anonymous caller know to talk to you?"

"He claimed he was calling every main office of the Agency, looking for a group that investigates rebel farmers."

"Rebel farmers?"

"His term."

"So you told him you thought he meant anarchists?"

"Hell no. You think I'm stupid? I told him I didn't know of any such group, but if he would give me his information, I would ask around and pass it on."

"Cute. Also risky."

"Too true. I could definitely have lost him there, but he stayed with me."

"Trace?"

"No trace. Throw-away cell phone."

"Shit. And had he really called any other FBI offices?"

"As far as we can tell, no. He knew he wanted to talk to me all along."

"Ah *hah*. You think he told you the truth?"

"Only one way to find out."

"Are we invited?"

"It wouldn't be a party without you. Give me your cell phone number, and I'll call you as soon as we have a command post set up at the site."

"Give me yours, just in case you forget."

"Your lack of faith is shocking."

"Darth Vader said that, I think." They traded phone numbers, and he hung up. Then he called Webb on the interoffice phone.

"Abby, my dear, one of us must live right. You won't believe the call I just had."

Chapter Eighteen

All Roads Lead to Albuquerque

Doug and Sancho pulled into Albuquerque in the late morning, nine days and a few hours before the meeting with the anarchists. Later that day, they found jobs at a place called the *Restaurante Del Camino Real,* though the street it was on was named no such thing. It was on one of the many short, narrow side streets that were arrayed around the large, central, open-air market that formed the center of Albuquerque's Old Town. It was a small café, with seating for thirty people inside and rough wood picnic tables for twenty more on the sidewalk in front. The entry door looked out on the back of an adobe church that was flanked on either side by enclosed shops selling phony Kachina dolls, silver and turquoise jewelry, tooled leather goods, and other tourist baubles. The scullery in the back of the building had a small window that looked out across an alley and onto a highway, where a furniture store on the far side of the road displayed a homemade sign that proclaimed:

GOD BLESS AMERICA
SPEND MONEY

The owner of the café was a short, humorless man named Carlos. Sancho said he looked more like a real Spaniard than a Chicano, which was probably why he looked so mad all the time and also why he had no shoulders to speak of. Doug shrugged and said he would take his word for it. Carlos said that since there were two of them, he could only afford to pay them five dollars an hour and they should be damn glad to get it. These were tough times, after all. He paid in cash, once a week, and he didn't ask for Social Security numbers. They could also get paid every day, but then he would deduct ten percent "for the extra consideration." Doug instantly hated the man. Sancho didn't seem to care about him one way or the other.

Doug was amazed at how quickly they settled into the new routine. He couldn't imagine who had done all the work before he and Sancho came along, but there seemed to be no extra staff afterwards. The minutes were a hundred seconds long, but the day flew by.

The house specialty was a Navajo fry bread taco. The owner himself made the filling, and nobody else was allowed to see what he put into it. The pantry shelves were full of a mind-boggling array of spices and condiments, most of which were just there to mislead any spies who happened by. It was Doug's job to make the fry bread, which he mixed in a huge stainless steel bowl four or five times a day and kneaded by hand. He wasn't supposed to call it kneading, though, because "kneading makes it tough." It had no yeast in the batter, only baking powder, and it did not need to rise for any set amount of time. Whenever he had an order, he would tear off a handful of the rubbery dough, pat it into the rough shape of a bun, and throw it into a deep skillet with a thick layer of hot oil in it. Carlos told him the bun should be the same size as one of the diner's saucers, but he didn't say how thick it should be. The thickness Doug chose must have been all right, because it was one of the few things he didn't get criticized for. It took him several painful burns to learn how to drop the bread into the pan without splattering hot oil on himself, but he finally got the hang of it. If he put the edge closest to him into the pan first, the splatters would all go away from him. At one of their breaks, sitting on some vegetable crates and drinking cold soda pop behind the building, Sancho said, "You wanna know the first rule of working in a restaurant, man? It's that no dish you're working on and no manager that's bitching at you to hurry up is worth getting yourself hurt or burned over. Okay?"

"Now's a good time to be telling me that."

"Hey, you ain't even started around the knives yet."

"I can hardly wait."

Besides frying the bread and assembling the tacos, Doug was also the grill man, frying eggs in the morning and burgers all day, and it cost him most of his first day's wages to replace all the items he cooked wrong.

"So I'm the *sous chef*?" he had said to Carlos.

"The '*soo* chef'? What kind of hoity-toity joint you think this is? You're the goddamn fry cook, is what you are. When you ain't doing that, you help your buddy over there bus dishes and wipe tables, and you both get your asses here at six sharp, every damn day, and clean veggies and wrap the silverware in napkins. You get paid for eight hours, but you stay until all the cleanup is done at the end of the day, too. We close the kitchen at two."

Sancho bussed dishes, collected food scraps for the big disposal in the scullery, and ran the café's aging dishwasher, which probably leaked more hot water and steam than it used on the dishes. Only the dining room was air conditioned, but he didn't seem to mind the heat in the workrooms, and Doug noticed that he often hummed a tune as he worked.

The kitchen had a wall separating it from the dining room, but the pass window was big enough to give an almost unrestricted view of the customers. Sometimes, if he wasn't too busy to look up, Doug would watch as a waitress carried a dish he had made over to a diner who then took a big bite and sometimes either smiled or nodded pleasantly. And sometimes he found himself humming a little tune, too. Maybe Sancho's talk about hard work had been partly right, at that. *You make things with your hands and then you watch people enjoy them,* he said to himself. *How bad could that be?* At the end of the day, his shoulders and back felt as if they had been hit by a ten-ton truck, but somehow that seemed okay, too, almost like a badge of accomplishment.

Doug and Sancho continued living in their vehicle, though they would park it someplace different every night. Sancho said that if their camp started looking really settled, some kind of authority would pounce on them and make them get a room somewhere with indoor plumbing and rent. And that was one of the better things that could happen. They could also get run out of town altogether or thrown in jail. They found a couple of truck stops that still catered to over-the-road truckers who didn't have small homes on their rigs. There, they could buy cheap, hearty food and a hot shower and even a sauna for a small fee. Sometimes they used the shower to wash out one of their few changes of clothes. It was all a bit ragged-edge, but it worked.

As they got closer to the time of the meeting with the anarchists, they thought less about finding ways to cope with the needs of daily life. After the meeting, they didn't know where they would be, but they were pretty sure they would be gone. Doug wondered if he would wind up splitting up with Sancho. A part of him didn't want to. To his own surprise, he had come to regard the young man as a friend. To his even greater surprise, he found himself occasionally imagining the two of them staying where they were and working at the *restaurante* for a long time. And maybe that cute little Latina waitress really did smile at him when his back was turned. And maybe, just maybe—the owner hollered at him for daydreaming again, and he sighed and dropped another lump of dough into the hot oil.

* * *

Most of the cafe's customers were tourists, so Saturday and Sunday were its busiest days. For the hired help, the end of the day Sunday was payday. To give himself and the staff a bit of rest, Carlos closed the place on Mondays. He usually spent the day drinking beer in the darkened dining room. He didn't care how anybody else spent it. Sancho persuaded Doug they should do something that tourists do, take in some local sights.

"I thought we were going to fit in by working."

"Well, we don't got any work today, man. We got to fit in somehow else."

"So what are you proposing?"

"About fifty miles west of town, there's a pueblo city on top of a real high mesa. I heard some of the customers talking about it. They called it Acoma, the Sky City."

"And why do we want to go there?"

"'Cause it's a neat place, okay? And all work and no play makes Juan a dull boy, and if we spend the day drinking or shooting pool, we're gonna get in a shitload of trouble. Man, I got to explain *everything* to you?"

"So it seems. You think the Suburban has got another hundred miles left in it?"

"Sometimes you just got to live dangerous."

Chapter Nineteen

The Road to Sky City

Agents Webb and Connelly got to Albuquerque two days before the expected meeting of their persons of interest. The mobile command post was already set up. After the disaster in Long Beach, the agents from the San Francisco task force were cautious to the brink of paranoia. The next time they met an enemy in the field, they wanted to have the high ground, if only figuratively, and plenty of firepower. So for the Albuquerque operation, they had brought six agents other than Webb and Connelly and had set up a command and surveillance post several days in advance. It was in a ten-year-old Dodge step-van with blackout glass on the cab. It was painted with the logo of a TV station from Santa Fe, which they hoped would excuse all the antennae and parabolic dishes on it. They also threw a lot of dust on it, added a few dents, and gave it a flat tire, in the hope of explaining why the vehicle never moved or seemed to be active in any way. They wanted it to look one short tow job away from the junkyard.

Inside, they had all the best electronic communications and surveillance gadgets the Bureau had to offer. Besides being tied into their own headquarters, they had direct links to city and state police, sheriffs, and even the National Guard. They had monitors set up to watch not only local security cameras, but even the NMDOT traffic cams on the highways. And they had photos of Jake Wolf, courtesy of the US Army, and of

Doug Wright, courtesy of the Department of Defense. So far, though, all they knew about Wright was that he used to work for TechnoDyne Systems, which was how he had come to be photographed and fingerprinted, and that he had originally been hired to work on antiballistic missile systems. Being vetted for the job was how he had come to be in the FBI database in the first place. But what he did exactly, nobody knew, nor why he would now be associating himself with a possible bomb builder. As far as they could tell, he hadn't had a regular job for months.

By pure chance, Doug's photo was lying on the work counter in the van when the FBI technician was showing off his new video links to Webb and Connelly. Agent Basten was looking over his shoulder like a proud mother.

"Jesus Christ, that's him!" said Basten.

"Where? Who?" said the technician.

"The guy Wright. Anyway, I think it was him. He just came on that camera, driving a beat-up SUV of some kind." He pointed at one of the many monitors. "Can you replay it?"

"For the whole past day, if you like. And it keeps recording while we do, too."

The technician backed the footage up a few minutes, and soon they saw Doug driving into the camera again. They froze the image, enlarged the license plate, and made a print of it. Then they watched the vehicle drive off the screen a few more times.

"I would say you're right," said another agent. "Where is that?"

"Historic Route 66, westbound," said the technician. "It links up with I-40 a couple miles west of there."

"That heap of rust probably can't go very fast," said Basten. "Let's get somebody after him, now. Four somebodys, in fact. In two vehicles, so you can box him in if you need to." Four agents immediately dashed out of the van.

"Run the image once more, will you?"

The technician did.

"Who's the other guy with him? That's not Wolf, is it?"

"No, this is somebody we haven't seen before."

"Well, get what you can in the way of image capture, and let's start doing some probing. Somehow I don't think our boy is likely to be giving rides to total strangers."

An hour later, the agents who had pursued the SUV reported in by radio from the Acoma visitor center lot.

"We've got the vehicle, but there's nobody in it. It's in the lot of some kind of tourist gift shop. How do you want to play it?"

"Loud and pushy. Go ahead and show a presence. Intimidate the locals; let them know they don't want to hide these guys."

"You got it."

It turned out to be more than fifty miles to the high mesa with the tourist attraction, but Doug and Sancho found it with no problem, and the Suburban ran as well as it had since they first got it. The mesa was almost 400 feet above the flat desert floor and capped with clusters of low buildings, all the same gray-brown adobe color. They could see it for miles before they got there. But they couldn't drive directly there. Instead, they had to park their vehicle at a visitor center and gift shop and buy a ticket for a bus ride to the tiny city. Doug also bought a big serape in a bright red and turquoise pattern, and he put it on at once.

"You're getting good at this game," said Sancho.

"I figure now you can find me in a crowd if you have to. But somebody looking for the old me won't glance twice at this."

"I like it, man. It looks good on you."

They rode a nine-passenger van up a steep and winding road to the top of the mesa with four other tourists, a sullen

Indian driver who didn't talk, and a female Indian guide who did enough talking for both of them. She said the city was originally a fort. "From there, the Acoma warriors could defend the People with their arrows from anybody who came across the plains to hurt them. For six hundred years, the fort was impregnable. Then in 1598, the Spaniards came under Don Juan de Onate. The Acoma fought long and well, but the Spaniards dragged a cannon up the side of the mesa and opened fire on the city, and we lost the battle. Before that, there were almost 2000 people living here. Only 250 survived. And after the battle, the Spaniards took away all the children twelve years old or younger and sent them off to be raised by the Catholic missionaries. The People never saw them again."

"Dirty bastards," said Sancho.

"We don't use that kind of language," said the guide. "But yes, that's what they were."

The van stopped in what passed for a town square and disgorged its passengers.

"It looks like there are still people living here," said Doug.

"There are some, yes," said the guide. "There have been people living here continuously for over a thousand years now. It has an ancient feel to it, don't you think?"

Doug said nothing, but he silently agreed with her. The place was strangely magical, even a little surreal. He wrote that off to the tilted perspective of the streets and buildings that were nothing resembling level or plumb.

"This place is weird," said Sancho.

"You're the one who wanted to come here."

"And I was right, too. But it's just kind of—"

"It feels like we were meant to come here."

"I was going to say that, man, but I thought it would sound stupid. It does kind of seem that way, doesn't it?"

"You were right the first time; it's weird. But I think I like it."

"Listen, Dougie, if something goes wrong Wednesday, if you got to run and you need my help, you come here, okay?"

"How will I get here? They don't let outsiders on the road up the mesa."

"You'll find a way. Okay?"

"Okay. Even if things go right, I don't know what's going to happen. For sure, people are going to want me to go somewhere with them and do a job. And I have no idea how long it will take."

"I got that already. And I can't come."

"Probably not. But when I finally get the big payoff, I want you to have part of it."

"Hey, I promise you I'll do more good with it than you would. So what do we do?"

"This is Monday. Skip three weeks, but then come back here every Monday. On one of them, I'll be here."

"Hokay."

Near one edge of the mesa was a building that did not match the style of the others at all, a large church with twin truncated adobe bell towers and massive proportions.

"That is the church of San Esteban del Rey," said the guide. "The Spaniards made the People build it in the sixteen hundreds sometime. But the People made all the frescos on the walls and the other decorations, too, and the Spaniards were too stupid to see that they put in all the symbols and figures from the old religion, so they would not be lost. And when they made the big wall around the church courtyard, they left a hole in it, right by the steepest part of the cliff. Do you see it? That is so the spirits of the lost children from the Battle of Sky City can come back home again."

For reasons he could not explain, that made Doug want to cry.

But Sancho wasn't crying or even listening. He was looking over the top of the courtyard wall at the desert below.

"Nice view, isn't it?"

"Yeah, nice view. You can see the visitors' parking lot real good. You see what I see, man? Two big black suvies with dark glass just pulled up, one right on each side of our Suburban."

"Oh, shit."

"Big-time, man. It's not like there wasn't any place else they could have parked. You got your gun with you?"

"Yeah, I do. I couldn't get the lock on the driver's door to work right, so I didn't want to leave it in the vehicle."

"That's good, man, 'cause I don't think we want to go back there."

"How do we avoid it?"

"You'll figure something out."

"Oh, *I'll* figure something out. You like that strategy a lot, don't you?"

When the tour van returned to the visitor center, they didn't get on it, saying they would wait for the next one. It took several more vans and several hours before there was one returning without any other passengers. As it wound back down the steep road, Doug made his way to the front and talked to the driver, the same sullen-looking one they had started with.

"I'll give you a hundred dollars to take us to Albuquerque instead of where you're supposed to go."

He shook his head no. "I get in too much trouble."

"Two hundred."

"Cash now?"

"Cash now." Doug reached into his pocket.

"I got to pretend I don't know where you went to?"

"No. Tell people whatever you want."

"Okay. Let's see the money."

Doug fanned four fifty-dollar bills in front of him, then tucked them into the driver's shirt pocket. "Those people who came in the black SUVs, what did they look like?"

"Like white folks who thought they were real important. Three men and a woman."

"Anything else?"

"Yeah, they had black nylon jackets with FBI on the back. And they were asking about you."

"Did they say our names?"

"No, they just said they wanted the guys who came in the Suburban. Acted like they thought we were hiding you, or something. Real pushy smartasses."

Doug made a show of adding another fifty to the wad and patted the driver on the shoulder. Then he went back to the rear, where Sancho was watching the road behind them.

"You hear that?"

"Yeah, man. When did the F, B, and I get into this game?"

"That's the best question I've heard in years."

"What's the answer?"

"I have no idea."

"So what do we do?"

"We go back to town, just like before. And we lay low, just like before. If they knew where to find us at the *restaurante,* they wouldn't be looking for us here."

"I'm starting to get real antsy for Wednesday."

"Can't argue with that."

"If nothing else, it'll be fun looking at Carlos' face when you tell him to stick his lousy tacos up his ass."

"That should be worth remembering, yes. Sometimes it's fun being a fugitive."

The van turned onto the main highway before it got to the visitor center on the other side. It headed east and was not followed.

"You figure we're safe now, man?"

"I don't think I'll ever feel safe again."

* * *

Back at the FBI surveillance van, neither the reports from the field nor the later patient waiting produced anything. When the visitor center closed for the day and the staff went home, the place was deserted.

Chapter Twenty

Matchbook

The next day dawned bright and clear, with the promise of boiling heat later. It matched Webb's mood: hot and disagreeable. Agent Basten had not called for an analysis on the incident at Acoma, but Webb was determined that they would have one, anyway, and Connelly agreed with her.

"What did you find out about the vehicle?" She stirred the black coffee in her waxed paper cup vigorously with a wooden stick, even though she had not added anything to it, then tapped the stick pointedly on the rim.

"Registered to an Emiliano Campos, with a rural route address about a hundred and fifty miles north and west of here. If there's anything significant about him or the rig, we're not finding it, but we're sending somebody out to talk to him anyway." Basten's tone was defensive, which seemed totally appropriate to Webb and her partner.

"Is the thing still sitting in the parking lot at the visitor center, or didn't you check?"

"I did check. I do a few things right, you know. Apparently Wright left it there, so we have no handle on where he went next at all, and we—"

"He came back here," said Webb. "If he has some kind of meeting tomorrow, he's not going to abort it just because of a few agents that he managed to lose like an expired lottery ticket."

"Agreed. So yesterday was a non-incident, and you needn't get your nose out of joint about us starting anything without you."

"You promised to call us when you were set up, and you didn't."

"Okay, I admit it."

"Then consider my nose out of joint. What about the guy in the vehicle with Wright?"

"We're coming up dry on him. Not in our systems at all."

"Those guys in our central lab can identify a specific lemming in the middle of a herd of a thousand," said Connelly.

"You're not pushing them hard enough," said Webb.

"We don't have enough juice," said Basten.

"Then get it. Tell them we think the vehicle *might* be carrying guns or bombs, or whatever the favorite flavor is these days."

"Man-portable missiles is the current hot-button item."

"See? You're more resourceful than you thought you were."

"But we *don't* think that," said Basten.

"I only said 'might.'"

Connelly rolled his eyes, but it was clear that he was proud of his partner. "How do we want to play things tomorrow?" he said.

"Low key, at least to start," said Basten, obviously relieved to have a change of subject. "Our two targets are supposed to meet someplace in the market around noon. We'll put you two agents and two of our own over there an hour ahead of that, and—"

"Two hours would be better. We want to see if anybody else is setting up a net."

"If you say so. Okay then, how about you two at ten and two more at eleven, with a tested sound hookup. If you spot either guy, set up a standard shadow box on him, well back.

When and if the two of them get together, give us some direction so we can try to get a parabolic mike pointed where it can pick them up. If we don't get anything incriminating on tape, we let them both go their own ways."

"I think we have enough evidence to pick up Jake Wolf now," said Webb, "at least for questioning. And if he's who we think he is, we maybe don't care if we tip him off to the fact that we're interested in him."

"Okay, but we're not pouncing right away, understood? Give the two of them some time to get together and maybe say something worth listening to. And if Wright sees us snatch Wolf, then we'll have to take him, too, so make sure he's not too far away to snatch at the time we make our move."

"Make sure he's gone so he doesn't see us grab Wolf, but make sure he's not too far away so we can grab him, too?" Webb gave him two arched eyebrows. "This operation has got cluster fuck written all over it already."

"You wanted in, you're in. You want out, say so now."

"No."

"All right, then. Let's get you checked out on the com gear."

In the middle of the morning, Doug was in the alley behind the café, smoking a cigarette on his break. He had just taken up smoking, and so far, he didn't like it much. But he thought he would stay with it a while longer, just because people who smoked seemed to get more out of their breaks than he did. As he re-lit his cigarette for the second time, a familiar figure came around the corner of the building.

"They stay lit better if you draw on them now and then, you know."

"Jesus, Ben. I wasn't expecting you until tomorrow."

"I've managed to stay alive and out of jail for a long time by doing what people don't expect, Doug."

"I'm sorry to say I'm starting to know what you mean."

"What are you talking about?"

"Let's just say it's been an eventful trip so far."

"I'm sorry to hear that. Anything I should be aware of?"

"I don't think so. Well, maybe you should, at that. Yesterday I got followed out to a tourist site by some FBI types."

"Really? How do you know?"

"They had on their souvenir jackets, the ones with the team logo on them."

"Careless of them. Did you lose them?"

"Yes. At least I think so."

"That's okay for now, then. Who's the Latino kid you've been camping out with?"

"Just somebody I picked up on the road. He helps me rob convenience stores."

"How convenient. Is he anti-ZOG?"

"I doubt it. He's pro-little people, but I don't think he's really anti anything."

"Then he can't come along to the site."

"He probably wouldn't want to. How's the money situation these days?"

"I promised it and I got it. In fact, I got more than we needed. Do your job right, and there'll be a nice bonus for you. Do you still have the matchbook?"

"From Dirty Dick's in Omaha? Yeah, I have it. What's it for, anyway? Is that a fallback meeting place?"

"As a matter of fact, there is no such place as Dirty Dick's. That's how we're sure nobody but us has the matchbooks. Very limited edition. You could call it a collector's item. Yours is your pay voucher. When you get our hardware up and running, I'll tell you where to go to cash it in. Meanwhile, don't lose it. If we get split up somehow, it will show you where to go."

"But you just said there is no Dirty Dick's."

"And that's why the matchbook won't tell you to go there. Learn to pay attention, Doug. Sometimes things are not what they seem."

"What they seem is awfully melodramatic."

"Well, you signed on for a melodramatic world, didn't you? Anyway, the money is set to go. Are you ready to deliver on your part?"

"Yes."

"All right, then. Be in the square tomorrow at noon."

"Not now? What are we waiting for?"

"Follow the plan, okay?"

"I'd really like us to go today."

"Why?"

"Um, well . . . It's just, you know, the FBI and all, and . . ." For a fleeting moment, he considered telling Ben about Mr. Black and his minions. But then he would also have to tell him that Mr. Black knew the time and place of the Wednesday meeting. The more he thought about it, the less he could think of any easy way to do that. So he shut his mouth and hoped for the best.

"Tomorrow," said Ben. "Noon. Just watch your back. You'll be fine. If the feds are there and they spot you, get the hell out, fast. Trust me, I'll find you and pick you up when the time is right."

Carlos stuck his head out of the kitchen door and growled, "How long you think your break is, until tomorrow? Talk to your friends on your own time." Doug threw his cigarette in a dusty tire track in the alley and turned to go. Ben was already gone.

Back in the kitchen, there was only one order clipped to the metal carousel in the pass window. It was for *huevos rancheros*. Doug put the toast down first, then cracked three eggs into a bowl and beat them with a wire whip. He smiled a little as he did it. It had taken him a few days to learn that eggs actually cook faster than toast does. One of his father's favorite sayings flashed into his head, quite unbidden. *There isn't any job so simple that there isn't a smart way and a stupid way of doing it.* Jesus, agreeing with his old man! What was next, drinking beer at some bowling alley?

He finished the order and put it up, steaming, on the pass window. "Order up!" he cried. "Rita?"

But Rita was nowhere to be seen, nor was Maria, the other waitress. He thought it would be a shame if the eggs got cold, so he decided to deliver the plate himself. The ticket said the customer was out on the "patio," which was more prosaically known as the public sidewalk.

The lone customer was a woman at the far end of the dining area, and Doug got almost up to her table before he bothered to look carefully at her. When he did, he froze.

"You should put that plate down before you drop it," she said, looking up from under a broad-brimmed straw hat. "Here." She pointed at a spot on the table in front of her.

"I didn't think I'd ever see you again, Brenda." He put the plate down and added utensils and a napkin from his back pocket.

"Long Beach isn't all that far away, is it?"

"It sure seems like far. It seems like the far side of the moon."

"You were planning on going back eventually, weren't you?"

"I'm not so sure anymore. But I mean, um . . . What are you doing here?"

"Mr. Black thought it would be best if the first agent you met here was not somebody you would immediately run away from." She pointed silently at her wristwatch, which was rather large for a woman's, then made an "itsy-bitsy spider" motion with her hand on the tabletop, letting him know she was carrying a bug. He nodded his understanding.

"Why would I run away?" he said.

"How should I know? You know how those folks think."

"Yeah, I guess I do." He found that it was hard to keep his voice from trembling. "But they're okay with me, yes? I'm not in any trouble?"

"I didn't hear them say you were." But silently she gave him a very dour look and a subdued nod, yes.

"Great." Nothing about it was great. "So what's the plan?"

"I give up. What's the plan, Doogie?"

"Tomorrow at noon I walk away from this job and go strolling around the square, and my man, Ben, picks me up. After that, I don't know what happens."

"That's if your man shows." She arched her brow in a silent question: had he already seen Ben? He pretended he didn't notice.

"Yes, if he shows."

"Anybody else?"

He hesitated.

"You'd better tell me, Doug."

"Yesterday I got followed by the FBI for a while. I don't think they trailed me back here, though."

"That's more like it. See? Confession is good for the soul."

"What do you mean, confession?" He was glad to feel his face flushing at that. "It's not like I contacted them."

"Relax, it's just an expression. Are these eggs any good?" She added ample amounts of salt and pepper from the battered cut-glass shakers on the table.

"They're very good. I made them myself."

"Really? I'm impressed."

An angry Carlos suddenly appeared in the front doorway, shaking an accusatory finger. "Now you take a break with a customer?"

"Eat shit and die," said Doug, but very quietly.

"What? What was that? You looking to lose your job, you lazy bastard?"

"You have no idea," said Doug. He kept his back to Carlos.

"You look different," said Brenda.

"That's probably just the newly stooped shoulders and the bandanna on the head."

"*Hombre*! You better move it!"

"No, it's something else. You don't look so much like a loser anymore."

"I'm talking *now*!"

"Really? Wow. What a thing to say. Thanks, Brenda." He headed back inside, infuriating Carlos even more by moving slowly and giving him a calm smile. *Impressing the girls and learning the ways of passive rebellion? What a strange trip this has been.*

"See you tomorrow," said Brenda behind his back.

Doug paused for half a step, suddenly feeling as if he had about two pounds of ice in his stomach. The agents of Mr. Black had reacquired him, even before the scheduled event in the square. And they were definitely back in the game. Worst of all, Brenda had confirmed that he was solidly on their shit list. What the hell was he going to do now? *See you tomorrow,* she had said. He couldn't think of any way to change that.

Chapter Twenty-One

Dogs in the Marketplace

D-day morning at the *restaurante* had begun normally enough, with Sancho and Doug sitting on crates in the alley and peeling carrots and potatoes. The only thing different was that Doug had brought his backpack. After he had stared silently at his moving hands for a while, he put down his knife, reached inside the pack, got a thousand dollars and the keys to the Suburban, and gave them to Sancho.

"It's been a hell of a trip, Sancho. Thanks."

"Hey, *de nada, amigo*. Anytime." He stuck the keys in his back pocket and the money in his underwear. Doug smiled slightly, noting how many things he still hadn't learned about survival on the fringe.

They shook hands. It occurred to Doug that it was the first time they had ever touched. Somehow, that seemed wrong.

"Don't forget about Sky City, okay?"

"No way, man. Hey, you know what you ought to have in that backpack? You ought to have the biggest fry pan Carlos has got."

"What on earth for?"

"In case somebody tries to shoot you in the back sometime."

He laughed, then thought about it a moment. "You know, that's not such a bad idea."

"All my ideas are good, man."

"I guess maybe they are at that." He slapped Sancho on the shoulder, and they picked up their buckets and went inside, where their boss was just unlocking the front door.

"I don't believe this shit," said Carlos. "You getting mail sent here now?"

"I have no idea what you're talking about," said Doug.

"No? Well, somebody stuck an envelope under the door with your name on it, like this was your house or something. I don't want no more of that shit, *comprende*?"

"Okay. Give it to me, please."

"Later, maybe. You got to learn a little lesson first."

"Now. Or else you won't get the use of that hand back for a month." He took a step forward and shifted easily into a judo stance.

Carlos saw the look and the stance and immediately backed down. "Okay, okay! We don't need no rough stuff here. Take your damn letter."

Doug snatched the envelope away from the smaller man. It had nothing on it but his name, written in what looked like a woman's hand. He stuffed it in his back pocket without opening it.

"You looking for a big crowd today, Carlos?"

"Yeah, sure, I guess. I don't know. Like usual, I suppose. Why?"

"Because about a quarter to twelve, if you want to keep putting out the food, you'd better put on an apron. I'm leaving."

"Bullshit, you are. You walk out on me, don't bother coming back."

"That's the idea."

"You can't do that! I got no money to pay you off, for one thing."

"That's okay. I took one of your skillets and a big knife. I'll call it even."

"What if I raise your pay some?"

"Wouldn't matter. I have to go meet my stockbroker, and he won't wait. Sancho, there, would probably help you out, but I doubt that he's going to do two people's jobs for the same wages." He looked over at Sancho and winked.

"Double," said Sancho, grinning.

"Seven-fifty," said Carlos. "That's fair."

"Double."

"Eight and a quarter. Nobody's worth more than that."

"Hokay, I leave with Doug."

"Nine. All right? I'll give you nine bucks an hour, but only for today."

"You mean only until you hire another guy."

"Think you're smart, don't you?"

"You bet," said Sancho. He looked as if this was the most fun he'd had in years.

"All right, we'll say nine bucks an hour *for a while*. Okay?"

"Sure." He returned Doug's wink. "For a while."

Doug chuckled. But he was also surprised to find that now that the time had come to tell his belligerent boss to stuff his lousy job, there was no satisfaction in it. Carlos was already out of Doug's mind. With no more power over him, he also generated no emotions in him.

At ten minutes before noon, Doug put on his serape, shouldered his backpack, and walked out the front door. He had never felt so exposed in his life.

By 11:50, Agent Webb felt as if she had checked out every souvenir in the market at least twice. It was getting harder to continue to look interested.

"Is this thing still working?"

"We're reading you five by five," said a voice in her ear. Well, at least something was going right. The equipment was the best she had seen. It was almost invisible, and the sound quality was excellent. So if the operation went totally down the toilet, it wouldn't be for technical reasons. She wished she had as much faith in her fellow agents.

The market looked normal enough to Doug, though it seemed somehow brighter than usual, the colors in sharper focus. And had it always been this noisy? A thousand voices of vendors, beggars, tourists, strolling musicians, ranging from bored to fascinated to desperate in tone, blended into an incomprehensible drone. Behind him, the bell in the church tower tolled noon, and he felt stupid to find himself immediately glancing at his watch anyway.

He didn't see Ben anywhere. Now and then he would stop dead in his tracks and carefully scan the entire market, a full 360 degrees. But he mostly didn't like doing that. He thought it made him look conspicuous. He preferred looking out of the corner of his eye while he pretended to be interested in something else. He had to admit, he didn't see much that way. But he didn't really see much, period. Ben had said he would find him. *Where the hell was he?* He started looking at his watch much more often than was necessary or natural.

He reached under his serape and pulled the matchbook out of his pocket. Ben had said it would tell him where to go, but not to Omaha. He studied the outside and found nothing unusual about it, other than the size of the breasts on the nude model. He opened it up.

"Hey, *amigo*, how about a light, huh?"

He whirled to his right and saw a dark-skinned Indian approaching him with a thin cigar in his mouth. How the hell had he gotten so close without Doug noticing? He didn't know if he should tear off one of the matches or not.

"Um, these don't work. They got wet."

"They don't look wet to me."

"Well, they are." He reached in his pocket and pulled out some bills. "Here, take a couple of bucks and go buy yourself a throwaway lighter."

"*You* go buy one, asshole *tourista*." He spat on the ground and walked away.

A moon-faced woman at one of the stalls tugged at Doug's arm. "I sell you a lighter for two dollars," she said, holding up a Bic covered with pieces of imitation turquoise. She gave him a toothy smile.

"Yeah, okay, *señora*. I need a sombrero, too. Something big and floppy. It's too hot out here in the sun. What have you got?"

"Very nice," she said, holding one plain hat and one with elaborate designs painted on it. The plain one was a reasonable fit, and he bought it and kept it on, pulling it low on his brow. As he was paying for it, he glanced over at a woman who was looking at jewelry a few stalls away, a pretty, thirty-something petite blonde in a very tailored white linen suit. When she leaned over to replace something in the display, her jacket fell open, and he got a glimpse of some kind of plastic ID badge. He didn't recognize her as any of Mr. Black's people, so that left his new friends, the FBI. *Shit!* One of the maxims from his surveillance classes flashed into his mind. *If you think you've been made, you have. If you think you are being tailed, you are. Concentrate on what you can get away with doing in plain sight.* And what the hell might that be? He found that his mind didn't work nearly as well in the field as in the classroom. *Where the hell was Ben?*

Webb saw him before he spotted her. Two stalls away, person-of-interest Douglas Wright was trying on straw sombreros. She bent down and picked up a turquoise and silver bracelet from a display and held it up in front of her face, as if scrutinizing the detail.

"Tallyho," she said quietly. "Goose Number Two at my nine o'clock, wearing a red and green serape and carrying a dark blue backpack. No, now he's wearing a sombrero, too."

"What color?"

"Straw color. No design on it."

As Wright turned toward her, she put the bracelet back where she had found it and shook her head and smiled sadly at the hopeful woman who was trying to sell it. As she was straightening back up, her suit jacket fell open for a brief moment, and she realized with horror that she was still wearing her ID badge. *Shit!* Had he seen it? She said nothing about it to her electronic audience. Wright strolled carelessly away from her, occasionally nodding to the people who were crouched on the ground by their stalls. She let him get forty or fifty yards ahead before she started working her way in the same direction. And then she stopped.

"Connelly, are you reading me?"

"Loud and clear."

"Are you seeing what I'm seeing?"

"Looks like our boy has somebody besides us following him."

"That's sure what it looks like to me."

"What the hell are you two talking about?" said a voice from the van.

"Goose Number Two has another tail. Two men. Tall, athletic, not very tan. They're dressed like locals, one in a jacket that's probably reversible, and one in a serape. But they stand and move like agents. Now and then they talk into their collars and make eye contact with each other."

"Is one of them the guy we saw on the traffic camera?"

"No, no way. And none of them is Goose Number One, either. These are totally new players."

"Have they spotted you two?"

"No way to tell."

"Assume they have. Drop back to the south perimeter and let Fox Three and Four take the lead. Keep looking for Goose One."

Doug continued to walk around the square, because that was what Ben had told him to do. But Ben had also said if he saw the feds, he should get out of there. But where? He continued walking in a way he hoped looked aimless, though he was beginning to work his way to the outer perimeter of the market, where he might disappear into some dark alley. Twice he dared another look at the matchbook. He probably looked at his watch every minute and a half. He couldn't help it.

On the second look at the matches, he saw that two of them, tucked away in the back row on the two outer corners, had numbers on them. One six-digit number on one paper match shaft and a seven-digit number on the other one. He called up everything he could remember from yet another of his classes, one on memory devices, and tried as hard as he could to memorize them. Then he also remembered the letter he'd received back at the *restaurante*.

He put the matches in his shirt pocket, pulled out the envelope, and tore it open. Inside was a short message on some hotel notepaper, in the same hand as the name on the outside. *I can't take this crap anymore. When the balloon goes up, I will already be gone. I thought you might like to know. Good luck.* It wasn't signed, but he knew it was from Brenda. Where, he wondered, was "gone"?

Webb and Connelly stayed well separated and continued to pretend to browse through tourist wares, mostly keeping their backs to their quarry. Neither of them spotted Jake Wolf.

Ten minutes later, nothing had changed. Wolf had not appeared and Wright continued to walk aimlessly around the market, though now he seemed to be working his way toward the outer edge of the big square. His two sets of followers trailed behind from different directions. Now and then Wright reached under his serape and took something small out of a shirt pocket and seemed to study it. He checked his watch more and more frequently. His movements were becoming jerkier.

"Subject is turning at the southwest corner of the open market, heading north," said one of the FBI tails into his collar.

"How far behind him are the unknown shadows?" said Basten from the command post.

"Thirty yards. They never get much closer than that."

"Okay, listen up, folks. Change of plan. Fox Three and Four, take a diagonal across the square and cut Goose Two off. When he gets opposite the first little side alley, snatch him as fast as you can. Get him out of sight of the tailers. And when you have them dumped, bring him over here. We're going to make him disappear for a little while and see what his friends do. Fox One and Two, stay where you are and continue watching for our other guy."

"Roger that," said Webb. She wondered if Agent Basten had ever run a field operation before. Under her breath, she said, "Stupid, stupid plan. We have no idea what we're dealing with here." Ten yards away, Connelly read her lips and nodded his agreement. They both looked across the market square, where the other two FBI agents were rapidly moving to cut off Wright. Then they saw the two unknown agents see the same thing. The unknowns both pulled out guns—semiautomatic pistols with large silencers—and held them loosely at their sides as they strode rapidly toward the coming merger between agents and subject. When they got within ten yards of the FBI men, they raised their weapons.

"Fox Three and Four, watch your sixes!" She couldn't tell if they heard her or not.

* * *

Doug looked up from the matchbook to do another panoramic scan of the area. There was still no sign of Ben, but coming toward him on a zigzagging diagonal were a pair of clean-cut men in suits that couldn't be anything but FBI agents. And coming up behind them, with drawn guns, were two more men that he recognized altogether too well. During his initial training and intimidation, they had both beaten him several times. Black's people.

Then all hell broke loose.

Chapter Twenty-Two

Into the Fire

"Down, down, down!" screamed Webb. "Shooters behind you!"

"What?" said Basten's voice. "What the hell is going on there?"

"We're under attack!" As she said it, she pulled her own Glock. But before she could assume a shooting stance, the two phantom agents had already fired several rounds. Both of the FBI agents out in the square went down, hit.

"Agents down! Agents down!" She tried to get a clear shot at one of the attackers, but now the square was in utter pandemonium, with people screaming and running in every direction. There was no way she could risk it. She waded through the crowd toward the two stricken agents, trying to keep track of where the shooters had gone, without much luck. They had already fled the scene, and Wright, also, was nowhere to be seen.

Webb and Connelly got to the fallen men at the same time. One had been shot twice in the back and once in the head and was already dead. The other was still alive, bleeding from multiple wounds in his back.

"Basten, do you copy?" said Webb. "We need some paramedics here, ASAP. And some more firepower couldn't hurt, either."

Her earbud was silent.

"Did you copy that or not?"

More silence. Connelly repeated the call on his own microphone, but he didn't get any response, either. Webb took a cell phone out of her purse and called 911 for an ambulance. Then she said to Connelly, "I'll stay here with this guy and try to stanch the bleeding. You go see what happened to our com link. Tell Basten we're butt-naked out here, and we need some reinforcements. And watch your own ass on the way. We don't know which way those guys went."

As Connelly ran off into the frenzied crowd, she grabbed a bunch of clothes from a vendor's stall and started applying pressure bandages to the wounds she could see. After a while, the cloth was not dripping so much blood, but she couldn't tell if that was because she was doing a good job of keeping pressure on or because her man had already died. Sweeping the scene in all directions to see if the gunmen had come back, she noticed something on the ground near the spot where Wright had been standing when the shooting started. Something small. Not a cell phone. Something smaller than that. She made a mental note to go look at it when she got a chance. As she continued to apply pressure to the wounds, she felt something metal press against the back of her neck. A gun muzzle, definitely, and it was still hot. So at least one of the shooters had not fled.

"Don't look around," said a deep, slightly hushed voice. "Give me your gun."

"You'll never get away with it," she said. "There are—"

"Give me your gun if you want to live. Now."

She handed her piece, butt first, over her shoulder, absolutely certain she was about to be killed anyway. She imagined she could hear the trigger mechanism being slowly drawn back. She wondered how fast she could pull out her backup piece and chamber a round in it. *Not nearly fast enough.* But then the unknown player made some kind of jerking movement, and the pressure on her neck was suddenly gone. Then the man was running away, plunging into the chaos of the crowd. She got a final glimpse of him by the edge of the public square, where he tossed her gun into a trash can and kept on running. Something had scared him off, but she had no idea what it was.

Doug ran as fast as he could. West, into a maze of small passages between weather-beaten leaning buildings. There was more gunfire, this time without the silencers that the first shooters had used. As he emerged from one passageway onto a short side street, he saw four gunmen pouring machine gun fire into the sides of a TV step van parked at the curb. He turned and ran back the way he had come, and some bullets slammed into the side of a building next to him. He turned at the next junction, and at every one after that, until he had no idea where he was anymore.

He stopped in deep shadow to gasp for air and check his back. As far as he could tell, there was nobody behind him. He took a few more deep breaths, pulled his sombrero down once more, and emerged into the brilliant sunlight again, on a street he did not recognize. He tried to walk with a slightly more slouching posture than he normally did. A block later, a newish Ford Ranger pickup with an extended cab came screaming around a corner and skidded to a stop in front of him. He reached over his shoulder into his backpack, groping for his gun. All he found at first was the handle of Carlos' big skillet. Then the passenger door of the pickup flew open, and he saw Max, Ben's right hand man, sitting behind the wheel.

"Get in, quick!"

He scrambled onto the seat, and before he got his door fully shut, they were off in a cloud of dust and gravel. He recognized the unmistakable blurbling sound of a very large, well-tuned engine winding up at the low end of the RPM range, where the torque is overwhelming. No way the Ranger had come from the factory with that kind of engine. It had to have been made for a police cruiser or a big V-10 three-ton rig.

"Get in back and stay down, out of sight," said Max.

He did.

The paramedics from the local fire department got to Webb before Connelly did. She was ashamed to find that she had tears running down her face, and her voice was shaking badly. She showed them her ID, told them the minimum they would need to know for the moment, and watched helplessly as they put the wounded man on a stretcher and wheeled him away, already attaching IV tubes. Another EMT asked if she needed any attention, and she told him no. He looked skeptical, but he left her.

A minute later, Connelly came back, still with his weapon out, at the high port position. He was out of breath and had sweat pouring down his face and into his collar.

"What's the story, partner?"

"You aren't going to believe this, Abbs. It's a goddamned massacre. They—somebody—hit the command post. They put about a thousand rounds into it from the outside, then sprayed the inside for good measure. Everybody is dead."

"*What?* Basten?"

"Everybody."

"It should have been me, too. One of the shooters just had me dead to rights, but something scared him off." She took her backup weapon, a compact .32, out of the holster that was strapped to the inside of her ankle and chambered a round.

"You and me, Abby, are the entire FBI task force at this point. So watch your back."

"This is a nightmare."

"I wish it was. You can wake up from a nightmare."

Webb scanned the entire market square, her .32 "last-ditch gun" tracking where she looked. There was no sign of the shooters or anybody else out of the ordinary, though there was still enough chaos that it was hard to be sure. As she looked to the north of the square, something flashing caught her eye.

"There's somebody in the bell tower of the church, with either some binoculars or a rifle scope. That must be what the shooter saw. He'd have been no match for a sniper."

Connelly turned his eyes and his weapon that way.

"I can't see anybody."

"Shit. Neither can I, now." She put her gun down at her side, walked back over to the spot she had looked at earlier, and bent down. Connelly followed her.

"What are you doing?"

"Picking up something. I think our man Wright dropped it when the action got heavy."

"What is it?"

"Looks like a matchbook."

She went over to the trash can and got her Glock back. Soon the scene was flooded with local uniformed police officers. Webb had no idea what to tell them. Nothing she had just seen made any sense to her at all.

Doug stayed down as he had been told. They went careening through Old Town, swerving around other cars and sometimes barely missing pedestrians. They stopped at the back of the adobe church by the café where Doug and Sancho had been working. The passenger door opened, and Ben dove in. He had some kind of high-powered rifle with him. Before he finished pulling the door shut behind him, Max was off again, getting clear of the old part of town, even as police cars all around them were heading the other way, toward the center of the market. Soon they were well away from the area, and Max reverted to driving like the most uptight and law-abiding of citizens, obeying both speed limits and traffic signs. Finally, they took Highway 448 north at a sedate 53 miles per hour.

Ben looked over his seat back into the rear passenger area and said, "You can sit up now, Doug. How are you doing?"

"How am I doing? I'm scared shitless, that's how." It was the right answer if he were still trying to play the part of an innocent civilian with no special training. But it wasn't totally untrue, either.

"Relax. The fun part is all over now."

If only I believed that.

Chapter Twenty-Three

New Horizons

"Are we really clear?" said Doug. "Nobody doing a loose tail?"

"Not loose or any other kind. Trust me, I'd know. All we have to do now is cruise. What's in the pack?"

"Huh? Oh. Socks, underwear, maybe a shirt, plus a big frying pan, a kitchen knife, and a .45 semiautomatic." He took the straps off and handed the pack over.

"What kind of semiauto? Anything good?" Ben put the pack on his lap and opened a zipper.

"No. It looks like a Colt Model 1911, but it's really just a cheap knockoff. The brand stamped on it is Hitasu or some stupid thing like that."

"You ever use it?"

"Not yet. But I was starting to wonder if I would have to, back there. Who the hell were all those shooters, anyway?"

"You don't know?" His voice was slow now, and careful, as if he were faking being casual. To Doug, it dripped menace.

"Why should I know?" But his thought was, *oh shit, he's on to me.* He hoped it didn't show on his face.

"You're answering a question with another question. That's not a sign of good faith, Doug." He was studying Doug's eyes intently now.

"Without the question, then, I don't know who they were."

"It looked to me like they were protecting you." The stare and the slow speech continued, even as Ben pulled the .45 knockoff out of the backpack.

"Are you crazy? They were shooting at me, too, you know."

"Really? Then they weren't very good shots, were they? Or was that just a little street theater?" He was pointing Doug's own gun at his head now, without checking to see if it had a round in the chamber.

"What are you accusing me of?" *That's it, Wright. You're dead meat.*

The stare continued in silence for what seemed like an eternity. Doug remembered something from his training about withstanding interrogation. *Never volunteer information if you're not actually being asked a question. It's a sure sign that you're hiding something or lying.* He said nothing, and he made a conscious effort not to hold his breath.

Finally, something changed, something offstage that Doug couldn't see. Ben smiled slightly and put the gun back in the pack. "With any luck, before you ever have to use this, we'll have gotten you something better."

"I'd just as soon pass on that whole scene, if it's all the same to you. I didn't sign up for urban guerilla warfare. I haven't even practiced on the video games." *My God, am I safe after all?*

"That's okay, because I'm not paying you a million-plus dollars just to play hired gun. Not that kind of gun, anyway."

"Not that I've seen the million. No offense."

"None taken. But I haven't seen what you can do yet, either. No offense. We had another guy for a while, younger than you. Not a missile engineer exactly, but a real computer genius. He couldn't make any sense of the system at all. Couldn't tell it where to go, he said. Very sad, the way he turned out."

There was no doubt in Doug's mind that the last statement was a threat.

"Just exactly what kind of system are we dealing with, Ben?" He said it with deliberate slowness, as if he were gingerly poking at some kind of sleeping beast, one that he really didn't want to wake up. He had thought about this moment many times, knowing that he had to play it exactly right, or he was doomed. He had to seem surprised—no, astonished—to hear that Ben had a nuke. He also had to allow himself to be talked into working on it, but with great reluctance.

Ben's eyes flashed with triumph as he enunciated each word and letter as a separate sentence. "Second. Generation. Minuteman. I. C. B. M."

"You can't be serious." He let his jaw drop, and he conjured up the memory of the night he was abducted, hoping it would make his face turn pale.

"Why can't I be serious?"

"Because it's not possible. Only the government has those things."

"Don't ask me how they lost this one, but I have it and it's the real thing."

"In a silo? You can't just launch one from some cornfield, you know."

"In *my* silo, that nobody else knows about."

"Holy son of motherfuck. Solid fuel?"

"Solid fuel. One owner, very low mileage. Air conditioning and cruise. Original factory warranty. Can you talk to it?"

He took a long time to answer. He bit his upper lip and stared off into space, focused on nothing. Finally he said, "A million plus, you said."

Ben shook his head yes and kept his eyes on Doug's. "A million five."

"I want the money before you launch." *So I have time to tell the boys in black where it is, dear God, please.*

"It's already waiting for you."

Doug appeared to think some more, then nodded very slightly, let out a sigh, and nodded more definitely.

"All right, then. Yes, I can talk to your missile. But not with today's computers."

"We got our first guy a machine that could play floppies. We even got some floppies for it to play, from the archives at Los Alamos. We took a big risk getting them, almost lost a man. He still couldn't do it."

"He was probably thinking in terms of a total computer system. Back when your bird was new, they didn't have that. They had mixed mechanical and electronic systems. Sort of like a computer running an abacus running a steam engine. And there were no satellite navigation systems or GPS devices, either. People used programmable calculators to solve the trajectory equations, which were absolute monsters. Then they tied them to arbitrary gyroscopic bearings."

"Arbitrary? Why arbitrary?"

"Because when something is starting out going straight up, it has no bearing except 'out.' You have to give it some reference heading that it can read."

"Funny how I didn't hear any of this from our other guy."

"Well, you said it yourself; he was young. Techies nowadays think any hardware more than two or three years old is from the Stone Age, and they don't know shit about it and don't care, either."

"That fits, come to think of it. So what do we need, if not a big computer?"

"We need a store that sells antique electronics. One that caters to surveyors and building contractors would be good. We want a programmable calculator, not a computer as such, with at least twenty digits in its addressable numeric registers. And we need to go to a city that has a technical university and look for a used bookstore."

"Why not a new bookstore?"

"Because we want a textbook in something called geodesy. Nobody teaches the subject anymore. But somebody who once took a class in it would definitely sell the text, because it's the most boring stuff in the whole damned world."

"Couldn't we go to a university library?"

"Maybe. But if we have to ask for an archives search, then we'll leave some kind of record of it and maybe of ourselves, too. On the other hand, if we buy an old book for cash, who the hell would remember or care?"

"So, where are you thinking we'll find all that?"

"Which way are we heading?"

"North."

"For the book, maybe Colorado Springs. The Air Force Academy probably taught a course in geodesy at some time or other, maybe still does."

"And for the other thing, the calculator doohickey?"

"I don't know. I'm thinking we go online and look for a place that services early electronic surveying instruments and plotting devices. The bigger the place, the better. We're going to ask them to rummage through the dustiest part of their warehouse, and we want them to have some hardware there that they've forgotten. That could be anywhere in the country. But there will be one or more, somewhere. That stuff was good. It worked. And in some places, people are still using it."

"And sometimes they need spare parts." Ben smiled.

"You bet they do."

"You know, Doug, I'm starting to get a good feeling about you."

And Doug was starting to relax for the first time in as long as he could remember.

As they were clearing the northern outskirts of the metro area, Max suddenly slowed down. Ahead of them, on the right-hand side of the road, there was a body lying on the shoulder.

"What the hell?" said Max.

"Don't stop," said Ben. "Don't even slow down. We didn't see it."

Max sped back up, and as they got closer, they could see that it was a woman. Her face, which was pointed at the sky, was beaten horribly, and her clothes were covered with blood. She looked as dead as anybody Doug had ever seen. But even at fifty-five miles an hour, he recognized the pale blue raincoat and matching shoes, from that first terrible night in the interrogation basement. It was Brenda.

"I don't get it," said Max. "What kind of an idiot dumps a body right out on the main highway?"

"Somebody who's still out ahead of us somewhere," said Doug. But what he thought was *Somebody who wanted me to see it. Somebody who wanted me to be very, very impressed and scared shitless. Somebody who wanted me to know this is what happens if you go off the reservation. But how the hell did they know I'd be heading north? I didn't know it myself.*

"He's right," said Ben. "And the police could be setting up a roadblock to catch them soon, too. That might not be so good. Take the next side road."

They took a secondary county road forty miles east, then turned and headed north again. They went through Santa Fe, and an hour later the desert began to give way to the foothills of the Colorado Rockies.

Chapter Twenty-Four

Old Tech

Doug had a hundred different emotions competing for space in his head, including several varieties of fear. Brenda had gone rogue and had even been foolish enough to say so in writing. And for that they had killed her brutally, smashed her like a bug and made sure Doug would see her body. How the *hell* did they keep finding him? They wouldn't kill him yet, not before he had led them to Ben's missile site. But after that? Were there really fifteen more sites, or was that just a handy lie to keep him full of optimism? Maybe once he delivered, he would wind up just like Brenda. Or maybe they would just make him *wish* he were dead.

On the other hand, if he threw in his lot with the farmers and made the missile work, Ben seemed likely to pay him off and send him on his way. That is, *if* he could find a place to run that didn't lead straight back to Mr. Black *and* if he could find a way to make sure the missile never got launched. He would have to decide soon. Which horse should he back? And which one was more likely to let him live?

Meanwhile, he was wrung out. He suddenly wanted to sleep more than he could ever remember. He took the knife and frying pan out of his pack and dumped them on the floor. Then he used the pack as a pillow and made himself comfortable across the back seat of the pickup, with his serape as a blanket.

He dreamed of a Sargasso Sea of discarded robots, with a young boy wandering through it, looking for a specific one by name.

When he awoke, he had slept so deeply that at first, he couldn't remember where he was, or even who he was. It was pitch black outside, and they were still moving. Now Ben was driving while Max slept in the tilted-back passenger seat. Doug had no idea what time it was. He had a fancy watch that not only glowed in the dark, it even lit up, but he had quit wearing it when he and Sancho got to Albuquerque, thinking it was too conspicuous. Maybe it was in his pack; he wasn't sure. He looked out and saw that they were on a winding road in rugged mountains. To the left, far below them, were the twinkling lights of some town.

"Durango," said Ben, as if he had been watching him. "Are you hungry?"

"I could eat the asshole out of a skunk."

"That's one I hadn't heard before. Do all engineers talk like that?"

"Not even slightly. That was my old man talking. I think it was his substitute for saying grace."

"What did he do, your old man?"

"Auto worker. Forty-eight years on the line for GM."

"Did they screw him over?"

"Actually, the union took care of him pretty well. He would have gotten a nice pension, but he died on the job."

"Well, there you are, then. Screwed him over, after all."

There he was, indeed. Sometimes Ben talked like a totally rational person. But just like Max, sometimes he could only see things through one very heavily tinted pair of goggles. And in that view, even a powerful union couldn't save you from the evils of Big Money, in an entire world gone so wrong that it couldn't be fixed. It had to be destroyed.

***

They ate at a twenty-four-hour pancake house in Durango. Doug had steak and eggs, and they were both overcooked. "Tell the cook to move over to the edge of the griddle," he told the waitress. "You can't do eggs over medium on the hottest part. They'll get wire edges and rubbery middles every time."

"Yes, sir."

"Besides being an engineer, now you're an expert on frying eggs," said Ben. "I'm impressed."

"'Anything worth doing' and all that."

"I just hope working at that joint hasn't ruined you for the important work."

"The day I quit being an engineer, I'll be dead." *Or maybe what I really mean is the day I start being a real engineer, I will come to life.* "But don't expect the work to be fast."

"What are you saying?"

"Most people have this idea of how things work at a silo, though we haven't even seen any images of them since the movie *War Games*. They think the crew gets a call from NORAD telling them to change their target from Moscow to Iran, say, and the techies punch a few buttons, and it's done. Or one computer talks to another computer and everything happens like magic. And the President or the head of SAC or NORAD, or whoever has the big stick this month, shifts from, say, the 'Hong Kong Gambit' to the 'Siberian Flank Initiative,' and everything is ready to go again. Same game. All new goals. It doesn't work that way. Or at least, it didn't when the Minuteman series was new."

"So how did it work?"

"Not very well, mostly. First of all, the number of people who know where *any* missile is targeted is very, very small."

"Starting with the guys in the silos, I assume."

"No. Not starting or ending with them. The silo crew never knows where its missiles are headed. Never. And neither do their commanding officers or their commanders' commanding officers."

"But how do they—"

"Somebody would come in and do the settings for them, using a master plan that was seldom seen and never talked about. There used to be something called the SIOP, or Strategic Integrated Operational Plan. It was a list of all possible nuclear targets, with priorities assigned to each of them and actual targets selected."

"How many targets did it include?"

"Thousands."

"Jesus."

"Exactly goddamned right. Keeping the thing up to date was a nightmare. Changing it for any other reason was almost unthinkable. And the list of people authorized to see it kept shrinking, but even so, the number of people who *had* seen it kept growing. Finally, in 2003, they did away with it altogether."

"And replaced it with what?"

"Nobody knows."

"*What*?"

"Well, all right then, *I* don't know, okay? But I do know that changing a target is something done mechanically, on site, not electronically from some remote location. Always was, probably always will be. If you punch a bunch of buttons, some machine somewhere can read what you punched. And somewhere else, some bad people might just have that machine. Security people go nuts over that kind of scenario. But if you physically move some switches and wires, that's strictly between you and the machine."

"And then the machine knows where to go?"

"Sure, why wouldn't it?"

"How?"

"It doesn't know names, not of the target or any other place. It only talks numbers. See, for any path in the world—any orbit, trajectory, arc, or even straight line—you can write a formula, okay? A mathematical description. You fire a simple cannon ball, its path is y equals a-x-squared plus b-x, plus c. You plug in a,b, and c, and you've defined it completely, and you know how to aim. A rocket trajectory is more complicated, of course, because part of its path is under power, so it's accelerating, but it basically comes back to the same equation in the end. The problem comes when your playing field goes global, and you have to mathematically define your position and that of the target."

"Why is that a problem?"

"Because they've never been mapped in the same system. There are all kinds of map projections. There are state plane coordinate systems and regional systems and flight chart systems and the Coast and Geodetic Survey system, and so on and so on. Worldwide, there's thousands of systems. And none of them is really accurate except over a very small area, because the earth not only isn't flat like a map, it's not even a true sphere. It's more like a sagging pumpkin, and there's no way it matches any mathematical formula. And worse yet, the elevation of the surface varies by more than five miles, and that's in relation to something called 'mean sea level,' which is not even the same on both sides of the planet."

"Well, shit."

"Exactly."

"But people can target missiles," said Ben. "They do it all the time, don't they?"

"Yes. And they've been doing it for over fifty years. It's easier now than it used to be. But for an old system, you have to revert to the old ways."

"Which are what, Doug?"

"Some mathematician with the patience of Job invented an imaginary mathematical surface around the outside of the earth, called the geode. Then he created a formula that lets you plug the longitude and latitude of a place, plus its elevation, into the equation and project it onto its true astronomical position on the geode. And then, in turn, you can answer all kinds of tricky questions like what's the true distance from Pago Pago to Skagway or how the hell do I fire a missile from Omaha and hit Moscow. No way any technician at a silo could do it. He would just be given the numbers by somebody else, and he would mechanically plug them in, probably with a second or even third person checking his work. Or he might not even get to do that much. He might just stand aside while some high-powered outside mystery people with sterile coveralls and stainless steel briefcases come in and do the whole thing."

"And how does anybody know if it's right?"

"They don't. They think they do, but they really don't. The only way to truly find out is to make the shot. There are people who claim that back in the early days of the Cold War, the whole business of targeting was a colossal bluff. We didn't know what we were doing, so we faked it. And we figured the Russians were faking it, too."

"So where would the missiles have gone if they had ever been launched?"

"Nobody really knew. Maybe within a hundred miles of their targets, maybe the middle of the ocean."

"Jesus. And while people in the countryside were losing their farms and committing suicide, we were paying billions for that shit."

"That's about it." Doug didn't feel obliged to mention that his own very attractive salary had come out of those same billions, a generation later. The state of the art for ICBMs was a lot better by the time he was on board, and it wasn't really his area of practice anyway, but the government was still paying huge sums of money for systems everybody knew wouldn't work.

"Well, then I think we have all the more right to steal one of the fuckers, don't we?"

Max, who had said nothing the whole time, grinned and nodded.

"So how long will it take you to work out these used-to-be-phony numbers, Doug?"

"I honestly don't know. I've never done it before. I've only read about it. Where's the target?"

"Can't you guess?" He picked up a corn muffin and held it in front of his eyes, as if he were contemplating a globe. A smile was beginning to creep onto his lips from some deep well of cynicism.

"No, I really can't."

"I want to hurt some real bad people, real bad. Now how do you suppose we do that? Do you think that Con Agra or Citi Bank care if I blow up a bunch of stupid little kids in Oklahoma City or shoot some agents in Waco, Texas? Do you think their stock would go down one single point? No. What would hurt them? What would they miss the most?"

"Um. Washington? But they have so many defense systems that—"

"Bigger."

"*Bigger*? What's bigger than Wash—"

Ben continued to give him an intense stare and a wry smile.

"Oh, my God. Wall Street?"

"Give that man a prize. We are going to utterly incinerate Wall Fucking Street."

"Holy shit." His mouth stayed open, and it wasn't an act. Finally he managed to say, "That's about as big as it gets, all right."

"We're talking about the dawn of a whole new era, Doug."

"The freight train in the gully," said Doug, and his eyes glazed over. He didn't know how he should appear to react. Should he look shocked? He probably did, without even trying. The whole undertaking had suddenly quit being even slightly abstract.

"Just like I told you. Can you do it?"

"Technically, it's actually a little easier to figure than a foreign target, being on the same continent as we are. You did say you're paying me in cash, didn't you?"

"I did say that, yes."

"Because after we do the deed, securities aren't going to be worth the cost of a match to burn them up. And electronic bank accounts will probably be frozen worldwide."

"Cash."

"All right, then." He heaved a huge sigh. "Do we have Internet access?"

"We can get it on my laptop at one of those wi-fi places."

"Good. That will let us find our used technology store."

"Why find a store? Why not just buy the stuff online?"

"And have them send it where?"

"Good point. Find a store."

"After we get our hardware, we also need to get access to Google Earth so we can get the longitude and latitude of our target. Then I'll need several days, maybe even a week or two, to crunch numbers and check them, plus whatever it takes to figure out the wiring at the site. That won't be mathematical, just tricky."

"It takes what it takes. As long as you realize you don't get paid until you're all done, I'm not worried about it. Let's get going."

On the way out to the pickup, Ben took something out of his pocket and threw it through a storm sewer grating. "Your new cell phone," he said, "from your backpack. You won't be needing this one any more, either."

Chapter Twenty-Five

Aftermath

The media, of course, went crazy over the shootings in Albuquerque. Fortunately, the local police department had a chief of detectives who loved to be in the spotlight, so Agent Webb, for the most part, was able to stay out of it. That, if nothing else, earned her high praise from FBI headquarters. It also earned her a new job, heading up a task force with the specific aim of finding out exactly what had really happened. Not that there weren't plenty of other people concerning themselves with that question as well. Albuquerque became a magnet for all the groups that blamed and hated the feds for Ruby Ridge, Waco, and half a dozen lesser-known incidents. And the shooting site drew almost as many people from Homeland Security, looking into said groups and occasionally making somebody quietly disappear.

The most common media slant was that the gunmen had been terrorists, though nobody specified if they were foreign or domestic. One newspaper called the incident "Fedster's Last Stand," and another simply labeled it an FBI massacre, without bothering to note in the headline if the feds had been killers or victims. Both reporters and ordinary citizens, who had no hard information whatsoever, nevertheless had strong opinions about what had started the shooting.

Webb managed to stay out of the public debate for the most part. She went back to her old office in Kansas City, but the resources that were now at her immediate disposal were mind-boggling.

"I want a team of technicians taking apart that step van ASAP," she told Connelly.

"What for? To learn that somebody shot it?"

"No, to see what's left of the equipment inside it. There was about a million dollars worth of recording equipment there. I want to know what it recorded, every bit of it. And I want somebody looking at what any and all satellites were watching in that part of the woods on that day. By God, we are going to get a look at these phantoms."

But for reasons she could not easily articulate, she did not turn the book of matches from Dirty Dick's over to the FBI lab. She knew she should. In fact, she could lose her job over an omission like that. They had already exiled her to the lousiest duty station anybody could think of. There was no form of discipline left but firing her. But she had some creeping issues of trust. For now, at least, she wanted to be the only person who knew about the matches.

Two days later, a truckload of equipment and data discs found its way into the office, some of it smashed almost beyond recognition but most of it in fairly decent shape. Webb had a bunch of technicians set up extra temporary monitoring devices, and she and Connelly started looking at videos and listening to radio traffic. The van itself had not had any cameras monitoring it, so they didn't get a look at the actual assailants. But some of the audio recordings were interesting, to say the least.

Half an hour into the surveillance operation in the open market, somebody unknown had broken into the agents' conversation.

What was that? said an unknown voice. *What did you call the target?*

Goose Two, of course.

That's not what we agreed to. Why did you change it?

That's exactly what we agreed to. Have you gone nuts?

Get off this frequency, said a third voice, also unknown. *We've tapped into the cowboys' line.*

Roger that. Switching to Guard Three. Out.

"Now what do you make of that?" said Webb.

"CBers? Hunters? Boy scouts? Who knows?" Connelly shrugged.

"None of the above," said Webb. "They not only had our frequency, they talked like us. *They talked like us, Frank.*"

"What are you saying, Abbs?"

"I'm not sure yet. What did we get from satellite imagery?"

"On the original operation, we didn't have enough clout to retarget any satellites to that area."

"No, I wouldn't suppose we did. But there ought to be—"

"But somebody did."

"Somebody?"

"Can't tell who. But there was high-rez surveillance going on at Old Town for four hours on the day of the incident, at just the right time."

"Have you seen it?"

"I scanned it, is all. You can see the firefight—"

"You mean the turkey shoot. That was no fight."

"Whatever. Anyway, you can see it, but the angle is bad. No faces. You need a broader physical and movement profile to ID anybody. If you pan back, you can also see some chopper activity."

"You mean like TV eye-in-the-sky stuff?"

"Not TV. This is an unmarked Bell Jet Ranger. Black. No numbers, no insignia of any kind."

"Get hold of the FAA. If the thing was within the positive traffic control area for the Albuquerque airport, they have to have known about it. And you can't operate any kind of aircraft below two thousand feet in a metropolitan area without their approval, unless you want to risk getting shot down. I want to know if that thing belonged to some government entity besides ours."

"Are you saying we got taken out by another agency?"

"It sure quacks that way, doesn't it?"

"Oh, boy. Just purely oh, boy. That's monstrous, Abbs. That's pure Third Reich stuff."

"Maybe. Until we're sure, this is just between us."

"If it's true, what do we do? And who the *hell* do we trust?"

"I don't know. Right now, nobody. Let me ask you something else altogether. You ever do one of those puzzles where you fill in categories to fit numbers? You know, like, 'What has 52_s in 4_s?'"

"No. What on earth are you talking about?" He looked at her as if she had gone a little crazy.

"I'm talking about a puzzle, a game. The answer to that particular item would be a deck of cards."

"The hell you say."

"Sure. It has 52 cards in four suits. That's an easy one. Sometimes they—"

"Oh, I see. That's an *easy* one. You play some weird games, Abbs. Does this have anything to do with what we're working on?"

She sighed, reached into a pocket, and produced the matchbook from Dirty Dick's.

"I don't want to hear what you think of the naked woman on the cover. Take a look inside."

"Where did you get this?" He looked at both the front and back covers, then opened the book up.

"That's what I picked up off the ground in the market in Old Town."

"Right after the shootings? The thing you thought our subject Wright might have dropped?"

"The very one."

"My God, Abbs, you should have—"

"Sent it to the lab, I know. Are you going to turn me in?"

He looked at her for a long time, then back at the matchbook, then at her again. Finally he said, "Oh, what the hell? It's only a career."

"What does that mean, exactly?"

"No, I'm not going to turn you in. But don't invite anybody else into this game, will you?"

"Good idea, agent. Now look at the numbers on the matches. Two sets, one with seven digits and one with only six."

He looked. He looked at each one of the matches in the book, being careful not to fold them, then focused on the two with the numbers again. He went over to his desk and took out a pencil and notepad but threw the pencil at the wall.

"Shit, I don't even dare make any notes, do I?"

"Nope."

He put his feet up on the desk and stared at the two matches, his brow deeply furrowed. Finally, it smoothed out again.

"It's a place."

"How did you get that?" She went over and looked at the cryptic object again, as if it might have somehow magically changed while it was in his hand. The numbers still read 1033515 and 472251.

"The first three digits of the seven-digit number are less than 180, and the other four are two pairs, each less than 59. On the six-digit number, the first two are less than 90 and the other four, again, are two pairs, each less than 59."

"And you said my games were weird? Why break it apart like that?"

"It's longitude and latitude, Abbs, to one-second accuracy. Latitude never goes to more than six digits, because at ninety degrees north or south, you're at a pole, and it starts back towards zero. And longitude never goes to more than seven, because at 180 and zero, zero, zero, zero, it goes from east to west or vice versa, and starts back down."

"My God, you're right. Do we have an atlas?"

"Is that the highest tech tool we can find?"

"If we want to keep it to ourselves, it is."

"I hear you, partner. One atlas, coming up."

"It's actually four possible locations." He put a big, dusty volume down on the desk and looked at the matchbook again, as if for the first time. "We don't know if it's north or south latitude, or if it's east or west longitude."

"Where are the four places?"

"Offhand, the northern US Great Plains, the middle of Mongolia or Siberia, the south Indian Ocean, or someplace in the Pacific about a thousand miles west of Cape Horn. What do you like?"

"Whoever wrote it down assumed the reader would know which one it was without being told." She picked up the pencil he had thrown and began chewing on the eraser.

"Probably. So? I wish you wouldn't do that, by the way."

"So the people our murdered task force was watching were pure-corn home grown. I'm thinking US heartland. And the Bureau can afford more pencils. Anyway, you threw it away." She continued to bite methodically, not quite breaking the rubber surface.

"It's still two possible locations. If it's straightforward degrees, minutes, and seconds, that's one spot. But if somebody's being cute, it could also be decimal degrees to four places, which would be something else." He flipped through the atlas, tried Montana first, and then paged forward to North Dakota.

"But both of those are close to each other, yes? How much is one degree?"

"A minute of latitude is the definition of a nautical mile."

"Was that an answer?" She bit the eraser off. "Now give me one in English."

"There are sixty minutes in a degree. So even if our two answers differed by a whole degree, they couldn't be more than sixty nautical miles, which is about seventy-five ordinary miles, apart. But they only differ by about a tenth of that."

"But you just had to complicate it, didn't you? Smartass. Okay, show me where we're talking about."

"The Theodore Roosevelt National Park in North Dakota." He pointed to a corner of the two-page map. "Mostly wild. Rolling prairie and some badlands, coming up close to the foothills of the Killdeer Mountains."

"A place where you need a permit to even be in the general vicinity," she said.

"That's if you're a law-abiding citizen."

She nodded. "And enough people *are* law abiding that traffic to the area ought to be damn thin. It would be a good place to hide something or somebody."

"Want me to get hold of Parks and find out exactly how thin?"

"No. Not yet, anyway. This could be a huge break. For now, I don't want anybody knowing that we're interested in that location. I mean anybody. Maybe whoever belongs to that matchbook will assume it's just lost. Meanwhile, we need some ground truth. Where can we plug into Google Earth without leaving any record of it?"

"Public library?"

"Do you have a card?"

"I do."

"Well, God bless Andrew Carnegie. Let's roll."

Chapter Twenty-Six

Crunch Time

From Durango, they drove up into the San Juan Mountains and then into the Rockies, crossing the Continental Divide somewhere near a town called Salida and heading back down toward Colorado Springs. Ben was tireless. Sometimes he would let Max drive, but Doug never saw him sleep or even look bored. Doug himself slept a lot, but he always woke up feeling as tired as before he had started. It was different from when he was on the road with Sancho. That had been an adventure. This felt more like being driven to his doom, and all he wanted to do was check out of the whole scene.

At Colorado Springs, the only bookstore that handled technical texts was the one attached to the Air Force Academy. But it was open to the general public and had what they wanted, a brown, unimpressive little volume simply titled *Geodesy*. It had been printed in 2010, but it was actually a reproduction of a 1952 text. As he leafed through it, he saw that it also made numerous references to a 1926 work. Original pay dirt. There was also a 2009 book on the subject, which included a lot of references to trajectories. Doug bought both of them, along with a book on celestial navigation and another on fluid mechanics. He also bought a spiral-bound notebook that had every right-hand page printed in graph paper and two Pentel drafting pencils with extra leads.

"What the hell do you want all those for?" said Ben.

"The notebook and pencils for notes. The other books are just smokescreen."

"I like the way your mind works. How about a little pornography, while we're blowing smoke?"

"They don't have any. I looked."

"Figures. It wouldn't go with the saltpeter regimen of the cadets in the school, I suppose." He flipped through one of the geodesy books a bit and made glowering faces at the pages of diagrams and numbers.

"The supposed anti-aphrodisiac in the food? You think they really do that, or is that just urban myth?"

"I think the government will do anything they can think of that's sneaky and mean and fucks somebody up."

"Yes, you do think that, don't you?"

"You don't?"

"I have to admit, I'm starting to."

At a nearby Starbucks, they used Ben's laptop to find the kind of hardware store they wanted, a place called Albinson's in Minneapolis, Minnesota. Getting the longitude and latitude of the New York Stock Exchange proved to be a bit trickier, though. Doug could download a simple version of Google Earth easily enough, but he could immediately see it wasn't going to be accurate enough for what they needed.

"Aw, shit. We need Google Earth Pro."

"So get it." Ben looked at the screen for the first time. "Why is that a problem?"

"It costs four hundred bucks."

"Who cares? You're about to be a rich man, aren't you? Put it on one of your credit cards."

"My what?" Doug's hands froze above the keyboard. He felt sick to his stomach and he involuntarily turned his head away from Ben.

"The ones in your wallet. The Visa and Mastercard."

"Oh. Well, um, they probably don't work." *Except to summon Mr. Black and his troops.* "I don't remember the last time I made a payment on either of them."

"Oh, really? But you still keep them?"

"Well, yeah. I mean, they're mine, after all. Maybe someday I'll get them reinstated."

"Funny thing. That's what our last guy said, too."

Doug stayed away from that topic completely. "We can probably get what we need at the same place we get the calculator. I'm sure we can." He remembered his training and said nothing more. Ben allowed him to leave the subject there. Doug couldn't decipher his expression, but he was pretty sure he was now on dangerously thin ice with both his employers.

They got back in the pickup and headed east. About seventy miles out of Colorado Springs they hooked up with Interstate 70, and soon the land around them turned as flat and brown and featureless as a dusty tabletop.

They passed into Kansas, and Ben stopped on the shoulder and gestured toward the northeast, where a seemingly endless array of spinning white wind turbines marched off to the horizon.

"What does that remind you of, Doug?" He squinted a bit, and his face looked grim and sad at the same time.

"Um. A wind farm?"

"Yeah? That's what it's called, all right. It reminds me of a cemetery. Like Arlington, say, with one white marker for each soul that isn't around anymore. Soon there won't be anything else here."

"Excuse me, but what else was ever here?" He didn't want to offend Ben, but it seemed to him that Kansas had always been mostly empty space.

"Farms, Doug. There used to be a farm every quarter mile. People came here once to homestead 160-acre parcels and make a life. But sooner or later, the Big G, Greed, got to them all. It wasn't just the banks. The farmers cannibalized each other. When a bank foreclosed on a farm, the neighbors lined up to buy it. They paid too much for it, but the banks went ahead and loaned them the money anyway, knowing they could foreclose on the same piece of land over and over. And after each time, another house and barn would get bulldozed and another family would move away or scatter to the wind. After a while, there weren't any neighbors anymore. The whole Great Plains is being depopulated, Doug. In twenty more years, it will be just like it was before the settlers ever came here, except for the white markers. Maybe I'll come back with a horse and a tent, live off the buffalo, if they come back."

"But *somebody* is still farming here, surely? Just in bigger parcels."

"They won't be for long." He pointed at the floor of the pickup. "Down there is the Ogallala Aquifer. Used to be, it was the biggest pouch of underground fresh water in the whole world. All of the cash-crop farms use it for irrigation. Only it's getting used up. It's thirty feet down now and dropping. When it gets a little lower, the pumps won't be able to pull the water anymore, and the farmers who are left will just lease their land to the wind-turbine people and walk away, let the prairie grasses take over."

"And where will they go?"

"To hell, mostly. What does it matter? Once you've lost the land, you're nobody anymore. And if you not only lost it but helped kill it, well, so much the worse."

He put the pickup back in gear and drove on in silence. Doug had no idea what to say, so he, too, was silent. He looked over his geodesy books, and he wondered if Ben would actually make the missile shot before he paid Doug off. When Doug had asked him, he had merely said the money was already waiting for him. That wasn't the same as saying he could get it right away. And that was not a trivial distinction. The only way he could keep Ben from blowing up half of New York and killing millions of people was to tell Black where the site was. But when he did that, he wanted to have the money in hand and already be on the move with it, because he was sure his leash would get pulled up short right away. So if he were going to work both sides of the street, take Ben's money and disappear, but also stop the launch, he would have to at least set things up so the shot *could* work. He wondered if he could. And he wondered if he dared to either do it or not do it.

Looking at the pages of formulae, he could see that nobody, not even he, could tell just by looking if a set of numbers to match those equations was phony or not. And that was assuming he could figure them out in the first place. He didn't scowl as Ben had when he looked at the pages, but he felt like it. The geode was one tough nut. There were formulae that took three lines to write, and if you got one term, one number, one plus or minus sign wrong, all your calculations would be worthless. And the time to decide which horse to back was getting closer.

The road was empty except for an occasional battered pickup or a tractor pulling an empty wagon. They blew across the featureless prairie at a steady hundred miles an hour and topped off their gas tank at every station they came to. The local radio stations featured evangelist preachers, radical right-wing political commentators, or country music. After a while, Ben turned it all off. They crossed the Missouri River at Kansas City and headed north on Interstate 35. Soon they were driving through rolling green country, with neat little sets of buildings and fenced pastures with mixed livestock types. Sometimes there were forests that came right up to the roadway ditch. Doug tried to see if Ben had a look of approval on his face, but he couldn't tell.

In Des Moines, Ben finally declared a rest stop, and they checked into a hotel for the night. Doug had a double bed all to himself, while Ben and Max took turns sleeping in the other one or standing watch. Nothing had ever been said about Doug being a prisoner, but he assumed he would be in a lot of trouble if he got out of their sight for very long.

The next day they ate pancakes and sausages at an IHOP and got back on the road. By late morning, they were crossing the Minnesota River, heading into the outskirts of Minneapolis. The place they wanted was just west of downtown, and they found it with only a few curses and vulgarisms.

"Fucking towns that grew up along a river are all laid out the same."

"How's that?" said Doug.

"Like a goddamn maze," said Max.

"I disagree, guys," said Doug. "I think it's a government conspiracy."

"You're full of shit," said Max.

"Well, yeah." He shrugged his shoulders. "I just thought it might cheer you up."

The sales clerk at Albinson's was pure gold. He acted as if it were perfectly normal for somebody to be looking for some thirty-year-old hardware, and he knew exactly what he had in stock. "I just took in a Hewlett Packard 97 desktop model from a surveyor who was retiring. Mint condition. It's got a full set of surveying and mapping programs on magnetic cards, a battery pack and adapter that are like new, and lots of ribbon for the calculator printer. If you need another battery, you can't get them from HP anymore, but Batteries Plus can make you one. Takes them a couple days. Non-lithium, so they don't have any weird habits."

"I probably won't need another one. How much for all this fine stuff?"

"I won't break up the set. Give you the whole works for two hundred even."

"Throw in a couple of pads of programming paper?"

"You got it. I can probably find some blank magnetic cards, too."

"Done. Just one other little thing. Do you have Google Earth Pro on any of your computers?"

"Sure. We have it on all of them. We let the customers play with it while they're waiting their turn. I can't sell it to you, though. That's strictly a franchise subscription app."

"I just want to use it for a few minutes."

"Right over there." He pointed to a laptop on a service counter.

It took Doug less than five minutes to get what he wanted, and he heaved a huge sigh of relief. They were in business. He made the first entry in his new notebook.

On the way back out to the parking lot, Ben said, "You look like a little kid with a new toy, Doug."

"I feel like one. You know, I haven't used a calculator like this since I was in high school. Man, they were high-tech back then. Still are, in some ways. If all you're doing is crunching numbers, not mixing any non-math operations with them, HP's goofy system called 'Reverse Polish Notation' still beats anything on a PC. I can't believe how easy that was. Did you see all the goodies they had? What a place!"

"Now all we need is somewhere for you to work."

"Yes we do."

"What does it have to have?"

"A nice big desk or table, light, and electricity. Oh, and a coffee maker of some kind."

"You'll have to learn not to be so demanding, Doug."

"I'm trying."

"We'll look for a place here in Minneapolis, I think. I have no footprints here, no history."

* * *

They wound up renting an artist's loft in a part of town that the local realtor referred to as Nowhere. "That's a not-quite acronym for 'North of Warehouse,' meaning the old industrial area just upstream on the Mississippi from the original milling district. The new development was supposed to be all upscale condos, but sales are in the tank, just as much as with any other housing. The developers are happy to get a short-term rental on one of the units now and then."

Ben told him they were in town for a short while to work on developing a movie, and he showed the man a California ID and paid for two months' rent in cash.

Their unit was on the fifth floor of an eight-story brick building. Through occasional breaks in the surrounding skyline, it had an obscured view of the river and the rail and barge traffic. It was only partially completed and only the finished parts had cabinets and furniture. The living room and kitchen had been showrooms for the project, but the other rooms had bare floors, exposed studs, and rough brick exterior walls. Doug liked it. They got a desk and chair, lamps, and some hide-a-beds at a thrift store and moved in.

Doug wasn't told that he couldn't leave, but he took it as a given. Ben and Max were gone most of the time, but one or the other brought him takeout food at least twice a day. At night, Doug slept in a back room, but one or both of the other two men would be out patrolling the area all night. Sometimes they went out to breakfast together.

At least once a day, Ben would burst into the unit and yell, "Bogies!" Then he would use a stopwatch to time how long it took Doug to get his notes and papers and calculator into a canvas duffel bag and get out the door. Ten seconds was the goal. It took Doug several tries before he made it.

"There are five ways out of this building, Doug. Take the time to walk them all, every day. I've given them all numbers, see?" He pushed a small hand-drawn map into Doug's hand. "That way we can tell each other which one we're going to, and it doesn't matter if we get overheard. Memorize them now. I'm also cutting a new back exit door out of the unit today."

Then Ben pointed silently to the bottom of the map, where there was a set of numbers that had nothing to do with the exits. Doug recognized them as being very close to the ones he had memorized from the Dirty Dick's matchbook, but not quite the same. "But that's not—"

"No, it's not. But it's your starting point. Take a day to memorize this, then burn it. It's okay to write it down in your notebook, but if you do, you can never let the book out of your sight again. Now get to work."

So now, at last, he had been trusted with the longitude and latitude of the actual missile site. The "starting point," Ben called it, meaning the point of origin of the launch. He had been given the Holy Grail and the secret handshake, all rolled into one. If he betrayed that trust, he would surely die for it. Well, if he betrayed it too soon. Timing was everything.

He began by simply reading the textbooks, taking his time, like any beginning engineering student, then pacing around and rephrasing what he had just read, saying it out loud, making it his own. At first it was very hard, like trying to stir up an old dog that had done nothing but sleep for years. But it got easier, slowly and then with increasing speed. After three days he was actually punching numbers into the HP 97, and after four days, he started to *feel* them. He wrote a program to take the geodesy equations and run them automatically, and he saved it on a magnetic card as a check on his manual calculations. But he soon got to the point where he could tell if he was doing something wrong even before the program said so. It was the point engineers sometimes referred to as CSL, or "Calculus, Second Language." In the days before engineers let computers do all their thinking for them, it was what all the good ones aspired to. He hadn't felt it for a long, long time. In fact, he had forgotten it. And God help him, he began to be very excited about Ben's project. It wasn't just a way to make a lot of money. It was salvation, in every way that mattered.

On the middle of the sixth day, Ben and Max came into the unit with two big suitcases full of something heavy.

"You're working too hard, Doug." Ben reached down and shut off the desktop calculator. "Take a break. It's a beautiful day. Go for a walk or something. Hell, go get yourself a beer. You've earned it. You can leave the notebook here. We'll watch it for you."

"How long do you want me out of here?" He was amazed. So he wasn't a prisoner, after all.

"At least three hours. I'd say go to a movie, but I don't think there are any around here. Take your gun."

"Who am I going to shoot?" He rummaged around in the backpack, found the .45, and stuffed it in a front pocket, where it fit very badly and threatened to pull his pants down.

"Probably nobody. But you're on the wrong side of the law now. Always assume that there's somebody out there who knows that and wants to take you down for it. Always know where you will run, how you will get away, no matter where you are. And never be afraid of killing somebody."

"Got it." *If only you knew.*

"I can see the gun in your pocket. That's no good. Tuck it in your waistband at the small of your back. Put a round in the chamber, safety on. Then put on a loose jacket."

"I don't have one."

"Take mine. Now, get the hell out of here."

* * *

He walked out into the neighborhood he had lived in for a week but had never seen, and he felt wonderful. He had done something he had quit believing in a long time ago. He had resurrected himself as an engineer. And there was still more to come.

He headed toward downtown and passed through an area that seemed to be full of nothing but strip joints and small art galleries, which struck him as an odd combination. He wondered if women found it easier to get their lowbrow husbands to go shopping for art if they both knew he would sneak a look into one of the other establishments along the way. He smiled and went on.

He walked down to the waterfront he had only been able to glimpse from the loft windows. Past a big cable-suspension bridge, he took the pedestrian walkway along an elaborate set of waterfalls that looked man-made. A sign proclaimed the Corps of Engineers lock and dam at St. Anthony Falls. There was a curved, multiple-arch stone bridge across the river, but he decided not to take it. There was no ship traffic in the lock, and he could only get so excited about looking at falling water.

"What the hell?" he said out loud. "Ben was right. I've earned a real break."

He went back the way he had come and turned into the first strip joint he came to. He took a seat by the runway, where a not quite over-the-hill stripper had just taken off her bra. He ordered an overpriced beer, then sat back in the edge of the general gloom away from the stage and ogled the dancer shamelessly. *You've come a long way, Dougie my boy. Used to be you were too shy to even go into a place like this.*

He tucked some money into the dancer's garter, finished the beer, and ordered another. His mood got better and better.

Then he heard the voice in the darkness behind him.

"Enjoying the show, are we?"
He didn't have to turn around to know it was Mr. Black.

Chapter Twenty-Seven

The Road to Dirty Dick's

No matter how long agents Connelly and Webb stared at the satellite image, it didn't make any more sense. In the middle of the North Dakota Badlands, where there shouldn't be anything but rocks, scrub brush, and prairie grasses, there was a building. It was hard to get a sense of scale in the image, but it looked about the size of an average house. It was one story high and had a shiny metal roof with a sign on one edge of it.

"I wish I'd brought a magnifying glass." She put her face closer to the screen and squinted.

"Wouldn't matter, Abbs. The pixels just aren't there to define anything as small as that sign. On our own satellites, maybe, but not here. And you said—"

"Spare me what I said. You think it looks like that sign could say Dirty Dick's?"

He squinted, too. "Sure. It could also say Daffy Duck or Dunkin' Donuts. So what do we do now?"

"We need eyes on the ground, John. Bad."

"How do we get them without involving anybody else?"

"Obviously, one of us has to go there."

"I was afraid you were going to say that. And just how are we going to do *that* without letting anybody else know about the matchbook or the name of the place?"

"That's the same question."

"That's because you didn't answer it last time."

"Well, it's a little tricky, isn't it?" She took out a fresh pencil and bit on the eraser. "You ever watch that TV show about the FBI agents who do nothing but profiling? They're always going somewhere in the Bureau's private jet. Wouldn't that be something?"

"I wonder if there's a name for that." He scowled.

"For what, traveling in a private jet?"

"No, for obsessively eating erasers. Farberlepsy or something. I think it's really a substitute for— "

"I don't want to hear what it's a substitute for. We can't both go and leave the task force office to run itself, but maybe one of us can sneak off for a few days."

"Or maybe not." He shook his head. "Not right away, but sooner or later, you will have to tell somebody where you went and why. The where isn't so bad, but the why is a real killer."

"Okay then, try this out. We pick somebody to hold down the fort for a few days, and we check out a bureau vehicle and head back to Albuquerque to have another look at the battleground and the road to it."

"And when we get there, we miraculously find the matchbook?"

"That will be our story, anyway."

"Hell, Abbs, if we're going to do that, we really can take a Bureau jet."

"No we can't, because I'm not really going. I'm heading in the other direction in my own car."

"Good grief. Have I ever mentioned that you have the professional equivalent of a death wish?"

"I think that has come up once or twice, yes. Are you in or out?" She quit biting on the eraser and gave him a look that she had always found to be highly persuasive.

"Let me get this straight. When the shit hits the fan—and the shit will definitely hit the fan—our story is that we thought we were being stalked by another agency."

"That's our story, yes."

"And based on that, we decided to be clandestine, unorthodox, and probably totally against all of our own regulations."

"By George, I think he's got it. So you're in?"

"And I thought my mother didn't raise any idiots. All right, I'm in." He sighed. "Just a few changes, though. First, don't take your own car. Take something that nobody in the Bureau, not even me, has ever connected you to. Same thing with your weapon."

"Where do I get a gun I can't be tied to? In particular, where do I get one on short notice?"

"I have several. What do you like?"

"I'll have a nice big backpack to hide it in, so I can take something with some serious shocking power. A big magazine would be good, too. I'm way too crummy a shot for a five-round revolver."

"How about a Beretta nine? Twelve rounds in the magazine and one in the pipe."

"I like it."

"You're really going to do this, aren't you?"

"I'm maybe even going to like it."

"Then I'll just say this once: be damn careful out there in the boonies, Abbs. Because your backup is going to be slow to nonexistent. And believe it or not, somebody cares."

"Why, Agent Connelly, I'm touched. Does this mean we're an item? Can I tell all my friends?"

"You don't have any." He gave her a playful cuff on the shoulder.

That afternoon she took a city bus to a used car lot and bought a ten-year-old Jeep Renegade. She paid for it with cash, but she registered it in her own name. She figured by the time the new title got the attention of anybody that might be shadowing her, she would already be back from her trip. Then she went to three different sporting goods stores and bought every piece of camping equipment that she could remember from her days as a Girl Scout in Upper Michigan. She also bought a few things that hadn't existed back then, including a hand-held GPS. It seemed like another world and another life, those long summers in the deep woods, and it was. But the experience had served her well and would again. She put all the gear in the Jeep and filled the remaining space with non-perishable groceries. She parked the Jeep a mile from her house, took a bus back to her office, and drove her regular car home. Before dawn the next day, she and the Jeep were on the road. As she crossed the Missouri River, she looked down and thought, *Funny thing, it looks just like the Rubicon.*

Chapter Twenty-Eight

Choosing Sides

Doug walked out of the strip joint in a daze. He wandered aimlessly, with no thought of where he was headed. He crossed a six-lane street against the light and was oblivious to the cars honking at him. At some point he encountered a panhandler, and without thinking about it he reached into his wallet and gave the man a bill.

"Wow, a fiver. Thanks, man."

"Yeah, right. Thank Sancho when you see him."

"Who?"

"Leave me alone, okay?"

But at some level, his mind was racing furiously, in the grip of powerful currents he didn't begin to understand. For weeks he had expected to be snatched, bagged, beaten, and brought to the edge of screaming terror. It was just a question of when. And more recently, he had wondered how much pain he could endure before he told Mr. Black the location of the ICBM silo. He wasn't even sure why he wanted to withhold that bit of information, but he did. He wanted it very badly. The timing of the telling was everything.

So it utterly amazed him when none of those horrible things happened. Mr. Black had only wanted to talk to him. But it was crazy talk.

"I don't know the location of the silo yet, I'm afraid," said Doug, "but we'll be going there soon." He thought about the telltale signs that showed when people were lying, and he avoided them all, except the one about not offering information that had not been requested.

"But can you actually make the missile work?"

"I think so, yes. I haven't seen it yet, but I have the navigation system figured out."

"Then the location of the silo doesn't matter," said Black.

"It doesn't? How could it not?"

"We are going to implement a slight change of plan, Mr. Wright. You see, as soon as the missile is out of the ground, a dozen different agencies and military units will know exactly where it came from, with no help from you. They'll swoop down on it and dispatch our domestic terrorists so fast, they will never know what hit them. I and my staff will not need to lift a finger."

"Am I hearing you right? You're actually going to let him launch?"

"No, I'm not going to just *let* him. I want him to."

"You *want* him to launch a nuclear missile?"

"Yes, but not at the target he gave you. You are going to change the numbers, you see. Then help him get it going, any way you can." He gave Doug a piece of paper with some longitude and latitude coordinates on it. It was hard to read in the dim light of the place, but he could see it defined someplace fairly close to the equator.

"Memorize that and destroy it. We've trained you for that, after all."

"Okay, sure. I don't recognize the location. Where is this?"

"Some people know those numbers by heart, Mr. Wright. It's been a thorn in our national side for almost sixty years now. That's beautiful downtown Havana."

"*What?*"

"Exactly. We are going to let our homegrown anarchists do what our government has lacked the will and the courage to do for decades. We are going to restore our sovereignty and our national pride. We are going to settle the score with those Communist bastards, once and for all." He got a far-off look in his eyes that Doug did not like at all.

"Sweet Jesus."

"Yes he is. If you get a chance, you might paint that on the nose cone. If it works out that we get to do it all again, the next target will be North Korea, but that's speculative at this point. Now leave. We should not be seen together."

Doug did as he was told. But it would be the last time he would. *That son of a bitch is even crazier than Ben! He's not only in the grip of a complete fantasy, it's not even today's fantasy. The goofy bastard is time-traveling, no less. And furthermore, when the Green Berets or the Navy SEALs or whoever come storming into the missile complex with all guns blazing, he isn't going to do a damn thing to help me. He isn't even planning on being there!*

He could understand Ben Savitch's anger and hatred, even if he didn't share it. The man had seen an entire way of life taken away from him and his people. No wonder he was a bit less than totally rational. But what had the Cubans ever done to Mr. Black? In fact, what had they ever done to anybody besides their own people? Black was stuck back in the era of Reagan and J. Edgar and even Tailgunner Joe, mindlessly in the grip of a fairy tale about evil empires and righteous nukes. And that made him not just crazy, but utterly unpredictable. Suddenly the choice of which horse to back was ridiculously easy. *The lesser of two crazies. The one who will give me money and maybe help me disappear. The one who believed in me, gave me a project. And by God, I'm going to do the project.*

Was there a way to do the project without also becoming a mass murderer? He thought about the early nuclear warheads and all their secret hardware, like weak-link/strong-link "fuses," and the so-called x-box detonator with its altimeter and proximity sensor, all powered by non-rechargeable, non-replaceable batteries. Would any of that stuff still work after fifty or sixty years of sitting idle? It seemed unlikely. *But if it does . . .* Well, that was another problem for another day. The present had enough of them.

He wandered aimlessly for another hour, thinking about how much to tell Ben. As fatal as it could turn out to be, he finally decided he would have to tell him everything. He straightened his shoulders, got his bearings, and headed back to the loft, his resolve increasing by the minute.

The place didn't look any different when Doug got back to it. Whatever Ben and Max had been doing there, they were done and were now chatting quietly over a fresh pot of coffee. Doug poured a cup for himself and sat down at their only desk. As softly as he could, he said, "Do we know if this room is bugged?"

"We didn't use to, but we do now," said Max.

"And?"

"And now it has listening devices," said Ben, "but they're all ours. What makes you ask?"

"We need to talk. Bad."

"Talk."

"You know that when you launch the missile, you'll have about a million armed troops pouncing on you instantly?"

"Yes. But we will have done what we set out to, and it will be worth the price. Don't worry, we'll find a way to get you out first. And we'll make sure you can go get your money."

"It's not just that, Ben. You and Max seem to know a lot about how to disappear and how to stay that way. I need you to teach me about that. The money alone won't do it for me."

"You're right, it won't. All right, I'll teach you some things. Anything else?"

"I'm afraid so." Doug took a deep breath.

"Well?"

"This isn't easy, Ben. And when I'm done telling you, likely as not you're going to kill me on the spot. But you've got to know. I work for an agency that has no name, one that's been looking at you for a long time now. I was recruited against my will, tortured and blackmailed."

"Of course you were. That's the way they always work."

"*What?* You mean you knew?"

"Not for sure, but you had all the signs. I was wondering when you were going to tell me. Max wanted to kill you a long time ago, but I told him you were going to have a change of heart. See, that's the first rule of how to disappear. You have to be a good judge of people. And I'm afraid I can't teach you that."

"But this agency, um, how can I say this? They're—"

"They're illegal as hell and they don't play by the rules."

"You know that, too?"

"There are more of them like that than anybody imagines, Doug. It's almost the new norm. You think places like Gitmo, where people just disappear forever, are accidents?"

"But, Jesus—"

"Doesn't go there. How are the numbers coming, by the way?"

He seriously considered laughing, crying, and collapsing, or all three at once. "They're done, basically. I'm just triple-checking now."

"Then you're done. I trust your figures. We'll leave the fancy calculator here; take only the notes." He studied Doug intently, possibly looking for some "tell." But there wasn't any.

"Okay. Thanks for the vote of confidence. What happens next?"

"Tell me about the credit cards."

He took a deep breath and squinted for a moment, dredging up the instructions that now seemed to be from such a long time ago. "If I use the Visa for anything at all, I will get six agents reporting to me within 24 hours. If I use the Mastercard, I will have armed assistance within an hour, but I don't know how many people that will be. The Macy's card isn't a credit card at all, it's a universal ATM card. It doesn't summon anybody. It just gets you money." He also told Ben everything else he knew about the agency, which was little enough.

"That tells me several things," said Ben.

"It does?" It didn't tell Doug anything.

"If your agency is as secret as they say, it has to be either a rogue group within a larger body, like the CIA, say, or else a small elite organization with no known address and no ongoing overt operations. Either way, it's not very big."

"Maybe not, but it's powerful and deadly. They were the ones doing the shooting in Albuquerque. I don't know who the targets were."

"I think the targets were FBI. Your dark agency didn't want them snatching you or me before we led them someplace interesting. But let's go back to size."

"What about it?"

"This agency is not so big that they have an operative in every town, just waiting for somebody like you to get in trouble. They couldn't. If your Mastercard can summon somebody within an hour, then they've had somebody that close to you all along, somebody shadowing you. More likely two somebodies. Super-secret agencies are also super paranoid. They almost never let anybody work alone."

"Except me."

"But they're watching you, so that doesn't count."

"Well, they certainly seem to know how to find me whenever they want to."

"Exactly. And what's the only thing you're still carrying that you started out with, way back in California?"

"My wallet?"

"That's right. With the credit cards in it."

"Oh, my God, yes. But you can't track a credit card until it gets used. Um, can you?"

"Maybe you can, with these. Let's see them. Are they fatter than a regular card?"

Doug laid his wallet on the table and pulled the cards out of it. All three of them were noticeably thicker than a regular card.

"All this time, I never noticed. Stupid, stupid, stupid."

"Beating up on yourself is always a popular sport, Doug, but it doesn't win any prizefights."

"So what do we do, put the cards on an outbound freight train?"

"Maybe not. Maybe we use them to summon your people."

"*What?*"

"Think small, Doug, remember? What if those six agents they say they will send you within 24 hours is all they've got? What if that's their entire field staff? We could set up an ambush, wipe out the whole damn outfit."

"Are you crazy? These people are ruthless. They're stone killers."

"What do you think I am?"

Chapter Twenty-Nine

Changing the Rules

Ben put a portable radio on the desk, turned it on, and found a station playing classic rock. They put the Mastercard on the desk, under the calculator. Ben insisted that they leave the calculator, even though it now had a magnetic program card in it with geodesy equations. Doug put the other two cards back in his wallet, and all three men left the loft by the new rear exit. The white truck with the big engine was waiting at the back door. Max got behind the wheel and started the machine, and they drove away slowly and quietly. Only two blocks later, they pulled into an alley between two vacant warehouses and stopped in front of a metal fire door.

"Leave your wallet with Max and come with me." Ben got out first and held the door for Doug.

The truck pulled smoothly away. Close up, Doug could see that the steel door that had appeared to be securely padlocked shut really wasn't. One half of the hasp was not attached to anything, and Ben quickly opened the door and motioned Doug to follow him through it. Inside, he pulled the door shut again and bolted it.

There were no lights, but clerestory cupolas high above them dimly illuminated the interior. The glass had been replaced long ago by corrugated fiberglass panels, and the light was muddy and green. The place could have been built as either a warehouse or a factory, but it was totally empty now.

Heavy timber columns and spacer beams soared up and disappeared into the dusty air under the roof. Pigeons roosted on the high beams.

Doug led the way to the only interior enclosure in the whole place, a wooden shack over against the far wall. Inside, there was a refrigerator, a bed, and a small table with a TV set on it. The TV was showing a black-and-white picture of the loft they had just left, with the radio and Doug's new HP calculator on the desk. A speaker somewhere was playing "Fixing a Hole," by the Beatles. Ben switched on an overhead light and closed the door behind them.

"Make yourself comfortable, Doug. I have no idea how long this might take."

"What are we waiting for?" He sat on the edge of the bed and looked at the TV.

"Max is taking your remaining credit cards on a nice little trip right now. I want to see what our spooks will do when they see you have left one of the cards behind."

"What if they don't do anything? How long do we wait?"

"Rule number two of how to disappear is this, Doug: teach yourself patience. Learn to be like a sniper in the jungle, ignoring the bugs and snakes and heat, waiting for the event you know is going to happen."

"It is?"

"You bet. You made it happen. And when it does, you will have stolen the initiative away from the enemy, and that's a fine thing to do. Going on the offensive is always good."

So they waited.

Four hours later the background music had shifted to "Get a Job" by the Coasters, and two men in dark clothes entered the loft, guns drawn, their eyes sweeping in all directions. Doug recognized both of them, but neither was Mr. Black. After a while, they put the guns away and simply searched.

Place is completely empty. I think they're long gone.

Find the card yet?

Yeah, it's here, under that funny adding machine. Not like a place it could have accidentally been dropped.

Why would he leave the one but take the others?

No idea. What do you want to do?

You know what we do. We leave the place the way we found it and report back to Mr. Black.

The two men headed for the main door.

"Just two," said Ben. "And they're not going to tell us much of anything. That's too bad. Still, initiative is initiative."

He pulled out a cell phone and touched a few buttons. The image on the TV screen went blank at the same time that a huge explosion somewhere outside shook the walls. A thin cloud of brown dust came drifting down from the ceiling, and Doug opened the door to see if their building was still standing. It was, but the green clerestory panels were cracked, and some of them had fallen.

"Now be honest with yourself, Doug. Doesn't that make you feel better?"

Chapter Thirty

The High Road

An hour or so later, Max reappeared with the truck. Whether that was by prearrangement or Ben had somehow summoned him, Doug couldn't tell. They drove in the opposite direction from the bombed-out loft and were soon on a tangled maze of interstates, making their way through the city and off to the northwest.

"Where did you leave Doug's credit cards, Max?"

"Town called Alexandria."

"I don't know the place. Any good for an ambush?"

"No. Too dense, too many people, too many blind spots."

"Can you pick the cards up again?"

"Sure."

"Let's do it. Then we'll head farther west. You want to do a good old-fashioned ambush, go to the Badlands, yeah?"

"Every time," said Max.

Doug grinned for a moment, then had a sobering thought. "Back at the loft, we most likely missed the one we really wanted to kill, you know. That's unless he was close enough to get hit by some flying debris."

"Who's that?"

"He calls himself Mr. Black. He's some kind of high-ranking agent, maybe even the head honcho himself. I saw him when I was off on my walk, when you and Max were wiring the loft."

"That's okay. When we actually use the cards you have left, it should call up a real party. I'm betting he'll be there. Fiddle the right tune, and the devil himself will show up."

"And then we kill him?"

"At least once," said Max.

The smile returned to Doug's face.

At the city of Alexandria, they drove into the center of the old downtown. Max parked near a public mailbox and got out. He scanned the streets in all directions while he pretended to mail a letter. Then he squatted down and took something off the bottom of the box. Back in the truck, he pulled the duct tape off the two cards and handed them back to Doug.

Driving away, Max circled several blocks in different directions before he went back to the highway. Doug recognized the pattern from his surveillance training, and he wondered where Max had learned it.

"If we've been made," said Max, "it's not by anybody in a vehicle."

"I agree," said Ben. "There's no tail I can see, either. If our Mr. Black is still dogging Doug's trail, the explosion must have at least distracted him for a while. Does this town have an airport?"

"It's probably a little one." Max nodded.

"Airports are the last places on earth that still have pay phones. Find it."

"I saw a sign as we were coming into town. It's this way."

The airport had two runways, crossing each other at about a hundred and twenty degrees. It also had a tiny terminal building with a control tower and half a dozen scattered hangar buildings, most with low-wing Pipers or high-wing Cessnas in front of them. There were also planes staked down on the sod, with no hangars, including a pair of Champion Citabrias, shiny new from the nearby Belanca factory, and a brawny-looking twin-engined amphibian.

Max and Doug waited in the truck while Ben went inside to use the phone.

"You know how to fly, Doug?"

"Not legally. I had a private license once, but flying got to be too expensive to keep up just as a hobby, so I let it lapse."

"What does that mean, 'let it lapse'?"

"You have to log a certain number of hours every year to keep the license current. I couldn't afford it."

"But you could fly that stuff out there?"

"Maybe not the amphib. That could be complicated. But all that other stuff, sure. Light planes are all the same, really. The only important thing that differs is the stall speed, and even if you don't have an operating manual, you can go up a few thousand feet and fool around and find out what it is."

"Why do you have to know?"

"Because a landing is really just a controlled stall. Any fool can take off. But it's good being able to land."

"Yeah, I guess it would be. Sometimes I wish I could fly. Ben does, you know."

"Really? No, I didn't know."

"Sometimes I can't believe all the shit he knows how to do. He's really smart."

"What does he fly?"

"He has some kind of bush plane stashed away somewhere. He says stealing airplanes isn't as easy to get away with as stealing cars, so he keeps one of his own."

"You're right, he's some kind of smart guy."

Ben was in the terminal over an hour, and Max watched the road into the airport with a pair of binoculars. When Ben finally came out, he had a bounce in his step and a pleased look on his face.

"How many troops did we get?" said Max.

"At least six, maybe more."

"Heavy hardware?"

"Very heavy. Head north, nice and easy, Max. Pick a place you like to stop for the night. Some of our people have a lot farther to come than we do, so we have a day and a half to get to the middle of North Dakota."

Max got back on I-94, took the big machine up to exactly the speed limit, and locked in the cruise control.

One day later, Agent Webb was two hundred and fifty miles to the south, unaware that she was duplicating the route of the agrarian anarchists. North of Des Moines, at the turnoff for Cedar Rapids, she stopped at the same rest area where they had regrouped and taken their new orders after the armored car job. As they had agreed before she left, she called Agent Connelly on his cell phone at the prearranged time of 6:30. Both their phones would have a record of the call, of course, including what numbers were connected, the length of the call, and where they were. But as long as they didn't text or leave any voice mail, there would be no recording of the actual conversation. It wasn't ideal, but it was the best they could do on short notice.

"So far so good?" she said.

"So far so good. Nobody thought it was even slightly odd that we were going back to Albuquerque. Are you in Frostbite Falls yet?" That was their pre-agreed phrase for Minnesota.

"Still about fifty miles out. I'm thinking I'll stop for the day in another hour or two. This vehicle is a real back-breaker."

"Don't tell me about it. And don't stop any place where you have to register and give a license number."

"I'll camp in a park somewhere. Or maybe park in a camp. I forget which."

"That'll work. Eat something besides erasers, okay?"

"Anything else I ought to know about?"

"Absolutely maybe. I checked back with our office, figuring I don't care if they know where I am, unlike some other people I could name. Seems there was a bomb in Minneapolis the day before yesterday."

"Another bank job?"

"No, so we don't have automatic jurisdiction. Empty building, supposedly, but two people were in it. A local cop called our central lab to ask if they had ever seen an explosive device with pieces of something ceramic in the detonator."

"You mean a spark plug?"

"We don't know that. Our lab techie danced around with the cop for a while, trying to get him to say 'spark plug' without being prompted, but he wouldn't do it. Then our man said we could analyze the remnants for them, but only if the FBI is officially invited in on the case. He couldn't get the guy to say that, either."

"Shit. Do we know where the site is?"

"All we know is it's in the old north end warehouse district. Sounds like it was a big blast, with multiple charges, so it should be easy to spot."

"Maybe I'll go through Minneapolis tomorrow and give it a highly uninvited and unofficial look."

"I didn't hear that, of course," he said. "And yeah, I think that would be worth doing. Who knows, it might even give you an excuse for being where you are."

"Wouldn't that be something, though? Talk to you tomorrow."

"Same time?"

"Same time." That meant that she would call him exactly an hour later the next day. Any other time, and he would know she was under duress. He would not call her at all unless there was some kind of trouble.

* * *

Just over the Minnesota border, she allowed herself a thirty-mile detour east to the deep, wooded valley of the Root River. She made camp in a little county park just outside the tiny town of Spring Valley, next to the river.

She had bought a porterhouse steak and some cloverleaf dinner rolls at a grocery store in town, and she made a fire pit on the sandy riverbank and started some charcoal briquettes in a perforated tin can. Then she pitched her dome tent, shook out her sleeping bag, and generally made things orderly.

A hundred yards downstream, there was another, bigger tent. Two young couples who looked like farmers were sitting in front of a fire, drinking something from a bottle in a brown paper bag and beer from long-necked glass bottles. She took out her binoculars and looked them over long enough to decide they were harmless.

When things were ready, she cooked the steak with the coals suspended above the meat on a grate, as she had seen it done on a Food Network program. It was perfect—slightly charred on the outside, red and dripping warm in the middle. She opened a cheap bottle of cabernet sauvignon, buttered a roll, and savored the meal. "Honest food" was what they had called it back in her teen years, the stuff that you could only have the first day out in the woods, because after that, the lack of refrigeration would be an issue. So the first night was a feast and a celebration. The rest of the trip, you ate canned or dehydrated goods. She smiled as she thought of that simpler, happier time.

She had camped with her Girl Scout troop many times, but she always preferred going into the deep woods alone. "Abby's looking for the truth of her soul in some hollow tree again," her friends would say. And maybe she was. She wasn't antisocial, but when her deepest energy wells needed recharging or she had a problem to solve, what she craved was solitude. And the solitude of the wilderness was the best. Not that she ever thought of making a career of camping. Even back in her scouting days, she knew she would become some kind of cop. No, that was wrong. Her father was "some kind of cop," a blue-and-black for thirty years on the mean streets of Chicago. He took great pride in being an honorable and honest man in a largely corrupt system, and she took pride in being his daughter. No, she wanted to be some kind of *super* cop, with cases that mattered.

Her father had died of a heart attack before she graduated from the FBI Academy at Quantico. But she knew he would be proud of her. Even though she had seen him spend countless hours staring into a glass of bourbon and muttering to himself, she was sure of it. "You work the streets, all you ever see is shit," he would say to the amber fluid. "Humanity at its worst. And you never get to do any good." Still, she knew. If he were still alive, he would be the proudest man on the planet. *My daughter, the FBI agent*. She needed to remember that now and then, especially when she was getting exiled to places like Kansas City. *And when you're working on a case like this one, kiddo.*

And what *was* the case, anyway? She was supposed to be running down the people who had massacred their agents in Albuquerque and who might or might not be the same as the people who had killed another agent in Long Beach. Instead she was going to check out a location from a matchbook that was *maybe* dropped by a guy who wasn't even one of the shooters. What did they know about him? He was a former aerospace engineer, literally a rocket scientist. Could that put him in Long Beach at the time of the first shooting? That part of the country was full of high-tech people like him.

That's it! He is *the link. Mr. Matchbook draws people who shoot our agents, draws them like flies. But they don't pick him up. They're shadowing him, waiting for him to lead them to something. And in the meanwhile, they don't want us interfering. I mean, they* really *don't want that.*

So did that make the shooters another agency? Maybe, maybe not. But she strongly suspected that the place she was going, after the side trip to Minneapolis, was where the matchbook man was supposed to lead them. Maybe he had even had something to do with the blast. She wished it were time to call Agent Connelly again.

She was about to have a last glass of wine when her reverie was broken and her attention forcibly drawn to the other campsite.

A lot of beer and whiskey had been consumed by then, and the party had turned rowdy. Somebody had brought out a boom box and put it on the ground between the two couples, playing heavy metal rock. It was so loud, they all had to shout to keep their conversation going, which they did. Webb was more than a little annoyed. The silence of the woods wasn't just nice; it was something to be respected, something almost sacred. And she needed it very much just then. She sighed, put down her wine glass, and walked over to them.

"Ladies. Guys." She nodded to each of them in turn, assessing both the mood and character of each face as she did so. What she saw did not impress her. One fat hillbilly with a John Deere tee shirt, so drunk his eyes were out of focus and his mouth was hanging open. One thinner guy with a badly trimmed moustache and a shirt with the sleeves cut off to show his muscles and some artless tats. He had a straw cowboy hat. The women were plain-looking, mousy types, both looking a bit nervous.

"You want to turn that down a bit so we can talk?"

They didn't. So she raised her voice.

"Look, I appreciate that everybody needs to blow off a little steam now and then. But this is my park as much as yours, and I didn't come all the way out here to listen to that bullshit excuse for music. So shut it off, cowboy, okay?"

Nobody spoke or moved. *Walk away, Abby, before you do something you'll have to regret. These redneck hicks aren't worth getting in legal trouble over.*

She turned and walked back toward her own camp, but the noise went on, and so did her anger. Then the sound level went up. She decided not to tolerate it, after all, and she turned again, glaring.

"Oooh, I'm scared," said the thin one. "You gonna turn us in now, or just rough us up some? I might just like that. I might like it a lot. You won't, though."

His woman reached across him and turned down the volume. "It really is pretty loud, Jimmy."

With no warning whatsoever, he slapped her in the face, so hard she fell backwards on the sand. She stayed there, sobbing quietly.

"Don't you *ever* touch my radio, woman. You hear me? I'll kick your worthless ass from one end of this woods to the other."

"I'm sorry, I just—"

"*Never.*" He was screaming now, working himself up.

And some black cauldron in the back of Webb's soul finally boiled over, flooding her with bittersweet, delicious anger. *That's all you get for slack, asshole.*

"I guess I'll just have to do the touching, then." She pulled the nine-millimeter out of the waistband of her jeans and calmly shot the boom box in its exact center. It flew off into the bushes and was immediately silent. All around the campfire, mouths hung open.

"If I hit that little thing, I can damn sure hit you, asshole. Think about it."

She turned and walked away, not looking back. Behind her, there was no sound but the crackling of the fire. After a while, the one with the radio said, "You better not sleep too sound in that cute little Gucci tent of yours, bitch. Because later on, I might just come over there, and—"

"You really shouldn't have said that, you know." She turned around and strode quickly back to the campfire. She stepped around it, and before the thin man could get to his feet, she smashed him in the face with her pistol. The sound of his nose breaking was sharp in the newly quiet woods.

"I'm afraid you're going to have to make a little trip to an emergency room now, cowboy. What a shame. I was looking forward to your visit."

She wished he would get up and try to attack her, but he rolled around on the ground, screaming in agony and spurting blood. She smiled, glad that he wasn't so drunk he couldn't feel the pain. *They say a broken nose is one of the most painful injuries there is. I hope so.*

Finally the screaming man's buddy hauled himself unsteadily to his feet, and he and his woman picked up their wounded companion and helped him over to a dirty pickup that was parked nearby. "Come on, Zhimbo. We gotcha now."

After they drove away, Webb walked over to where the other woman was still on the ground, though she had stopped crying.

"He's never going to change, you know. You need to get clear of him before he kills you."

"He's not so bad when he leaves the booze alone."

"But he doesn't, does he? And now that he's made you his personal punching bag, he's never going to leave you alone. Get away. Now would be a perfect time. Is that his red pickup over there? Take it and just go."

"You couldn't believe how long and hard I've wanted to do that. I really have. But where would I go? I've got no place where he wouldn't find me. And then he would *really* hurt me."

"Get to a big city. Rochester, or better yet, St. Paul or Minneapolis. Park his truck where it will get towed away. Then find any cop and tell him you need to go to a battered women's shelter. There will be one. And they will help you make a new life."

"Really?"

"It's what they do."

"You make it sound so easy. You with your gun and all your confidence. God, how I wish—"

"I didn't say it was easy, sweetie. I said it was possible. Also necessary."

"I don't know. It's awful scary. I never . . ."

"Everything is scary, sweetie. But staying where you are isn't just scary; it's a guaranteed disaster and a probable death sentence. Go. It could be the last chance you get."

"Maybe I could just . . ."

"Do you have any money?"

"Um . . ."

"Wait." She went back to her Jeep, unlocked it, and took two hundred dollars out of the glove compartment. It was most of her traveling money, but she could always stop at an ATM, and she figured the other woman couldn't. She went back to the other campsite and pressed it into her hand.

"I can't pay you back."

"Pay me back by having a life."

"I'll try."

"Try hard."

"Thank you." She stood up and gave Webb a hug. "Thank you so much."

"My pleasure." She left the woman staring dumbly at the wad of bills in her hand in the light of the dying campfire. She didn't know if the woman would find the courage to go or not, but she had done all she could to help her do so.

Are you proud of me, Daddy?

She struck her own camp and covered the remains of her fire with beach sand. She refused to let the two drunken rednecks make her afraid, but it was possible that they would come back not with reinforcements but with a sheriff's deputy or two. That could turn into a hassle she definitely did not need just then. She drove five miles or so into the countryside, turned into a machinery access road between two cornfields, and parked in a small grove. She slept uncomfortably in the back of the Jeep.

At dawn the next day, she drove past the campsite again before heading north. The big tent was still there but the red pickup was not. There was no fire.

You did good, kiddo. Really good.

Chapter Thirty-One

Looking for the OK Corral

The place Ben had picked for the ambush wasn't really the Badlands, but it was closer to them than to any major city. It was a town of fewer than a thousand people, with a three-block main street, a grain elevator, a lumberyard, two cafés, and one bar. It was 6:30 in the evening when they got there, two days after they had blown up the loft. The rendezvous point was the bar, but they went to one of the cafés first. They parked the truck in a mowed field behind the grain elevator, not really hidden, but not out in plain sight, either. They locked it and walked the three blocks back to the center of town.

The café had no name, just a sign that said "Good Food" and another that said "Breakfast All Day." A middle-aged waitress brought them one-page menus in plastic sleeves, put down three coffee mugs, and started to fill them.

"How did you know we wanted coffee?" said Doug.

"Around here, the guys either drink beer or coffee with their meals. If you wanted a beer, you'd have gone over to the Golden Nugget and had an overcooked burger and a brew. We got better stuff here. Best food in town."

"You got a hot beef sandwich with mashed potatoes and gravy?" said Ben.

"You kidding? Is this farm country?"

"Good to be home." He smiled. "I'll have it."

"Make it two," said Max.

Doug found himself smiling as well when he noticed that the menu included an Indian fry bread taco. He surprised himself by ordering it.

"Is this really home, Ben?"

"Close to it. I grew up on a farm about eight miles from here. I know every foot of the land around this town."

A few tables away, the three farmers Doug had seen that first night at the Launch Pad bar were working on T-bone steaks. Ben nodded to them once but did not go over to talk to them. Soon four more rustic types drifted in, two at a time. Ben nodded to them as well, though not too overtly.

The food was classic American comfort fare. They capped it off with slices of apple pie that were two inches thick and had a crispy, golden crust with a lot of sugar baked onto it. *Stoking up for battle,* Doug thought. And as foolish as the whole idea seemed, he was looking forward to it. Ever since his vehicle had exploded, he had been living outside the law and on the run, and he found that he was starting to like it more and more. He was also beginning to get a feel for Ben's ability to inspire men to do terrible and dangerous things for him.

"Now?" Doug opened his wallet to show the Visa card.

"Not yet. At the bar, after we've set a few things up. Then you might as well max out your ATM card, too. Getting antsy?"

"Yes."

"That's okay, as long as you don't go all blood stupid on me when the action starts."

"I don't think so. I think I'm all right with it."

"Good. So do I."

Half an hour later they were at the Golden Nugget bar. Their seven comrades filed in as well, and they put two tables together in a far corner and settled in. Nobody made any introductions. The newcomers regarded Doug with looks that ranged from curious to openly hostile. A bartender came over to take their orders, and Doug told him to put everything on one tab, which the bartender said he appreciated.

After they got their drinks and the bartender had gone again, Ben raised a double shot of Canadian whiskey and said, "Confusion to our enemies." The others raised their glasses as well and said, "Hear, hear" or "Amen to that" or just "Fuckin' A."

Ben spoke very quietly after that, and the rough-looking men leaned in to hear. "This man," and he put his arm around Doug, "is the one we've been waiting for." The men nodded solemnly and leaned closer. "But he has a bunch of spooks chasing him. Tonight we're going to activate their homing device and then set up a little party for them. Sometime late tomorrow, things should get real interesting around here."

"I'm interested already."

"Me, too. I'm overdue for some action."

"Bring it on."

There were more comments of the same ilk. Finally Ben gestured for people to quiet down, lowered his voice even more, and said, "Now here's how we'll set it up . . ."

They talked for another hour. Finally Ben turned to Doug and said, "Now." Doug went over to the bar and settled up the tab using the bugged Visa card. The operation was on.

The next morning, Agent Webb found the bombed-out warehouse easily enough. There was broken window glass in the streets for three blocks around it, and the block that held the bomb site itself was barricaded off with police sawhorses and yellow CRIME SCENE tape. She parked the Jeep in an alley and locked it up.

The building was a real mess, but it had not fallen down. The non-bearing brick walls on the blast floor were all blown out, but the concrete columns and beams had held, though some of them had their outer layers of cement blown away, exposing the reinforcing bars. There was nobody around.

The doors at street level were all locked, and she couldn't jimmy any of them open. But in the back, there was a steel fire escape that looked serviceable. She looked all around for disapproving eyes. Seeing none, she quickly ascended the rusty structure and ducked inside the blown-out floor.

There wasn't much to look at. There were only a few interior drywall partitions, and they had been flattened, along with some furniture and cabinets. There had not been a fire, only an explosion. Or rather, many explosions. Webb knew enough about aftermaths now to see that there had been multiple origins to the destruction, probably simultaneous. The lack of any black residue also told her that the stuff used was high explosive, rather than black powder or some kind of home-brewed fertilizer-and-oil slurry. That could be good, if she could get an assayable sample. Sometimes manufactured explosives could be traced.

Whatever remnants there had been of the explosive devices had already been removed. She took out a camera and shot a few frames, though she doubted that they would prove very useful. She began to think this had been a totally wasted stop, and she decided to get a sample of blasted mortar and then get out before anybody saw her.

Then she heard the steps ringing on the fire escape behind her.

She ran to the opposite corner of the building, where a concrete block stair shaft was still intact. The metal door on it was bent from the blast, and it dragged on the floor. After pushing it open a few inches with great effort, she backed up half a step and kicked it with all her might. On the third kick, it went flying open. And it revealed one of the creepiest men she had ever seen.

He was tall and on the far side of middle aged, though he looked quite fit. He wore an expensive-looking black suit that had been expertly tailored to hide a sidearm in a shoulder holster. His bald head showed an odd scar, from the top of the pate down to where one eyebrow would be if he had any, which he did not. And something about him, something Webb couldn't quite define, oozed both power and evil.

"This is a restricted crime scene. What do you think you're doing here?"

"Um, ah, yeah." She tried to give him an apologetic smile and failed completely. "It's my editor, you know? Told me to see if I could get any good pictures of the blast. I told him there'd be nothing left to see, but he—"

"You have some press credentials?"

"Well, I didn't think I was going to have to show them to anybody, so I left—"

"What paper do you work for?" He took a step toward her and she immediately backed away, trying desperately to remember the name of a Twin City newspaper. She couldn't.

"The Chicago *Daily News*."

"Oh really? And you are . . . ?"

"Leaving." She turned and was about to run, but the man from the fire escape was inside now. She recognized him. The last time she had seen him, he was throwing away her gun. He had let her live on that day. Would he do it again?

"She's FBI," he said, drawing his sidearm. "She was in Albuquerque."

Apparently that bit of karma, wherever it had come from, was all used up.

"How very unfortunate for her. She should have stayed there."

"You want her dead?"

"Not yet. She has some things she's going to tell us first. Things she's going to beg to tell us, in fact." He gave her a long, appraising look. "Empty your pockets, miss."

She hesitated.

"Oh, come now, do I really have to stuff my hands into your pockets? Let's be a little professional here, shall we?"

"I'd love to think you were. Why don't I?" But she took her wallet and ID holder out of her back pocket and handed it to him.

"Oh, I assure you we are. We will cause you great pain and even death when it serves any good purpose. But we never do it for fun, and it is never casual or random."

"Well, I feel so much better, then."

"What you should feel, um"—he looked at her Department ID—"Agent Webb, is very, very afraid. I'll take the gun and the car keys, too, please."

She handed them over. But they didn't make her turn out her pockets, so she managed to keep the Dirty Dick's matchbook. "Look, this is probably a simple jurisdictional mix-up. What agency did you say you're with?"

"The one you never heard of and never will."

"Maybe you could just—"

"Cuff her."

As the man from Albuquerque was cuffing her hands behind her back, there was a chiming noise in the big man's pocket. He pulled out a cell phone and answered it by simply saying, "Go." Then, "When?" He listened a while more, and his face darkened. "And you're just telling me *now*? You will regret that, I promise you. Where is he, exactly?"

He listened a bit more and disconnected without saying anything else. Then he dialed another number and said, "Fuel for four hundred miles. On the pad and ready to lift off in fifteen minutes." To the man behind Webb, he said, "Our boy has called for the cavalry."

"Where?"

"The middle of nowhere."

"My favorite place. What about her?"

"We have to move now. She goes along."

They escorted her down the stairs and two blocks away, where a black SUV was parked at the curb. They had their guns holstered, and each of them held one of her arms tightly. The bald man pressed a remote control, and locks snapped open and lights flashed briefly.

"You know what's wrong with these vehicles, Agent Webb? There's no trunk to throw you in. I will, however, insist that you lie down on the floor in back. Stick your head up in plain sight for even a second, and I will hit it with a sap, which I promise you will not like. Are we clear?"

"Crystal. You are kidnapping me. That gives me automatic jurisdiction in my own case, by the way."

"What we are doing is *arresting* you. But aren't semantics entertaining?"

Chapter Thirty-Two

Vortex

Doug floated in heavy, oblivious REM sleep. He dreamed he was moving through deep space at terrible speed. Not in a spacecraft or even a pressure suit, as an astronaut would, but as a disembodied all-seeing intelligence. Planets and stars rushed up at him with frightening velocity, then quickly streaked past, first into his peripheral vision and then lost behind him. Far ahead of him, a spiral nebula came into focus and rapidly grew. As he got closer to it, he could see that it was spinning slowly. It was unimaginably big, and he was headed straight for its black, empty center. The outer arms of the nebula streaked past him like huge neon clouds, and his speed seemed to be increasing. Closer still, the image suddenly morphed. Instead of a galactic cloud formation, it was a powerful hurricane over the ocean, seen from great altitude. He continued to hurtle forward, into the eye of the storm. But the sea inside the eye was not calm. Instead, there was a huge black whirlpool, sucking in all the objects from the surface of the water. He acquired a body again, and the body was thrown into the boiling sea. He floated without any effort, with his head above the water. But no amount of kicking or stroking he did could keep him from the dark, swirling vortex. Soon he was over the rim and descending. He saw pieces of ships poking out of the surface here and there, and other bodies. Ben was there, looking unruffled as usual, and Mr. Black and some of his agents, with looks of varying degrees of horror on their faces. The pretty female agent from Albuquerque was there as well. He couldn't read her expression. For some reason, he was moving faster than the rest of them, passing all of them by.

Down and down they all went, until the sky disappeared behind them. At the bottom of the vortex, something was glowing. Something big. Farther on, he could see what it was, and he smiled knowingly. Gleaming white and illuminated by huge floodlights, it was an ICBM. Small jets of steam vented from the nose cone, and there were alarm bells sounding everywhere, drowning out the noise of the storm. He had forgotten that the missiles were always painted white. Everything in the nuclear arsenal was shiny and spotless and clinical-looking. The phrase *whited sepulcher* came into his mind unbidden. Then he thought, *No, that's wrong. A sepulcher merely contains something dead and rotting. But this thing holds evil itself, the power to destroy worlds. And it is definitely not dead. A live demon in a deep hole.* And the demon wanted him. It wanted all of them, but him most of all. The others, it would merely devour and spit back out as empty, charred husks. But it wanted him as a lover and a savior. It pulsed and vibrated. It *yearned.* It knew that he would finally bring it fully to life and would unleash it on the world.

Somebody was shaking his shoulder.

"Huh?" He threw off the Mylar sheet that the anarchists used to hide their infrared heat signature from prying eyes in the sky, and he sat up. Ben was looking at him from the front of the truck.

"That was quite a sleep, Doug. For a while there, I thought you were dead."

"I think I was." He looked at his watch. He had taken his turn at standing guard through the long night of nervous waiting and then had crashed into a solid six hours of much needed sleep.

"It's a good sign, you know, when you can sleep before combat. It means you won't rattle when the shit goes down."

"Is the shit about to go down?"

"Well, the first of them are here, anyway. We'll wait a while and see if there are more before we open fire. Unless they try to go away, that is."

Doug picked up his newly acquired Savage Model 10 carbine from the floor and got out of the truck.

They were parked in a shallow drainage ditch that ran alongside a railroad track. It was dry at the moment. It was high summer on the prairie, and the whole state was dry. The train tracks made a gentle curve and joined a spur line that ran past the grain elevator in town. A train had been there most of the night, loading closed gondola cars with the bounty of the prairie. The anarchists and their vehicles were spread out along the outside of the curve, well down in the ditch, where they couldn't be seen from town. On the other side of the tracks, three hundred yards away, sat a battered and dirty Dodge sedan with Doug's wallet in the trunk. It also contained two very well-concealed microphones.

Doug unfolded a small, collapsible periscope and took a quick look over the railroad embankment.

"Six of them," said Ben, "just like you were promised. They have a lot of handguns, but no heavy weapons that we can see. One of them has a sawed-off shotgun. They've been straggling in for about ten minutes. We'll give them another twenty, if they stay where they are."

Arrayed against the six men and their pistols were two M-60 machine guns, an assortment of high-powered rifles with sniper scopes, like Doug's, and a trench mortar. The mortar was for directional control. Nobody imagined it was accurate enough to home in on such a small group. But if the agents tried to run back into town, it could block their path and drive them back into the ambush. Ben's people all carried one or more sidearms as well as their long guns. Doug had been given a nine-millimeter Glock to replace his unreliable Colt knockoff. He didn't like it much. He thought it looked like a toy, and the balance and weight were all wrong. Nobody expected to use the handguns. The plan was that they would kill all the agents from a nice, safe distance.

Doug had a look through the periscope. "Looks just like you predicted it, Ben." The agents were all milling around the empty car as if they were not sure what to do next.

"Then it's time to be damn cautious, because nothing is ever *just* like you predicted it. Listen, if anything goes haywire here, you get the hell out, you hear? Of all of us, including me, you're the one person we can't afford to lose. If things go south, get yourself to the coordinates on the matchbook and wait for whoever of us is left."

"I don't like deserting you. I can handle myself." He didn't mention the additional problem of no longer having the matchbook.

"You got it or not?"

"Yes."

Over the tracks and across the field, one more agent joined the original six. Ben took a palm-sized device out of his pocket, and he, Doug, and Max listened to the conversation around the Dodge.

Anybody in the car?

Not that we can see, but the signal's coming from the trunk.

So why didn't you open it?

Could be booby-trapped. We'll wait until Black gets here, let him make that big decision.

Yeah? Well, I guarantee you won't see him opening it himself.

I'd watch that kind of talk if I were you. He knows everything.

Seems to, doesn't he? When's he get here?

I dunno. Soon.

In the Jet Ranger?

Nah, he thought he might need some extra firepower, so he took a Huey.

Those things are antiques.

They work. When the last Blackhawk gets hauled to the junkyard, it'll be carried under the skids of a Huey.

Yeah, yeah. Like you ever flew any of them.

I've seen what they can do. That's enough.

On the other side of the tracks, the listeners exchanged a look. Max produced a pair of binoculars and began scanning the sky. Soon he said, "Could be an inbound chopper coming from the southeast. Two, maybe three miles out."

"Just one?"

"That's all I can see."

"Then we attack now. Wipe them all out quick, and then we can give the chopper the attention it deserves. Otherwise, we'll be trying to shoot in two directions at once."

Which is the definition of an ambush, thought Doug.

Ben pushed a button on his listening device, and the Dodge sedan was thrown into the air by a ball of fire. Up and down the line, men moved from their concealed positions to sniper benches on the rail bed and opened fire.

Agent Webb was handcuffed to the floor in the back of the black Huey. Her abductors had not bothered to blindfold her, which she did not take as a good sign at all. *They don't care if I know where I'm going, because they are never going to let me leave there alive.* She had no illusions about miraculously getting any help from her agency. After all, she had deliberately dropped off their radar, and not even her partner knew where she was now. If she was going to be saved, it had to be by her own hand. And it probably had to be soon, before they had made her even more helpless.

The inside of the chopper was filled with a solid atmosphere of incredibly loud machine noise. The two agents and the chopper pilot wore throat microphones and big headphones that completely covered their ears and shut out all sound but their own speech. It put them in another world, she thought. Even though they were seated close by, they really weren't seeing her anymore. She remembered something she had once heard from her father, the cop.

"I never completely trust handcuffs," he had said. "They mostly work because the people wearing them believe they do. But of all the locks in the world, a handcuff is the easiest one to pick. Any kind of a bent piece of metal will do it. A paper clip works fine."

She didn't have a paper clip, but she had a belt buckle. Very slowly, moving only her hands, not her arms, she began to slide the belt around. Now and then it snagged on one of the belt loops on her jeans, but she finally got the buckle around to the small of her back. She unfastened it and groped for the prong on the buckle. Then she groped for the keyhole in her left cuff. She had no idea what the inner mechanism looked like or how it worked, so she simply wiggled the slightly hooked piece of metal in every way she could, hoping it would trip the lock. After what seemed like hours, it did. She noted the successful motion, and she changed hands and undid the second cuff much more quickly. *Nice work, agent. Now what the hell do you do?*

She looked around for something she could use as a weapon. There was nothing lying around loose anywhere. In fact, somebody had probably gone to some trouble to make sure of that. There were a couple of metal chests bolted to the floor and a first aid kit attached to the rear bulkhead, but once she made her move, she wouldn't have time to go rummaging in them. *Remember your combat training, agent? That disagreeable little asshole who loved to perform judo on the women said, "You always have a weapon of some kind."* The only thing she had was the handcuffs. They would have to do. Maybe she could use them like a set of brass knuckles.

Suddenly the other two passengers touched their headphones, then jumped up from their seats to look past the pilot and through the windshield. They looked away almost at once and moved back to throw open the side doors on the chopper. From one of the metal floor chests, they produced safety harnesses, swiveling gun mounts, and some kind of belt-fed heavy machine guns. Then they assumed gunners' stances on either side of the fuselage, with one foot on the floor and one outside, on a step on the landing gear. Somebody was about to be strafed. The pilot put the nose down, and they dropped to treetop level. Not that there were any trees on the brown prairie below.

As the gunners opened fire, they streaked low over what might have been a wheat field. The aircraft slowed a bit and swung its tail back and forth. *How fast are we going now? Doesn't matter. It will have to do.*

The open side doors were huge, designed to let several soldiers get in or out of the aircraft at once. The agents were at the front ends of the openings, their attention directed ahead. Nobody was watching Agent Webb at all. She decided to forget about trying to attack the agents and concentrate on getting out of the chopper instead. She held onto the cuffs, though she had no idea what they might be good for. She looked at the backs of both men again to be sure they were looking away from her. Then she stood up, sprinted the two steps to the threshold, and threw herself out into the slipstream. She cleared the skids and concentrated on tumbling and keeping all her joints loose, her knees together, and her arms protecting her face. After what seemed like an endless fall, when she couldn't tell which way was up, she landed like a ton of bricks and got the wind knocked completely out of her. She felt as if she had been hit by a truck, but she didn't think she had broken anything. As soon as she got her breath back and saw she could stand without too much pain, she ran.

A quarter of a mile away, a freight train was pulling away from a grain elevator. She headed for it. The chopper did not come after her.

Chapter Thirty-Three

Out of the Maelstrom

They couldn't tell if the car bomb had killed anybody. The agents in black trench coats were all prone on the ground in whatever small depressions they could find. Some of them were firing their weapons, but they were woefully out of range. On either side of Doug, the heavy machine guns had opened up and were spraying the field, but it didn't seem to be having much effect.

"They have some kind of body armor." Ben put a new clip in his assault rifle and took careful aim, working from a prone position with the train rail as a bench. "Aim for their heads."

Doug used the spotter scope on the side of his rifle to home in on the agent closest to him, then took a better look through the more powerful main scope. He recognized the man. It was one of the goons who had beaten him in the basement in Long Beach. That seemed like a hundred years ago now, but he still remembered it all too well, and he still hated the man. He set the range on the scope and put the crosshairs on the center of the agent's face.

He started to squeeze the trigger, smoothly and slowly. And stopped. For some reason, his finger wouldn't go any farther. *This is real, Dougie boy. All the fantasies and the games are over. This is not all those other people in Albuquerque, it's little you, and you have the power to kill somebody. Jesus H. Awshit.* Suddenly he knew he couldn't do it, not even to the asshole who had hit him with a rubber truncheon until he had hurt more than he had ever believed possible. And just as suddenly, he knew that he could. He could shut off all his emotions, plug in his neural memory, and do what needed to be done. His instructor had been wrong, after all.

He took a new aiming point, a foot to the left of the man's head, and fired. It was just a bare spot of dirt, but he stared at it as he fired and afterwards. A tuft of dust told him that his sights were set dead on for alignment but a bit short for range. He chambered another round and aimed at the agent again, this time putting the crosshairs about two inches higher than the spot he wanted to hit. He squeezed the trigger quickly but smoothly. Suddenly the man's head exploded, but not because of his shot. His landed a half a second later, in the middle of a gooey red mess. The agent had been hit with a thirty-caliber round, and his head had burst like a ripe watermelon. Doug's shot was totally redundant.

He felt cheated. *Ben has taken away my sin before I even finished committing it*. Somehow, there seemed to be something profound, even prophetic in that statement, but he couldn't quite put his finger on it.

The farmers' heads all turned suddenly as off to the right, they heard a long blast from a locomotive horn. The departing train was gathering speed and coming straight at them.

"Everybody off the tracks!" Ben sprinted back down into the ditch.

As Doug turned to follow, he took a last look over his shoulder and saw two Hummers emerging from behind the grain elevator, armed figures sticking out of their sunroofs. He looked over at Ben, who nodded. He had seen them, too. Before the train cut them off from view, the Hummer crews opened up on the rail embankment with heavy machine gun fire.

Down in the ditch, the ambushers were met by a hail of fire from the chopper. Doug dove behind their truck and was surprised to see that the heavy bullets did not go through it. *No wonder it needs such a big engine! That mother is carrying armor.* He looked down the ditch and saw the mortar crew get killed. They were cut down by both guns from the chopper, and then it hovered over them for a moment while somebody dropped a grenade on them. He couldn't see the big machine guns anymore, so he assumed they had found some kind of cover.

The chopper did a one-eighty and headed back down the ditch. Ben emptied a clip at it and put a spider web of cracks in the windshield, but it kept coming. Soon the world was full of bullets. Both the heavies on the chopper were still firing, and with good effect. And soon, the train would be past them, and the guns on the Hummers would reach them, too. Doug, Ben, and Max scrambled under the truck, but the whiff-whiff-whiff of shells hitting the ground was still much too close. One of them hit Max, and he cried out and dropped his rifle.

"Next time he's concentrating his fire someplace else!" shouted Ben.

"What?"

"Get out of here, Doug."

"But I'm—"

"Hop the freight and don't look back. We've been in worse spots than this before. We'll be okay."

They chanced a look back at the chopper. It was taking hits from somewhere behind it now, and little pieces of machinery were flying off the engine housing. It turned again and headed back away from them.

They climbed out from under the truck. Ben opened the door, dragged Doug's backpack out of it, and tossed it to him. Then he looked cautiously over the top of the truck box. When the chopper started strafing a vehicle farther down the ditch, he shouted, "Now!"

Doug slung his rifle over his shoulder and ran up the bank, carrying the pack by a strap. At the first grain car he came to, he turned and ran alongside it for a moment and then hauled himself up onto a foothold. The hopper cars all had sloped ends, which overhung small openwork platforms with a lot of complicated framework around them. Doug threw his pack up on one of them and followed it. He went to the far side of it and hunkered down behind something that he assumed was some braking machinery. He shouldered the rifle again to see if he could get a shot off at the chopper. But he and it were both in motion, and he couldn't get a steady view of it in his scope, let alone figure out how much to lead it. Somebody didn't have that problem, though. He saw the Plexiglas windshield erupt with more bullet holes. And then, faster than he could have believed, it was all behind him, and the brown and green prairie was streaming past at an ever increasing speed. Armageddon was happening back there, but soon he couldn't even hear it over the train noise. He wondered where he was going.

Agent Webb had climbed on the train six or seven cars behind the engines. They were well into the big curve in the tracks by then, so there was no way the engineer could have seen her. And in any case, his attention would have been taken up by the gun battle that he was about to drive through. She was a bit surprised that he continued, but he did. He poured on the power, and the big diesels labored and belched black smoke as the train accelerated slowly at first, then with more authority.

When the middle of the train was between the two warring parties, she saw a man leave the group in the ditch and also jump on the train. And she recognized him. Mister Matchbook himself, attracting gun battles again and then leaving. She wondered if she ought to approach him. Unarmed and without her ID, it didn't seem like such a good idea. She wasn't sure what to do next. Maybe she should work her way up to the lead engine and try to find a radio. She would have to eat a sizeable portion of crow and confess a lexicon of sins, but she could definitely get some help.

When they got a few miles away from the gun battle, she was climbing up the ladder to the catwalk on top of the grain car when she heard a loud, high-pitched buzzing above the noise of the train. She jerked her head around and saw the black chopper flying parallel to the train, a thousand yards away. The engine was belching black smoke and the fuselage was yawing back and forth, on the verge of being totally out of control. It was very low and getting lower. She couldn't make out any of the occupants.

The chopper streaked past them, veered away a bit, and then slammed into the ground. There was a complicated noise of crushing and tearing metal, and then the machine was quiet. It did not explode or burn. And suddenly she knew exactly what she was going to do next.

Those sons of bitches have got my gun and keys and ID.

She looked for some soft-looking grasses or crops, gave up on that, and jumped down on the hard dirt, tumbling as she landed. She hit hard, but not as hard as she had jumping out of the chopper. She got up and ran to the wrecked Huey.

She did not give a second's thought to the fact that she was running back to the people she had just escaped from. She was mad as hell. They had blindsided her and taken away her autonomy and her power, and she knew she had a very limited time to get it back, or the incident would become a scar she would carry the rest of her life. That was another truth she had learned from her father.

Once there, she found a dead pilot and a badly injured young agent, but no bald man in a black suit at all.

"It was nothing personal, you know." Blood was gushing from the agent's neck, and he could barely speak. "Help me?"

"Where the hell is my gun, asshole?"

Chapter Thirty-Four

New Road Buddies

The unnamed agent had a huge, ragged cut in his throat from some stray piece of torn metal. He was holding it with both hands now, but even so, he was bleeding out fast. Webb pulled her gun and other possessions out of his coat pocket. She also took his sidearm and a smaller gun from an ankle holster and threw them out the door. Then she went to what was left of the rear bulkhead, where the metal first aid kit was attached. She opened the box and found that it was a bad joke. The biggest bandage in it was a three-inch square adhesive patch, and the tubes of disinfectant cream and bug-bite remedy were not going to be of any help to the bleeding agent. There was a pair of scissors in the box, implying that there had once been rolls of gauze. If so, they were gone now. She took the scissors and re-crossed the smashed compartment to where the agent had his legs sprawled out in front of him.

"The first aid kit is no damn good," she said. "I'm going to try cutting your trouser leg up to make some kind of bandage." The man did a very abbreviated version of a nod.

She worked fast, and soon she had several layers of cloth wrapped around his neck. She hoped it was tight enough to stop the bleeding but not tight enough to strangle him. Humanitarian concerns aside, she wanted him to live long enough to tell her a few things. She looked in his other pockets for a cell phone, but there was none. Her own was back in her jeep in Minneapolis.

"Why didn't you just let him die?"

She had never heard the voice behind her before, but she knew who it had to be: the *person of interest* from Albuquerque, the magnet for trouble. The Matchbook Man. She turned to face him, still hunkered down on the floor. He had a carbine and a pack slung across his back and a Glock nine pointed at her, but her instinct was that he was not going to use it. He just wasn't poised that way. And trusting her instinct was yet another thing she had learned from her father. At Quantico, they would not condone it.

Since he had approached her from behind, he had to be aware of her own weapon in the waistband of her jeans. She made no move to reach for it. "In my business," she said, "you have to be comfortable with death sometimes. But that doesn't mean I like it to be random or chaotic."

"And what business would that be, exactly?"

"I'm FBI."

"I thought, probably. You were shadowing me in the market in Albuquerque."

"Yes. What was going on there, anyway?"

"I'm not sure I know. Not totally, anyway. Where's Mr. Black?"

"Is that the name of the bald guy with the scar?"

He nodded.

"How appropriate. All I know is he was on this chopper and now he's not."

They both looked at the agent.

"He jumphed o . . ." His mouth filled with blood and he gave up trying to talk.

"Did he take his briefcase?" said Doug.

The man attempted a slight nod.

"Then he won't come back here. He'll try to connect with the rest of the agents back at the railroad siding, if any of them are still alive. Or he'll try to get to whatever he's got left for reserve troops."

"Who are they, anyway?" said Webb. "And what do they want?"

"Just exactly why should I tell you? You were shadowing me. For all I know, you want to arrest me."

"Maybe I do. Are you one of them?" She pointed at the dying agent.

Doug said nothing at first, then jerked his head and said, "Outside."

He followed her out of the wrecked chopper to a small knoll thirty paces away.

"I didn't want to talk in front of him," he said. "They think I'm with them, but when push comes to shove, I'm not."

"So why are they killing FBI agents? The KGB died out a long time ago. They were supposedly our last organized predators."

"Oh, these guys are US, all the way. Some kind of goofy self-appointed agency. It could be totally rogue. I can't tell. If it has a name, they don't tell it to me."

"But they tell you other things? You've talked to them?"

"Well, of course. Like I said, they think I'm one of them. Or they did."

"But you're really one of the others from back there at the shootout?"

"The farmers?"

"*Farmers*? Are you serious?"

"Well, that's how they started out, anyway, before the banks and the economy and the government and their own simple orneriness made them into anarchists. I'm not really one of them, either, though at the moment our interests sort of coincide."

"How's that?"

"They owe me money."

"For what?"

"You don't want to know."

"Have you killed any of my agents?"

"No. That was all Black's people."

"The one in Long Beach, too?"

"That one, I'm not so sure about. I didn't actually see it happen."

"But you were there, were you? Interesting."

"Probably it was Black," he continued. "The crazy farmers—"

"The ones who owe you money?"

"Yeah, them. They do a lot of illegal stuff, but as far as I've seen, they mostly don't go around killing people. Well, not *good* people, anyway."

"I see." She did not mention the armored car robbery in Cedar Rapids with its dead guards. "Maybe we can work something out."

"I seriously doubt that."

"I have something you need, I think." She stood up and reached into a hip pocket. "I'm not going for a weapon, okay?"

She took out the Dirty Dick's matchbook and held it up where he could see it. And his expression told her that they could indeed work something out.

"You do need this, don't you?"

He didn't answer for a long time, and she saw a lot of things wash over his face, probably including the knowledge that he could just shoot her and take the matches and the decision not to do so. Finally he said, "What do you propose?"

"Put the gun away first. You don't need it. I have a Jeep back in Minneapolis. I say we ride a grain train that's going to the flour mills there, get the Jeep, and go to the place in this matchbook."

"You won't be welcome there."

"Let me worry about that. Go there with me, tell me a few things on the way, and I'll give you back your precious matchbook."

"You left something out."

"What's that?"

"The part where I don't get arrested."

"You're right, I did leave that out. Okay, I'm going to take your word that you haven't killed any of my people. When we get to Dirty Dick's, or whatever is at that longitude and latitude, we cut each other loose. We never met. You have my solemn word on it. But it's like a 'Get Out Of Jail Free' card. It's only good once. The next time we meet, you're fair game."

"And so are you. Okay. Quicker to get a vehicle around here, though. It's at least seven hours back to Minneapolis by train, and another five by car to get here again."

"Are we in a hurry?"

"Maybe."

"That's not very strong. The Jeep has a GPS in it. We could use that."

"That's nice. But why is it all the way back in Minneapolis?"

"Because that's where this Black character kidnapped me."

"But you got away?"

"I jumped out of the helicopter." She nodded.

"Then Black will have somebody waiting for you back by your Jeep."

"He will?"

"It's what you'd do, isn't it? You lose your subject, you go back to where you first acquired her. Basic."

"Oh, shit. You're right."

"And next time, they might not let you get away. A GPS is cheap and common nowadays. If we hop a train to either Bismarck or Fargo, we can buy one there."

"I don't want to buy another car. My credit is maxed out now."

"That's too traceable, anyway. So's the title. Better if we steal some kind of off-road vehicle."

"You can't seriously be suggesting that an FBI agent should steal a car."

"No, I'll do it. I'm getting rather good at it, actually."

Chapter Thirty-Five

The Road to Armageddon

It occurred to Agent Webb that each step she took lately put her more into violation of every policy that the Bureau had and possibly took her farther into harm's way as well. And she was amazed at how much she didn't care. Redemption drove her now. Full reinstatement. Unlike Dorothy, she was not going back to Kansas.

The next train she and Doug caught took them through Bismarck. They jumped off near a tiny, abandoned-looking Amtrak depot, and in the long-term parking lot, Doug hot-wired a fifteen-year-old Ford pickup that had oversized tires and four-wheel drive.

"The older ones are easier to do that on," he said. "Also less likely to have any kind of alarm or tracking device."

"Thanks. I really needed that bit of information to complete my professional training."

"You never know."

They bought a good quality GPS and some assorted camping gear at a big-box sporting goods store and a bunch of groceries at a supermarket. Webb wanted to find a place to buy a cell phone, too, but Doug wouldn't hear of it. "You do that and all bets are off," he said.

"I have a partner that I trust. He expects me to check in with him every day, and I've already missed one. He will want to know that I'm all right."

"And if somebody is monitoring his phone? Then both of you immediately become trackable. Absolutely not."

"You don't really trust me, do you?"

"If you don't have a phone, I do. Your agency, never. Your partner will just have to live with a little anxiety for a while."

They also bought straw cowboy hats. The pickup had a gun rack in the rear window and a big brush guard on the rusted grille, and they wanted to look like its logical owners. Then they treated themselves to dinner at a rather strange diner that featured do-it-yourself wok cooking. They hung around until the town pretty much closed down for the night, and Doug swapped license plates with a similar vehicle in a downscale used car lot on the edge of town. Then they filled the tank with gas, grabbed a few hours' nap in some farmer's field, sitting up in the pickup, and finally headed west.

Webb drove for half an hour, and then Doug said he would take over.

"I'm not tired," she said.

"You're also not careful. You don't check your mirrors nearly often enough or vary your speed to see if the vehicle behind you does the same thing."

"Okay, here I am checking my mirrors. See me doing it? And there are no vehicles behind us right now."

"I'm serious."

"So am I. I'm acknowledging that I made a mistake, okay? I'm not as used to being on the run as you are, I guess."

"You won't get a chance to *get* used to it either, if you don't start watching your tail."

"I get it, okay? Who are we watching for, cops?"

"Them, too, but mainly Black's people. We didn't see his body, remember? We don't know where he is. Assuming he survived the chopper crash, he's going to want you dead because you've seen him. And me twice as dead because I double-crossed him."

"You did?"

"Sure. That gunfight back at the rail siding was an ambush for his people, and I set it up. No way he can shrug that off."

"How would he trail you here?"

"I don't know, but his people seem to be very good at it."

"Point taken. I just became paranoid."

He let her stay at the wheel, and they rode in silence for a while. Finally, she said, "You know, I had a theory about you."

"Oh, really? And what was that?"

"It was that you weren't really one of the bad guys with all the guns, but you attracted them, whether you meant to or not. But now you say the rogue agents thought you were one of their own. Why is that?"

He laughed out loud. "Because they ran me down, hog tied and branded me."

"What do you mean?

"I mean they kidnapped me, took me to a place just a little nastier than Abu Ghraib, beat the living shit out of me, among other tortures and humiliations, and told me I had to work for them."

"How could they do that if they're really a government agency?"

"How could you be naïve enough to ask such a question?" He gave her a pained look. "For as long as there have been agencies with no visible oversight, our government has been doing unspeakable acts in the name of national security. Your agency included. And if you don't know that, maybe you should consider a different vocation, because sooner or later, you will be asked to do something monstrous, something that violates every principle you have. And you had better know how you're going to deal with that."

"Maybe I'll just quit."

"Maybe you will. I'm just saying, figure it out now."

"Is that why you're out of a job, Mr. Engineer? Did they ask you to do something that violated your deepest ethics?"

"No it isn't and yes, they did. They asked me to do a thousand things that were against my personal ethics, and instead of quitting, I did them. And there's not a day goes by that I don't regret that, bitterly."

She was quiet for a long time after that. She checked her mirrors, held the battered pickup at exactly one mile per hour under the speed limit, and let the dark prairie roll past them along I-94. Finally she said, "Tell me about this Black guy."

"What about him?"

"Why did he want you? Surely he has plenty of regular agents."

"You bet he does. And a lot of resources. He wanted me because he knew the farmers would want me. And he wants me to lead him to them, because he wants what they've got."

"What would that be, besides blisters and cow shit?"

He laughed. "I'm only telling you this because you won't believe me anyway. They've got a Minuteman ICBM site."

"Lots of people do. You can buy them online nowadays. Nut-cake survivalist groups like them a lot."

"No, I mean they've got a *live* one, as in, 'with a loaded missile in it.'"

"That's insane."

"Yes, it is."

"That is stark, staring, over-the-moon bonkers."

"I said you wouldn't believe me."

"But you're serious."

"Dead."

"You've actually seen this thing?"

"No, but I know where it is. It's close to where we're going."

"Oh, my dear, sweet God."

"So, what are you going to do, G-woman?"

"I wish I knew."

There was another long silence. In their mirrors they could see the first purple and orange streaks of sunrise in a sky full of angry, wild clouds. If they were being followed now, they wouldn't be able to tell. There was enough light to let another vehicle run with its headlights off but not enough to make it show up in the mirrors. At the town of Belfield, they turned off the interstate and headed north on US 85. An hour later, as the surreal landscape of the edge of the Badlands came into full daylight, Doug said, "Time to get off the highway."

"We can take real roads as far as the entrance to Theodore Roosevelt National Park."

"Where there will be a bored park ranger waiting to take our names and ask where we're going and log in our license number. Get off the road now. Head northwest."

"This piece of junk doesn't have a compass. Watch the one on the GPS for me, will you?"

"You could be a real outdoorswoman and steer by the sun."

"I am and I do, smartass. You really like to throw out a challenge, don't you?" She made sure there were no other vehicles around, picked a spot where the ditch was quite shallow, and turned into the open country. Soon they could not see the road anymore or be seen from it. She held the speed below thirty and watched the rugged terrain intently.

"You didn't finish telling me what your part is in all this," she said.

"No, I didn't."

"Well?"

"Well, what?"

"You told me what Black wants. What do the farmers want from you?"

He sighed. "Oh, all right. They seem to think they've figured out how to launch the missile manually, without needing the original, encrypted computers."

"Have they really?"

"I won't know until I see the setup. It's possible. What they definitely don't know how to do, though, is set the target. And I do."

"I thought anarchists didn't care what they blew up."

"Well, these do. They want to destroy Wall Street."

"Wall Street. In New York." She gave him an exaggerated open-mouthed stare.

"That's the one."

"It just gets better and better, doesn't it? And you're going to help them do it?" She swerved to avoid a large rock and ran over a rattlesnake instead. "God, I hate those things."

"I don't think so. Back at the ambush, I found that I had a hell of a hard time killing even one person. I'm damn sure not going to kill a few million."

"Maybe you want me to arrest you, after all. Turn state's evidence? A nice, cushy witness protection site somewhere? You just told me if you don't show up, they can't launch."

"Not a chance. Your people might be good enough to protect you from Mr. Black, but there's no way I trust them to protect me. And anyway, I haven't got my money yet."

"How are you going to do that and still avoid triggering Armageddon?"

"Well, that part gets a little tricky."

Chapter Thirty-Six

Dirty Dick's

By the time they were within a few miles of their destination, the terrain had gotten so rugged that they couldn't average more than fifteen miles an hour. There was no trail as such, and they frequently had to backtrack when something that had looked like a good route was suddenly blocked by a drop-off or a huge rock formation.

"You know, this is really beautiful country," she said, "as long as you don't have to try to live on it or travel over it."

"Yes it is. It reminds me of the moon, only with a little more color."

"It also doesn't light up at night."

"You hope."

"What's that mean?"

"If somebody gets careless with that nuke, this area could get hot in more ways than just thermal." He checked the GPS. "We're within easy hiking distance now. Start looking for a big overhanging rock of some kind, one that we can hide the truck under. The skies have eyes."

She nodded in agreement. "Lots of eyes."

What they found was almost a cave, except that part of one side was open. The rock floor was not very flat and had a lot of small crevasses, but with Doug walking ahead to signal to Webb, they were able to creep carefully in.

"How do I shut this thing off?" she said.

"You see the wires that I twisted together?"

"Yes."

"Well, pull them apart, that's all."

"You can put them back together in the right way again?"

"I did it once, didn't I?"

She pulled on the wires, and the bellowing V-8 fell silent.

"I'm going to leave the rifle here." He opened the passenger door, took the deer rifle from under the seat, and put it in the rear rack. "If one of us winds up disarmed and on the run, we might need it." He took off the secondary spotter scope and put it in his pack, which he then shouldered.

"Shall we go off to see the Wizard?" she said.

"It sure looks like yellow bricks to me."

She handed him a bottle of water from a grocery bag on the floor. "Hydrate first. You don't know when you'll have another chance to do it."

"Good thinking. I take back what I said about you being an outdoorswoman." He opened the bottle and drank deeply.

"Which way are we going?" she said.

He showed her the GPS display. She got out of the truck, walked out into the sun, and took her watch off. "This time of day and this time of year, the sun should be at about half past four, and north will be at twelve." She oriented the watch, squinted at it, and pointed. "North is that way, toward that big, scraggly pine. We want to go ten degrees to the left of it. It's less than a mile."

"I'm impressed."

"You had that coming."

After fifteen minutes, the terrain flattened out a bit, and they were able to increase their pace. Soon the dark, squat shape of a building came into view. What Webb had not been able to see in the satellite view was that it had a large cantilevered shed roof on the back side. Underneath it, its tail half inside the building, was an airplane.

Webb squinted. "That has to be the ugliest airplane I've ever seen."

Doug took the scope out of his pack and looked. The plane was a tail-dragger, with a boxy fuselage, a long, slender nose, and gangly-looking landing gear struts with huge balloon-like tires. Parked behind it was a Jeep Grand Cherokee that looked new. "Out here," he said, "that could be the most beautiful airplane you'll ever see. That's a Pilatus Turbo Porter. Made in Switzerland. It's one of the best short-field and rough-field machines ever built. If we have to get out of here in a hurry, that's the baby we want."

"You can fly it?"

He shrugged. "Who knows? It's possible."

"Wonderful." Apropos of absolutely nothing, she pressed something into his hand. He looked down and saw that it was the matchbook.

They approached the building from the side. There were two windows in it, but they were blacked out. Around the corner there was a notch in the main building mass and then a weathered wooden porch, reminiscent of an old-time western saloon or ranch. On the porch roof was a rusted and faded sign crudely painted on corrugated sheet metal.

Dirty Dick's
No place for Pricks

"As promised," he said. He turned back to look at Webb and found that she was gone. He assumed she had decided to disappear and try to find her own way into the missile complex. So this had to be the point where all agreements between them were off. *Fair enough.* He thought it was nice that neither of them had found a reason to shoot the other. He shrugged and went around to the front of the building.

In the middle of the front façade, at one edge of the porch, was a wood-frame screen door that hadn't been painted in decades, with a solid, rough timber door behind it. They both opened easily, and Doug stepped into a storm-entry vestibule with another door at the end of it. The place was dimly lit by a naked low-wattage bulb in the ceiling. There were no windows, but the door and both sidewalls had fisheye spy lenses in them and slotted holes about two feet below each one. *In medieval castles, those would have been called murder holes,* he thought. *And for good reason.*

He tried the door and found it locked. Something behind the door made a faint whirring noise, after which the door made a loud metallic click. He tried the door again, and it swung away from him smoothly. He took a deep breath and went in.

The inside seemed cavernous, and even more poorly lit than the vestibule. It was also cold. The whirring noise, he decided, had probably come from the control motors on a 50-caliber machine gun that was mounted on the far wall and was tracking him. He walked farther inside.

Suddenly he was blinded by a spotlight that was mounted above the machine gun. He put a hand up to shield his eyes, and the spot shifted to the floor in front of him. Then it traveled away from him and to the left. He hesitated a moment, then followed it. It came to rest on top of a battered table that held a key ring and a note.

Take the Cherokee and go due north. Follow the stripe on the ground. You will be met.

He took a last look around to see if anyone was there, picked up the key, and headed back toward the door. The spotlight illuminated the dirt floor just ahead of him. Now that his eyes were more accustomed to the general darkness, he could see that there were a couple of jogs in the back wall, probably where the tail of the aircraft sat on the other side. There were also many more guns, mounted with tracking servos and cameras. *This whole place is nothing but a big killing box. It's probably lucky that Webb didn't come in here.*

Outside, he looked around one last time for Webb and called her name. Getting no response, he walked around the Pilatus, got in the Jeep, and started it up. It had a compass display built into the rearview mirror, and it was already reading north. He pulled out. He noted that the ground was flat for at least five hundred feet, which probably meant that the Pilatus could take off straight out of its hangar with no maneuvering whatsoever. It would go out straight north, no matter which way the wind was blowing.

"What goddamned stripe?" he said to nobody or anybody. And then he saw it. It wouldn't show up to a satellite, but up close, it was distinct enough, and straight as a laser beam. He took the vehicle up to a cautious twenty miles an hour and followed.

He drove between surreal rock formations with horizontal stripes of pink, orange, and rust red against a background of gray or brown. The tops of the formations often had mats of green or brown prairie grasses and small, scrubby trees and bushes. But the ground immediately in front of him remained barren and relatively flat, and the stripe he was following was always visible.

The sun was approaching its zenith and the sky was now mercilessly clear. The cab of the vehicle was starting to heat up, and he turned on the air conditioning. It suddenly struck him as hilarious that here he was, driving to the end of the world in air-conditioned comfort. *Maybe that's been the story of my whole life; I just didn't realize it before.*

"Agent Connelly here."

"It's me," said Webb without giving her name. "I'm not under any duress at the moment, but I had to call now because I don't know when I'll get another chance."

"I don't recognize the caller ID."

"No. It's not my own phone. Go ahead and find out whose it is, if you want, but don't bother with a location. We both know where I am."

"The place you set out to get to?"

"That's the one," she said.

"So what's happening?"

"Are you sitting down?"

"As a matter of fact, I am. Why?"

"Because I have a story that's absolutely going to knock you off your feet."

The flat area widened out, and a mile or so ahead, Doug could see the silhouette of a farm tractor. As he got closer, he saw a man standing in front of it. Closer still, the man began signaling him to turn, swinging one arm like a windmill and pointing with the other. Off to Doug's left, a huge pair of trap doors swung smoothly up. He drove between them, down onto a brilliant white concrete slab. Soon a round manhole, twenty feet in diameter or more, swung away to one side with a loud grinding noise, revealing a black hole in the slab and a ramp leading down into it. He turned on his headlights and drove in.

The tunnel sloped steeply down, then quickly turned into a tight left-hand helix. It had an arched roof and was too narrow for two vehicles to meet. In his mirror, he saw the manhole close behind him, blocking out the sunlight. It sounded like doom. He left his headlights on and kept going. He followed the curved path for a surprisingly long way, and he wondered how deep in the earth he was. He finally emerged into an underground garage with a slightly higher roof. Ben's shot-up white truck was there, along with several other vehicles.

One of the farmers Doug had seen back at the gun battle motioned him into a parking spot near the center of the room.

All the other vehicles were parked facing the ramp he had just come down, so he turned the Jeep around and imitated them. He shut off the motor and left the keys in the ignition. As he got out, he saw Ben and Max emerge from a small archway. Max had one arm in a sling. Ben came striding up to Doug and extended his hand. He was smiling, the first time Doug had ever seen him do that.

"Welcome to the end of civilization as we know it." He gave Doug a two-handed handshake.

"You get clear okay, back at the rail siding?"

"We lost a few men." Ben's smile faded, and he looked pensive. "But the agents lost everybody, so it was probably worth it. The only ones who got away were in the chopper. It was smoking when it went out of sight. And there was no second wave of reinforcements."

"The chopper crashed. Black was in it, but he managed to get away before it went down," said Doug. "I don't know where he went. The pilot is dead, and the other agent is hurt bad. Either he's in a hospital somewhere, or he bled out at the crash site and he's dead, too."

"You got off the train and looked?"

"Yes."

"Why? That was a hell of a chance to take."

Doug managed a shrug. "If he had still been there, I meant to kill Black."

Ben looked at him hard for a long moment, then nodded.

"Where's the phone?" said Max.

"What are you talking about?" said Doug.

"The phone that was in the Cherokee. Did you stick it in your pocket?"

"I didn't see any phone. Where was it supposed to be?"

"Not 'supposed to,' was. In a holster on the dash, right out in plain sight."

"Not when I got in, it wasn't." Doug shook his head. "No way." He knew perfectly well what had become of the phone, of course. He kept quiet about it.

"It was turned on," said Ben, "in case we needed to talk to you while you were driving here, tell you that you made a wrong turn or whatever. Max, did he talk to anybody on the way here?"

"Not a word."

"Okay, maybe it's just lost. Go up on top and try calling it, see if you can hear the ring. Then take two men and go back to Dirty Dick's, find out what's what."

Max pointed to two men and gestured to them to follow him. Then he left at a brisk trot.

To Doug, Ben said, "You've had a long trip. Do you want something to eat?"

"I want to see it first."

"It?"

"Yes, it. The beast that destroys worlds."

Chapter Thirty-Seven

Face to Face With the Demon

It took his breath away. It looked so much like the one in his dream that his mouth fell open. How had he known exactly what it would be like? Unlike the dream monster, it didn't make any noises, but it definitely radiated the fierce malevolence and longing. This thing was nothing short of the end of the world in a single object. It wasn't something from the dark side of the id; it *was* the dark side. And it was built to blast into the stratosphere and was getting impatient. He had to admit, though, it was beautiful. Frightening as the gates of Hell themselves, but definitely beautiful.

They had entered the silo through the huge blast door, ten feet square and three feet thick. It had hinges that could have supported a floodgate on a major dam and was painted with wide red and white diagonal stripes and radiation hazard symbols in black and yellow. Inside, Ben threw the main switch on a large electrical box, and the place lit up with a hundred floodlights. The silo itself was perhaps forty feet in diameter, with smooth walls painted a pale, glossy greenish blue. At regular intervals, lights were recessed into the walls, which towered above them at least a hundred feet. Below them, they went that far again, then disappeared in a curve that headed under their feet. That was the blast-vent end of the silo.

They walked out onto a catwalk that circled the missile just below its gleaming black nose cone. Below that point, the missile was white, just as he had seen it in his dream. It sat in the exact center of the silo. Far below them, its end rested on four stubby lugs that resembled blunt tail fins. They sat on heavy buttresses that cantilevered out of the walls, and they had hold-down blocks on top of them. Two more catwalks circled the missile at lower levels, connected to the one they were standing on by steel ladders with protective cages. Three sets of mechanical hands came out of the walls to hold the big missile upright, and a robot arm held a braided electrical cable that connected to the nose cone. The demon looked as if it could easily shake off all these petty devices once it decided to rise. This was clearly an entity that neither man nor machine argued with.

And you thought you would find some clever, undetectable way to disable it, Mr. Engineer? Dream on.

"What's its name?" said Doug.

"What do you mean?"

"Anything that impressive has got to have a name."

"Well, we used to call it the Savior, because when somebody saw it for the first time, they would usually say, 'Jesus Christ.'"

"Have a lot of people seen it?"

"Very few, Doug. You've just become part of an elite group."

"Lucky me." *You're doomed, you know.* "And you figure this thing is ready to fly?"

"That's what we think, yes. We've completely bypassed the original control panels. Everything that used to be controlled by a launch computer, we now have manual switches for."

"They have to be tripped not only in the right order, but with just the right timing, you know. The most critical event is pulling the stand-offs."

"What are they?"

"The big arms that keep the missile from falling over when it's just sitting there. You'll want some video cameras pointed at the restraint blocks down at the bottom of the rocket. When you see the ballast blocks start to roll back, you know the engine is up to full power and the gyros are using the eccentric thrust to keep it upright and stable. That's when it's time to cut it loose of everything."

"We can set that up easy enough. We've got a lot of video gear."

"You also want to be sure you've got a *written* procedure sheet."

"Got that. That was about all we were able to get from the floppies that our guy swiped at Los Alamos."

"Well, make sure the list also includes the things that were always manual, not run by the computer, even when they had one."

"Like what?"

"Like opening the launch door and the blast exhaust door."

"Oh, like that. Yeah, those would be bad things to forget, all right. Sounds like we're glad you're here, Doug."

"I'm kind of surprised to hear myself say it, but I'm glad, too." And in some ways, he was, though the larger part of his mind was desperately trying to think of a way out. He tried to remember how long it had been since he had worked on a real project with a real outcome, and people had accepted his expertise and his analysis and done what he told them to. Maybe he hadn't ever done it before, only dreamed of it. It was intoxicating, exhilarating. And it gained more momentum by the minute.

He pointed to a row of flush screw heads along a seam in the nose cone. "If you haven't already done it, you're going to have to take off all these upper panels, by the way."

"What for? Everything checks out on the master status board. That's one item that never got ripped out."

"There are things you can't check from there. There will be anywhere from a dozen to fifty batteries inside this beast, to run everything from the controls to the arming of the warhead. They'll be a lot of different voltages, but they should all be labeled. We have to check the charges on all of them. Any that aren't up to voltage, we need to replace. They probably aren't rechargeable, but there should be spares around here somewhere."

"There are," said a gangly, youngish farmer in white coveralls who hadn't spoken until then. "I've seen them. I wondered what they were for."

"I don't think we've met," said Doug, extending his hand. "I'm Doug Wright."

"They call me Hal," said the youth, taking the offered handshake. "After the computer in the old movie, you know? I'm the closest thing we've got to a techie whiz."

"He's damn good," said Ben. "He did most of the new wiring."

"Good to meet you, Hal." The young man looked healthy enough, but Doug noticed that he had a lot of slightly discolored patches under his skin, like smudges from some kind of ash that had not quite been washed off. He assumed Hal must have decided to have a look inside the warhead. If so, there was no hope for him.

"Listen, we should hot-wire the gyros and make sure they still work," said Doug. "I also need the panels at this level"—he slapped one close to them—"off."

"What's behind them?"

"Among other things, the onboard computer. This is where we will set the target coordinates."

"Can't that be done remotely?"

"Not without a bunch of double-encrypted passwords that we don't have. We're going to bypass all that and reset the target manually."

"Outstanding," said Ben. Looking down at the massive machine, he said, "You know, it's always disappointed me that it doesn't have tail fins, like Flash Gordon's ship. It doesn't look finished without them."

"The V-2s that we got from Germany after World War II had fins. They didn't always work so well. The fins had no effect until the rocket got up to speed, and before that happened, it could get headed off in a totally wrong direction. What all the world's rocket scientists eventually settled on was controlling the flight by precisely adjusting the exact direction of the thrust nozzle, many, many times a second. It's sort of like the old trick of balancing a baseball bat on your fingertip."

"Hell of a baseball bat, Doug."

"Hell of a fingertip, too."

"Anything else you need right away?"

"You said something about food, I believe."

"The kitchen is holding a T-bone with your name on it, my friend."

"Well, let it be held no longer. I could eat—"

"Yeah, yeah. I heard that one already."

As they walked back into the main complex, he heard Hal giving orders behind him. A steady stream of men passed them, headed for the silo. They all wore white coveralls, had dust masks hanging around their necks, and carried tools. *Farmers transformed into the most lethal and most sanitary technicians on the planet,* he thought. *How things do change.* He thought of the technicians at Trinity Site, near Los Alamos, working on the building of the first atom bomb. From the pictures he had seen, the civilians all wore white shirts and neckties, just like tradesmen in any craft back then. *What a totally lost age of innocence.* They hadn't yet invented the work uniform of the lethal elite, the unsung cold warriors. But they were transformed, all the same. *Hell, the whole world was transformed. It would never be innocent again.*

He thought about Agent Webb, wandering around outside somewhere with the cell phone from the Jeep. Was she about to call in an army of agents? He didn't think it would matter. This place had organization and security and momentum. Especially momentum. And it was highly defendable. If the feds showed up, all they would do was screw up his own escape, which, of course, would be way too bad. He needed to get out of there, soon.

The cell phone had a ring like a doorbell chime. Webb recognized Connelly's cell number and answered on the first ring, saying only, "That was fast. What have you got for me?"

"Orders from the Director."

"You ratted me out to headquarters? I don't believe this."

"Calm down. This situation is just too powerful for us to run it totally on our own. No matter what decision you or I make, it's bound to be wrong. I had to pass the responsibility upstairs."

"Do they know where I am?"

"They know where you were going, anyway. I couldn't pretend I didn't know."

"Well, know this, partner: the missile silo is not at Dirty Dick's."

"It's not? How close is it?"

"I don't know yet. But if we send in an army of agents here, all they will do is start a war in the wrong place. Meanwhile the farmers will go ahead and launch from the real place."

"Maybe. What other choice do we have?"

"I've got to find the silo and go in, super low-key, and stop the launch."

"How are you going to do that?"

"I don't know yet." *Maybe I should have killed the engineer. Maybe I still should. Our temporary truce is over now. But Daddy didn't raise any assassins. There has to be another way.*

"Well, whatever you're going to do, do it quick, Abbs. And preferably, not anything crazy."

"Copy that." She hung up.

"That wasn't very long," said Black. "Did you get her position?"

"I got it. It's about a hundred and forty miles from the shootout."

"That has to be the silo. The anarchists went there after the firefight, and either she followed them or they snatched her. And the 'person of interest' they're talking about is almost certainly our man Wright."

"So what do we do, Mr. Black?"

"Do? We go out there and kill them all, of course."

"Including Wright? You told me he was going to nuke Havana for us."

"Considering his actions back at the ambush, I think it's safe to say Mr. Wright believes he has successfully slipped his leash. If we can take him alive, he is going to be very sorry for that before he dies. But no way he lives, in any case. No way he was ever going to live, but especially not now. And no way the anarchists get to bomb what *they* want to."

"Got it."

The steak was delicious, and it had caramelized onions and fried potatoes on the side and a glass of some kind of red wine. But the intoxication Doug had felt in the silo was definitely wearing off. Less and less could he see any alternative to targeting the missile for New York. He would love to send it to the South Pole or the deepest trough in the bottom of the Pacific or maybe someplace where the radiation wouldn't matter, like Bikini Atoll or the original Los Alamos testing site, which had already been nuked to oblivion. But he only had one set of target coordinates in his notebook and no calculator with which to run any more. And he couldn't just send the monster off into outer space, because it didn't have enough fuel to get it up to escape velocity. The only way to do the job and get the money was to do the job and get the money.

And if he did, then what? The FBI knew his name now. Even if he got clear of the launch site and away, he was probably about to become the most hated and most hunted man on the planet. His money wouldn't help that. *I need to disappear completely, cease to exist at all.* He hadn't been very successful at that up until now. What could he do differently? If they'd caught bin Laden, they would catch him.

Chapter Thirty-Eight

Mobilizing for Doomsday

Agent Webb retrieved the deer rifle from the stolen truck, went back to the building called Dirty Dick's, and went away from it to the north, the way she had seen Doug heading in the Cherokee. She didn't notice the stripe on the desert floor right away, but the Jeep had left tire tracks in the dust that were easy enough to see. Later, when there was less dust, she had spotted the stripe and figured out its significance.

She had nothing remotely resembling a plan. Obviously, she couldn't allow an atom bomb to hit New York. But short of killing Doug, how could she prevent it? Furthermore, she needed to set up some situation where it would be blatantly obvious to the Bureau and everybody else that she was the one who had done it, had saved the day. Did that mean letting herself be captured again? *Rock and a hard place, kiddo, rock and a hard place. And they're coming closer together.*

She had hiked about a mile when the phone rang again. She froze.

The caller ID was not her partner's number, nor any other one that she recognized. Should she answer it? Was there anything to be learned from it that would be worth the risk of exposure? She decided not. She neither answered it nor shut it off. When it kept ringing after ten or more chimes, she switched it to silent mode and put it in her pocket.

On a sudden inspiration, she ran back to the building and picked up a couple of tumbleweeds. She thought about tossing the phone on the ground next to where the Jeep had been. Maybe whoever owned it would assume it had just fallen out of the vehicle and not been noticed. *And what if Connelly calls again to tell you what the Bureau was going to do next, and you miss the call? That wouldn't be so good, would it, Abby? But then, what is? You're in a lot of shit here.*

She headed back north at a trot, doing her best to brush out her footprints with the tumbleweeds. When she got to where her earlier set ended, she moved smartly away from Doug's tire trail. She found an area of ledge rock with no dust or soil on it and again went north.

A mile or so ahead of her, something, presumably a vehicle, was kicking up a cloud of dust. She looked around for a rock formation to hide behind. She picked a crevasse with deep shadow, poked her rifle around to make sure there were no snakes, and settled in with a tumbleweed on either side of her. The cloud got closer.

Doug had a second glass of wine after the steak and nursed it for a long time, deep in thought. Eventually the eager youngster called Hal came and joined him.

"I found four gyros. Is that enough?"

"Just right, Hal," said Doug. "Two for navigation and two for fine tuning the pitch and yaw control. Do they work?"

"I have no way of telling how fast they're spinning, but they seem smooth and fast."

"Do they run for a long time after you shut off the power?"

"Seemed like a long time, anyway, yeah."

"Then they are doing what they should."

"Do we care which way they point?"

Doug shook his head. "They should align themselves the right way shortly after they start up."

"Yeah, they looked like they did that. Two of them have vertical shafts, and the others are horizontal."

"Perfect. How about the batteries?"

"I found twenty-six and replaced seven so far," said Hal. "I'm still looking for more, but I think maybe that's all of the bad ones. I didn't look inside the warhead yet, though."

"No point in it. The batteries there are different. They're called thermal fuel cells, and they can't be recharged or replaced. There's a single copper wire that goes through the bottom shell of the warhead."

"I've seen it. What's it for?"

"It's called the 'hard safety.' The assumption is that if the missile gets dropped or bent or broken or blown up accidentally, that single wire will probably break and there will be no way the warhead can arm itself. But a few seconds after a normal launch, a tiny current will go through the wire. It will melt all the fuel cells, and—"

"*Melt*?"

"I didn't say I thought it was a good system, did I? Yes, melt. They melt and they go live, and after that, any time the bomb comes within half a mile of the ground, it blows."

"I like it. Now all we have to do is set the target."

Doug nodded solemnly. He pushed his plate away, stood up, and reached in his backpack for his notebook. "I'll need a couple of screwdrivers, the smallest you can find. Maybe a needle-nosed pliers too; I'm not sure."

"I've got a jeweler's repair kit I'll get for you. Are you going to do it now?"

"Can't think of any reason not to." *Other than just saying to hell with the whole mess and getting out of here*. But even as he thought that, something was eating at the fringe of his consciousness, something that might even turn into a plan for disappearing. *If the machinery for setting the coordinates is set up right, there might be a way to save New York and still live. If not, I'm screwed.*

"I'll go take off the last of the outer panels, then."

"You go ahead," he said to Hal's departing back. "I'll be right behind you."

Doug, my man, you are be about to become either history's greatest unknown hero or its most terrible villain.

Back at the catwalk, the curved panels from just below the nose cone were sitting nested neatly off to one side. Inside the space they had been covering was a perforated frame that looked like something from an old erector set. Inside that was a Gordian knot of tangled wires the size of a beach ball, with small sub-frames inside it, fitted with mechanical relay switches and other little machines whose purpose could only be guessed.

"So where's the computer?" said Hal.

"You're looking at it."

"Where?"

"This whole gnarly mess."

"Really? But there's no circuit boards. Come to think of it, there's no keyboard, either."

"That's right. It's a Turing-style machine. Not digital at all. It runs by electricity, but the computing is all done mechanically and matched against physical models and clockwork trip points. It has no memory, but it doesn't need any, either. In its day, it was really quite a brilliant piece of work. Legendary, even. I never thought I would actually get to see one up close."

Hal handed Doug a small case made of clear plastic, with a set of tiny screwdrivers, a miniature hammer, and a two types of pliers in it. "Hang on to those, okay? You drop a tool here, and you ain't ever getting it back."

They both looked down at the perforated catwalk deck and the gaping tunnel sweeping away below it. Doug put the case in his shirt pocket.

"So what do you do now, Mr. Engineer?"

I wish I knew. "Flashlight?"

Hal gave him a small maglight, and Doug traced a few wires with it, tentatively identified some of the little machines, and finally let the beam settle on a gray metal box the size of a paperback novel.

"Here, I think." He took one of the screwdrivers out of the case and began to take the cover off the box. The cover had a small chain on it so it couldn't fall out of the missile, and the screws were made so they couldn't come completely out of the case.

Inside the box were what looked like old-fashioned car odometers, made of banks of cylinders with numbers on them, each with its own tiny drive gear. There were four rows of them, and he could reach them easily. "Paydirt," he said. "Four sets of numbers. Longitude and latitude, in geodesic coordinates, for two places. Starting and ending points." And they were physically set up exactly the way he needed them to be. For the first time since he had been snatched from the bar in Long Beach, he had a plan and a hope. He didn't need another set of coordinates; he just needed a hell of a lot of nerve.

He opened his notebook to the right place, wedged it into the snarl of wires, and compared numbers. The bottom two banks of odometer dials corresponded exactly to his own figures for the initial point, and he mentally patted himself on the back for still knowing how to crunch a set of numbers the hard way. Then he took a deep breath and started turning tiny gears on the upper two banks. When he turned a gear, the matching numbered cylinder turned with it, showing where the gear was set. But if he held a gear in place with one screwdriver, he could turn the matching cylinder with another one, changing the displayed number without moving the gear. First he set the target coordinates to match the starting coordinates exactly. Now the missile would go straight up, out of the atmosphere, and straight back to where it had started. Then he held the gears for the target numbers in place and turned the cylinders only, so it looked exactly as if the gears were set to the New York numbers from his notebook. He worked as quickly as he dared, frequently consulting the notebook, being exactly sure of everything. He kept his body between Hal and the numbers. He wanted the kid to see his work, but not yet. When he got the last cylinder set, he became aware that he had been holding his breath.

Finally he stepped back and wiped the sweat off his face with his sleeve. He realized he had been trembling. He handed Hal the notebook. "Double check me, will you? There's no way we get another chance at this."

Hal traced the numbers in the notebook with his index finger and looked back and forth between them and the machine many times.

"The lines of numbers in the book aren't arranged in the same places as in the box," he said.

"Don't worry about that," said Doug. "I didn't know until I looked at the old settings where they would put the initial point and where they would put the target, or whether they would put longitude or latitude on top. Just make sure there are four sets of numbers *somewhere* that match."

"They're perfect," said Hal. He handed back the notebook.

"Let me see," said Ben. Doug didn't know when he had come up silently behind them. They gave him the notebook and got out of his way. He put on a pair of half-frame reading glasses and pointed a flashlight at the numbers in the box. Finally he said, "You're right; it's perfect. We're there."

"Would you like the honor of closing up the box?" said Doug.

"You do it," he said, nodding to Hal. "Put everything back together, and come tell me when it's done. Doug and I have some things to talk about. We'll be in the mess hall."

Doug gave Hal back the jeweler's tools. Ben handed the notebook back to Doug.

"I don't need that anymore," said Doug.

"No, I guess you don't."

The cloud of dust looked as if it went all the way back to Dirty Dick's. Then it returned, stopping at about the place where Webb had left the main trail. She waited. She decided that if she got caught, she didn't want to have either the phone or her agent's ID on her. She put them both in a hollow space in the rock face and covered the opening with a smaller rock that she thought she could recognize again. She put her handgun in another one. And she waited some more.

The dust cloud did not move away and she didn't hear anything. No voices, no motor, nothing. After fifteen minutes, she took a chance on peeking above one of the tumbleweeds.

And immediately felt a gun barrel against the back of her head.

"I'm half Cheyenne and half coyote," said the voice behind the gun. "I don't rattle and I don't miss. Let's have that rifle, nice and slow."

What was that plan again?

Ben and Doug went back to the mess hall, poured themselves mugs of coffee, and sat down. Ben produced a pint of brandy and put a shot in each of their mugs.

"I think you've earned that, Doug, my man. I had faith in you, and you came through." He raised his mug to clink it against Doug's.

"Not to be sounding too ungrateful, but I've earned more than that."

"Yes you have. You still have the matchbook?"

"I do have it." *Again, that is.*

"Here's what you do, then. After we launch the beast, go to Las Vegas—"

"Wait a minute. What do you mean, 'after we launch'?"

"I mean if something goes wrong with it, we might need you here to help fix it. Why does that surprise you?"

Suddenly Doug had a lump of ice the size of a grapefruit in his stomach.

"We talked about this, Ben. We agreed that there's no way to hide the launch, and it will draw more troops than an invasion of California by space aliens. I've got to be out of here by then. You said I would be."

"And so you will. Relax. You may not think I'm a very moral person, Doug, but I keep the values I was raised with. I am a man of my word. Once that bird clears the silo, every soldier, cop, black ops outfit, and spook on the continent is going to be headed here as fast as they can move. But it's not like they have branch offices just down the road, is it? Even by air, it'll take an hour or two for them to get here. If you take the plane, you can be a couple hundred miles away by that time."

Not if I wait for even ten minutes, I can't. By then, this whole site is going to be one big pool of molten glass the temperature of the sun.

"But if I leave now—"

"You're not leaving before the launch, Doug. End of discussion."

"You're the boss." *Oh shit, oh shit, oh shit. What's the plan now, smarty?* "You started to tell me about Vegas."

"Yes, I did. Get yourself there. Take Highway 95 out of town to the northwest. Just on the edge of town, where it changes from a freeway to a two-lane, there's a truck stop. A man named Harry Scully eats breakfast there every Tuesday and Friday at exactly seven o'clock. He sits in a booth by the door. Walk in at ten past the hour with the matchbook hooked over the top of your shirt pocket, so the picture of the woman shows. He will invite you to join him, and he will buy. He won't know your name. Just tell him you're the man I said was coming. Go wherever he takes you. Don't come back for your own vehicle, if you brought one. He will give you a million and a half dollars in totally untraceable small bills and will drop you off where you tell him. He will not help you vanish. He doesn't know how to do that. He can't get you new IDs, either. He's strictly a money man."

"That's enough. Harry Scully, you say."

"That's the man." Ben poured more brandy in their cups. "I'll probably be dead by then, but—"

"What?"

"Well, yeah. With a mob like we'll have coming here, you think nobody is going to come in with guns hot and brains shut off? They won't leave a prairie dog alive."

And that's why you weren't worried about the blast doors on the checklist, isn't it? You didn't ever intend to survive, anyway. He pictured the farmers working their way through the launch sequence and then calmly waiting for the rocket exhaust to fill the whole complex with lethal flames. Except that now they would shut the blast doors for his benefit. *Thanks, ever so.*

"Tell Harry thanks for all he's done for us," said Ben. "Tell him he's on his own now. He won't like that much, but he has to know. Do you know how to fly?"

"I can fake it."

"Good. Take the Jeep back to Dirty Dick's and take the Pilatus. I recommend you skirt the base of the Rocky Mountains, cutting daisies all the way. You can really get off the radar there, as long as you don't wander off into the control space for Colorado Springs. They may say it's only an Air Force school, but they lie. It's a fully operational air base. You have enough fuel to take you all the way to Vegas, but I'd stay away from airports if I were you. Land out in the boonies somewhere. There's survival gear in the back."

"Thanks, but I don't know how to start up a turboprop."

"In a lot of ways, it's easier to run than a piston engine. No choke, no carb heat, and once you've got a flame, no worry about magnetos. You have to be able to handle a variable pitch prop, though."

"That I know how to do."

"Then you're gold. There's a startup checklist taped above the windshield, and all the gauges and controls are labeled. Just remember to start it with the prop fully feathered. Otherwise, it takes forever for the turbine to warm up. The starter motor will run for a fairly long time, but don't worry about that. It will shut itself off automatically when you're up to the right RPM."

"What's my rotation speed on takeoff?"

"Don't even think about it. Roll out of the shed, lock the brakes, and let the propwash lift the tail a little. Then wind up the revs, take the brakes off, and just let that big engine pull you right up off the ground. It'll amaze you, I promise."

"Okay, I'll try it. When are you launching?"

"Soon, Doug. Very soon."

"So you're really going to go through with this?"

"I have to. It's the only dream I have left."

"Well, I can definitely identify with that." He stood up and extended his hand. "Goodbye, then, Ben."

"Good luck, Doug. Really." He took the hand and they started to shake but froze when they heard a door open at the other end of the room.

Max came through the door and strode quickly up to them. Right behind him, held by two other men, was a bound and blindfolded Agent Webb.

From the other end of the room, Hal came rushing up to Ben and Doug. "We're ready," he said.

Chapter Thirty-Nine

Countdown

Webb thought it was nice that this bunch of thugs had blindfolded her. Maybe they weren't totally bent on killing her. Not yet, anyway. But if they were all inside the missile silo, she couldn't see any way they were going to let her go. *And no way your belt buckle is going to cut through those ropes, either, Abby.*

"Is this the person who took our phone?" A voice she had never heard before. Deep, soft, almost gentle, but definitely in command. If they were in the demon's lair, this man was its keeper.

"She didn't have it anymore when we found her." That was the guy who was in charge of the men who had captured her, the one with his arm in a sling. "But yeah, she probably did. She claims she's an antelope hunter from Bismarck, but her driver's license says Kansas City."

"I didn't say I was from Bismarck, exactly," said Webb. "I'm staying with my uncle for a while. He farms just outside of Bismarck."

"What's his name?" The demon-keeper again.

"Adam Webb." She used her father's name because she knew she could remember it, even under stress or torture.

"What does he farm?"

"Um, wheat, I think."

"Winter wheat?"

"What do I know? I'm a city girl. He grows crops, okay?"

"Does he keep livestock?"

"No. Just a dog."

"Hmm."

"Sure looked to me like she had one of our rifles." Mr. Sling again. She noted with professional approval that they all refrained from using each other's names.

"I gave her the rifle." A new voice.

Merciful God, it's Doug Wright! Is he actually going to cover for me?

"She gave me a ride in her pickup from Bismarck to Dirty Dick's. I told her she could have the rifle if she would do that. Hi, Abby."

"Hi, Doug. Nice to hear your voice again."

"We didn't see any pickup," said the man with the sling.

"It's parked in some shade," said Doug, "under a big rock ledge. It's probably hard to see."

God, I love this man!

"So you're vouching for her?"

"Well, she's damn sure not one of Black's people, I guarantee you that. Send her out with me. How can it be a problem?"

There was a long pause while she imagined herself as a mouse running under the shadow of a hawk. Were they actually going to pull this off? Suddenly it struck her as ironic to the point of hilarity that she was about to be saved by the man she had considered killing. And she knew absolutely that even if she were free and had her gun back, she was not going to do it.

"Are you two, ah . . ." She imagined the one in charge to be making some kind of lewd gesture.

"A gentleman doesn't discuss these things," said Doug. "But, yeah. We are."

Another terrible pause. She noticed that she was holding her breath.

"All right, take her out. But she stays blindfolded and her hands stay tied until you're at least a mile from here. You can wait in the garage until the launch is over."

"No problem."

The hands that had been holding her let go and a different hand took her arm, much more gently, just above the elbow.

"Let's go, Abby."

"I love the way you say that," she said, half-whispering.

"How?" He matched his tone to hers.

"Like it's true."

"If we're quick, it is." He kept his voice low. She had no idea what he meant. In a normal tone of voice, he said, "I'd like my backpack."

"I'll go get it," said soft-voice. "Wait here."

The hand on her elbow tightened, and Doug's voice said, in a very low whisper, "Be ready to move, *fast*."

"What? What have you done?"

"Shhh."

Footsteps retreated and after a few minutes came back.

"Here you go, Doug. I threw in a few extra magazines for the Glock. I don't know where you're going after Vegas, but I think you might want them."

"It's probably like grandma's chicken soup: it couldn't hurt."

"Go. Godspeed. Max, go to the garage with them."

The hand guided her through passages where their steps echoed off the walls and finally into a hollow-sounding place that was cooler than the other rooms and smelled of gasoline fumes. Along the way, Doug pushed her into side walls several times. She assumed that was deliberate, and she played along by making little "ouch" cries.

"Look, Max, she's bumping into a lot of stuff. Do we really need the blindfold?"

"Ben said to leave it on."

"Why don't I just—"

She felt a tug at the back of the blindfold and then heard some scuffling noises. Her wrists were tied in front of her, not behind, and she snatched the blindfold off and whirled around in time to see Doug hit Max just below the ear with his elbow. Max opened his eyes wide, and his jaw dropped open. She was too far away to reach him with her hands, so she gave him a kick to the base of his nose, then another to the solar plexus. He dropped in his tracks. Doug grabbed the man's dropped handgun and said, "Run!"

"The Cherokee?"

"No," he said, "the white pickup. It's faster. It's got a souped-up engine."

They ran to the shot-up Ranger without checking on whether Max was down to stay. The keys were in the ignition, and Doug threw his pack on the center console and fired the big engine up. Webb managed to get in on the passenger side despite her bound hands, and before she had pulled her door shut, they were headed for the helix tunnel with a shriek of burning rubber.

Soon they were going through a seemingly endless right turn. Doug found that thirty-eight miles an hour was as fast as he could take the spiral road without skidding into the walls, and he held it at that speed.

"Is this really going to work, Doug?"

"We'll see when we get to the top of this ramp. If the big door is shut, we're screwed."

"Why didn't we just wait? I couldn't find a way to stop the launch, anyway. I've failed. Why don't we just sit it out?"

"We can't sit anything out."

"Why?"

"Because what goes up comes down."

Her eyes grew wide. "You mean *here*?"

"Exactly. We gotta get out of here, Abbs."

After what seemed like forever, they saw a light ahead of them, a round patch of daaylight. And it was getting steadily smaller from one side, like a high-speed solar eclipse. The ramp straightened out, and Doug put the pedal to the floor. The eclipse disc was sliding in from their right, and he steered as far to the left as he could without going up a wall. There could be no turning back now.

"Good bye, Doug. It's been—"

"Shut up, Abbs."

They lost part of the right front fender and a corner of the cab roof on the sliding lid, but they managed to smash their way through. Once out of the ramp, they went airborne, landing hard near the old farm tractor and nearly rolling over before all four wheels were back on the ground and Doug got them under some semblence of control again. He hit the gas, and the acceleration knocked her back in the seat.

He reached in back for his pack, fumbled around for a while, and finally produced a kitchen knife. He held it out in front of her, and she sawed her ropes against it until they fell off. As they were passing the place where she had been taken prisoner, she said, "My gun and my badge are back there. Can we go get them?"

"No way." He didn't slow down.

When they got to Dirty Dick's, he skidded to a stop in a cloud of dust, well off to one side of the Pilatus. "Run!" he said.

They ran to the aircraft, and Doug pulled out the wheel chocks. They climbed in, throwing the backpack on a rear seat. He strapped himself in, ran a fingertip over a handmade placard above the windshield, and began to throw switches and move levers. The big four-bladed propeller in front of them began to turn as the turbine wound up slowly with a high-pitched whine.

"They still haven't launched, Doug. I mean, we'd know it, wouldn't we?"

"They'll do it as fast as they can, especially now that we took Max out."

"And then how long will we have?"

"You have to realize, I only had two sets of coordinates to work with, Wall Street and here."

"Okay. So how long?"

"I don't have a calculator anymore. I could only do the math in my head."

"Damn it, Doug, *how long*?"

"Eight minutes, give or take about fifteen seconds."

"Oh, my dear God."

He let the plane roll out from under the roof and locked the brakes. He opened the throttle, and just as Ben had promised, the tail lifted up off the ground. He gave it full throttle and let off the brakes.

As they rolled out on their takeoff run, the northern sky was lit up by a massive column of flame, then another one next to it, with a tall, slender object on top of the bigger one, speeding faster and faster skyward. The demon was loose. They both looked at their watches.

Chapter Forty

Armageddon

Ben had been right about the Pilatus. It seemed as if the wheels couldn't have made even one full revolution before they were off the ground. Doug looked at the instrument panel and saw that the airspeed was swinging past 70 miles an hour and the rate-of-climb indicator was at 940 feet per minute. *God, does this thing even* have *a stall speed?* He remembered a phrase his old flight instructor, a former military pilot, had once used to describe an F-16 fighter. The plane went, he said, "upstairs like a homesick angel." Doug put them into a standard-rate left turn, and when he rolled out on a south heading, they were already 500 feet above the ground.

Webb continued to look at her watch. "Can't this thing go any faster?"

They had some headphones in the cockpit, but they didn't know where to plug them in or how to turn them on, so they settled for shouting.

"The gauge says it will do 144, but I've got to get some altitude first. When the first shock wave hits, we don't just want to be a long way from ground zero, we also want to be a long way from the ground, period."

"You lost me."

"We can't go as fast if we're climbing."

"Oh. Well, shit."

"All engineering is a compromise, you know."

"No, I didn't know, and I don't want to, either." She looked at her watch again. "Two minutes since launch."

"We'll be okay. But we need to find something to use to cover our eyes. If all we have is our hands, when the fireball first lights up, we'll go blind."

"I threw away my blindfold."

"That probably wouldn't be heavy enough, anyway."

"How about cutting up your backpack?"

"No good. It's lightweight nylon. In that kind of light, it will be transparent."

"Well what, then?"

"How about your jeans?"

"How about yours?"

"I'm flying here."

"Yeah, right. And looking for an excuse to look at—"

"Look, would you rather be immodest or blind?"

She sulked for a moment, looked at her watch again, and pulled off her hiking boots and her dark jeans. Then she grabbed the knife and used it to cut off one pant leg.

"Here, you dirty old man," she said, handing it to him. "Four minutes to blast."

He wished he had looked at the altimeter before they took off, to see what field level was. But he was sure they had at least three thousand feet between them and the ground now, and he put the nose down and let the speed build up. Then he set the elevator trim for level flight, so he could take his hands off the controls when it came time to hide his eyes.

"Three minutes." She started to fold her half of the jeans into a dense pad. "How far away will we be?"

"About ten miles, I think. That's not great, but it should be survivable."

"Wonderful. So we're out of the woods then."

"Maybe not. We've got two choppers inbound at nine o'clock."

"*What?* Army, you think?"

"Couldn't be. Not this quick. It's got to be somebody who homed in on your phone call. That would be either Black or your people. I assume you did make a phone call?"

"Um. Well . . ."

"Yes?"

"Two minutes to blast."

He folded the leg of the jeans several times and laid it down on his lap. "Get ready."

Machine gun fire began slamming into the back of the plane. He threw it into a hard left bank, turning toward the attackers and forcing them to scatter. He kept turning.

"What are you doing, Doug? You're turning back toward the blast!"

"I want our friends to be facing north when the time comes. They shouldn't be expecting the flash."

"But we're going toward it, too."

"What's our time?"

"Seven minutes past launch. Forty-five seconds out, soonest case."

"Call it at fifteen."

More bullets hit the airplane.

"Now!" she said. "Cover up."

He let go of the controls, pulled the blindfold down, and pressed the denim over it, using the palms of his hands for even more cover. The plane continued to shake with the hits. He counted the seconds. *One thousand fifteen, one thousand sixteen. Damn it, that's too long. Seventeen.*

At eighteen seconds, the cloth in front of his eyes turned light, and despite all the layers of cover, he could dimly see the bones in his hands. He started to count again. He figured they had a maximum of ten seconds before the shock wave hit them.

As soon as the light diminished a little, he uncovered one eye and grabbed the control yoke. The light was still painfully bright and seeming to come from everywhere at once, but he could make out the controls. He threw the plane into a sixty-degree bank. The machine gun fire had stopped.

He was wrong about the ten seconds. At seven, the shock wave hit them from behind and below. The sound was utterly deafening. He saw the floor pan buckle upward, and he felt as if he had been kicked in the ass by God's steel-toed boot. For a few seconds, he couldn't breathe. Outside, he saw that both wing tips had bent up, just outboard of the main struts. But the ailerons still worked, the engine had not quit, and they were still doing something resembling flying.

He uncovered his other eye. The light around the plane was now purple and sometimes orange, but it was not so painful. He checked the altimeter and saw that they were almost two thousand feet higher than they had been before the blast. He didn't see the choppers. With any luck, the pilots were totally blind and were either flying into the ground or climbing wildly up past their service ceiling and stalling out. He wasn't sure if his hearing worked or not, and he realized they should have put the headsets on, even if they couldn't make them work.

"Are you okay?" He looked over at her for the first time since the flash. She obviously couldn't hear him. Hell, he couldn't hear himself. She looked somewhat miserable but intact, which pretty well described how he felt, too. He tapped her hand to let her know it was safe to remove her blindfold.

He didn't know how long they had before they ran into the base surge. That was the mountain of air, blown away by the blast, rushing back to ground zero. When it did, he suddenly realized, it would sound exactly like the world's biggest thunderclap, which it was, in a way. He put his headphones on and motioned to Webb to do the same. He didn't know how much she knew about nuclear explosions, and he tried to make some gestures to tell her they had another shock wave to get through.

Then he saw that he didn't need to gesture. He could simply point. Ahead of them, a wall of dust a mile high that seemed to go from horizon to horizon was coming at them with terrible speed. *How can anything that big move so fast?* Two seconds later it hit them with an impact like flying into a mountain. The sound was terrible, even with the headphones on, and the plane reeled and seemed to be going backwards. Everything loose in the cabin was flying around in all directions, and he was utterly unable to tell which way was up. He finally oriented himself with a dim horizon outside and managed to get the craft upright. He knew he had to get above the fast-moving air mass, or he would be blown right back to ground zero. He put the boiling, writhing mushroom cloud behind him and gave the plane all the power he had. At six thousand feet he finally started to make some progress away from the thing. Maybe they were already dead of radiation poisoning anyway, but at least they were getting away. Below them, the sea of dust streaked past at an incredible rate, and there was a final thunderclap even louder than the last one.

They continued south at near-redline speed. Gradually their hearing came back. Better yet, Webb found a place to plug in the headphones and a way to turn on their throat microphones.

"So that's what Armageddon feels like," she said.

"Are you all right?"

"For a while I seriously wondered if my back was broken, but it's better now, and I can see okay, so I guess the answer is yes. Where are we going?"

"Away."

"Gee, really? I figured that much out all by myself, ace. You want to share a little more than that with me?"

"For now, that's all I've got. It'll be dark in another hour. We lost the gyrocompass and the artificial horizon in all that violent maneuvering, and I can only see clearly out of one eye.

I can't fly in the dark like that. So we'll get well clear of this area and look for someplace nicely in the middle of nowhere to put down for the night."

"And tomorrow?"

"I have to go get my money. I'll leave you someplace along the way, somewhere you won't have any trouble surviving. I expect that you have to go back to hunting me. I won't make it easy for you, but I won't hold it against you, either. We do what we have to."

"I don't have to start doing it right away, though. I consider our truce to be extended for the time being."

"Works for me."

"I haven't thanked you for getting me out of the silo, by the way."

"As funny as it sounds, I think maybe I should be thanking you."

"Oh?' She looked over at him and gave him the arched eyebrow that he was starting to think was her trademark. "How's that, exactly?"

"It's not so easy to explain."

"We've got an hour, you said."

He sighed. "Okay. A few months ago, I was a self-centered, self-pitying loser. I didn't think of myself that way, but I was. Since then I've learned a lot about—well, I guess about helping people who can't help themselves. A very good person named Sancho, among others, taught me. Back at the silo, it dawned on me that the farmers had always been bent on their own destruction. No way I could save a one of them, ever. And no way I could save the woman who tried to help me back in Albuquerque, either. She's dead now. Maybe I can't even save myself. But I could save one person. I could save you. So I did. And that was the best I have felt about myself in as long as I can remember."

"It didn't exactly leave me massively depressed, either. Where will you go after you get your money?"

"I don't know. Maybe someplace where I can help people."

"What does that mean?"

"I don't know yet. I'm still new at this. Every life I ever wanted is gone or was never there in the first place. And every job I ever did—well, you can see for yourself. I have to try something I've never done before."

"I'm going after Black," she said.

"Are you serious?"

"Deadly."

Forty-five minutes later they passed over a small town just off a major east-west highway. Doug took it to be Belfield, where they had first turned off the interstate in the pickup. He went straight for another ten minutes, putting some low buttes between them and the town, and looked for a field. They weren't hard to find. Most of the area was gently rolling grassland, with an occasional herd of cattle or bison. The bison seemed to be constantly moving, and when they kicked up a dust cloud, he was able to tell that the wind was out of the northwest. He rolled out on that heading and took the plane down to where the wheels were brushing the tops of the grasses. When he saw an area ahead that was flatter than most of the country, he chopped the throttle and dropped completely out of the sky. It took him a lot longer than he thought it should, because the plane had such a low stall speed that he had trouble getting it to quit flying and do a landing flare-out. When it finally did, his air speed indicator was showing just under fifty knots. It was dark on the ground by then. They had dropped below the last of the evening sunlight. He looked for someplace to hide the airplane, but there wasn't any. He let it coast to a stop, shut everything off, and climbed into the rear cabin to see what they had in the way of camping gear.

"This is really pretty good," he said. "We've got sleeping bags, food, water, all kinds of stuff."

"Can you sleep?"
"You better believe I can."
"Me, too. Zip the bags together, why don't you?"
"Really?"
"It's cold out here at night, smart guy."

Chapter Forty-One

Flight to Avoid

The next morning they built a fire well away from the airplane, heated water for instant coffee, and fried some canned sausages. They didn't have any bread, but they had taco shells wrapped in plastic. They put the sausages in them and added canned corn and salsa from little foil packets. The combination was surprisingly good. Or they were just extremely hungry.

"How serious were you yesterday, Abbs, when you said you were going after Black?"

"I told you: deadly. Why?"

"I'm thinking you might have to stay out in the cold to do it. Black seems to be awfully well supplied and supported. I think it's entirely possible that the higher-ups in your organization have more than a casual relationship with him."

"But his people have killed some of our people, for crying out loud."

"So? Maybe they were people who were finding out more than they were supposed to."

"That's pretty cynical, Doug."

"I've become that way, yes. And you should be, too. Do you have anybody back at your Fort Apache that you still trust?" He took a long drink of coffee and stared off into space.

"I trust my partner. Why does that matter?"

"I'm thinking that we need some of the Bureau's resources. To find Black again, if nothing else."

"Oh, and now it's *we*? What's your interest in it? You're about to become a rich man and disappear, you said."

"I did say that, yes. But there's something I need to do first." He stood up and began kicking dirt over the remnants of their fire. "Black tortures and enslaves people when he could simply hire them, and he orders mass murders and individual ones without hesitation or remorse, for reasons that are totally insane. And he took away every shred of dignity and security that I ever had. He terrorized me, completely. I've got to do something about that."

"Like put him in prison? But if he's connected as high up as you say—?"

"No. People like him don't go to jail, and I don't want him to. I want him dead."

"He might have died back at the silo, you know, in the blast."

"And he might not have. I don't want to hear that he's dead; I want to see it."

"That might not be possible, you know."

"No, it might not."

"I can't knowingly help you assassinate him."

"No, you probably can't. But you can do other things."

She blew out her breath and bit her lower lip. "Let me think about it, okay?"

"Take all the time you need. Take until seven o'clock in the morning, two days from now."

"What happens then?"

"That's when I get the money."

They landed the Pilatus in the desert north of Las Vegas.

"Shouldn't we wipe the plane down for fingerprints?" said Webb.

"What for? Even if we did, we don't have any bleach to get rid of our DNA. We could set the whole thing on fire, but we don't really care if somebody finds out we were in it, anyway. By the time they figure it out, we'll be long gone from Vegas."

"But if you want to disappear, this is the perfect time to do it. If we leave no trace of you here, then as far as anybody knows, you were simply incinerated in the bomb blast."

"I could have been. Unless you tell people otherwise."

"Maybe I won't be asked."

"You will."

"Maybe I have a bad memory."

"Really?"

"It's a funny old thing. Memory."

"I like it. Let's burn the plane."

They didn't have any tubing to siphon gas out of the wing tanks, so Doug simply punctured one of them from below with his fancy pocket knife. They took turns catching the dribbling fuel in cook pots and splashed it all over the inside of the plane. When they were satisfied they had it well soaked, they let the rest of the leaking fuel run into the dry ground.

"It would be nice if we had some kind of timer or fuse," she said.

"It would be nicer yet if we had an RPG and an air-conditioned Land Rover to get away in, but we don't. Start hiking."

He let her get about twenty yards ahead of him and then used one of their waterproof camp matches to light the airplane at the tail. He didn't wait to see how fast the fire spread. Fast enough, he was sure. It made a loud *whuff* noise, and he felt heat on his back.

They sprinted away for a while, ignoring the rapidly growing inferno behind them and the explosion that came a few minutes later. Then they settled into a fast walk and hiked into the city of Las Vegas. They heard sirens in the distance behind them.

"Where are we going?"

"After Vegas? That depends on what we can find out from your partner."

"What are we going to ask him?"

"Two things. I assume he can't trace the location of somebody who is listening in on his calls?"

She shook her head. "If you know an address or a phone number, getting the log of all past phone calls is the easiest thing in the world, and listening in to new ones is almost as easy. But you can't work it the other way and find out who is listening in on you."

"That's what I thought. Okay, when you call your guy, which we won't do until we're ready to leave town, tell him you're going to send him a couple of addresses to check out. He should not only check the incoming phone logs for those places, but also the logs of all the numbers that were called from there. If he finds what I think he will, the two of you could even wind up being big heroes. The trick is to get the addresses to him without letting any eavesdroppers know what they are."

"That would be a trick, all right. How do we do that? No way we can get access to a scrambler phone."

"Ever hear of the US Postal Service?"

She laughed. "I love it! Stone age communication is the last thing left that can't be hacked into. You said we needed two things from him. What's the other one?"

"I want to give him the name of a dead person. I want his Social Security number and all the information off his driver's license and passport, if he had any."

"What dead person?"

"I don't know yet. Somebody who was born about the same time as me and who died or disappeared just after he became an adult. I'll go to some newspaper office and check the past obits. Then I don't have to look for somebody to forge me a Social Security card or even a driver's license; I can just send for duplicates."

"That will still work? Won't the current files just show this person as being dead?"

"Not if he died long enough ago. Think old tech again. Everybody assumes that the minute public records became computerized, then every paper document ever filed away anywhere in the world immediately got magically transferred to an electronic database. But it didn't work that way. Plenty of records never got reformatted and never will. You think your grandparents' wedding license is in a computer file somewhere? The original blueprints for the Empire State Building? A 1927 New York phone book? No way."

"Yeah, but Social Security—"

"Doesn't have any more spare techie clerks than anybody else. When the brave new world order came along, they upgraded as far back as they figured they needed to and called it good enough. And it was, so they left it that way."

"I hope you're right."

"I'm betting on it. If I died back at the silo, I need somebody new to be. Right now, we need a motel. I don't meet my banker until tomorrow morning."

They found a Comfort Inn within easy walking distance from the truck stop Doug would need to be going to. They asked directions to the nearest post office and the nearest place to buy a cell phone. Then Doug used motel stationery to write down two street addresses and put them in an envelope with an address that Webb gave him on it.

"What are those places?" she said.

"Two addresses in Long Beach: the place I first got snatched and the place where they tortured me the most often.

I figure Black and his minions don't work out of any regular government building. But everybody has a home base somewhere. I favor the first one, the bar. It has a second story with no windows and a lot of fancy antennae on the roof. I used to think they were just there to make the place look tech-y, since its name is the Launch Pad. But they could be for real, too. And the parking lot there is where they killed one of your agents for no apparent reason. Think about it. Your people have followed all kinds of 'persons of interest' without getting shot at. But that night—"

"You think our guy was about to stumble into the mother ship, Rogue Spook Central."

"That's what I think, yes. It would fit. And if Black is alive, sooner or later, that's where he'll go. Anyway, it's all I've got."

"So let's go mail a letter."

After they mailed the envelope, they went to the truck stop and ate a late lunch. Doug found that he had acquired an abnormal passion for fry bread tacos, and he was disappointed that they weren't on the menu. He settled for a burger with Tex-Mex seasoning. Webb had a steak salad.

A big-screen TV on one wall was full of news coverage of a nuclear "accident" in North Dakota. There was no mention of a missile or a silo or terrorists or anarchists.

"My God," she said, "are they actually going to whitewash the whole event?"

"You mean lie to the public because somebody in the government lied to them? Gee, when has that ever happened?"

"But how do they explain an A-bomb in the middle of a national park in the first place?"

"They didn't call it an A-bomb. They called it an N-accident."

She groaned. "And I thought the intelligence business was full of misinformation."

"It has nothing on the news media. What got you into the cloak and dagger business, anyway? Did you get a junior G-man badge in a cereal box when you were little?"

She chuckled. "Something like that, I guess. I was raised by my father. He was a lifelong Chicago cop. So I guess I wanted to be some kind of super-cop, to make him proud."

"Was he?"

"I'll never know. He died before I graduated from the Academy. But I still try, you know?"

"I do know."

They finished their meal and went back to the motel. Inside, they locked the door, drew the drapes, and went to bed together, without even talking about it.

"I can't believe we did that," she said afterwards. "It's like it was automatic."

"I think it was. We've just escaped certain death several times over. That's a powerful aphrodisiac."

"You didn't think there was any magic there?"

"Damn right, there was."

"I thought so, too. Let's do it again."

"Which one?"

"Maybe both."

He sighed. "I'm sorry to say, we probably will."

"Shut up and fly."

The next morning, she waited in the room while he went off to see Harry Scully. An hour later, she heard a car door slam and peeked out through the drapes to see Doug get out of a battered and dirty sedan with two aluminum suitcases.

"We need a car," he said.

"Did you get your money?"

"One point five mil, all cash."

"Then you can buy one for a change. This is Vegas. Nobody raises an eyebrow over big amounts of cash."

He shook his head. "I don't have an ID."

"I do. And if we use my license, we will automatically have insurance, in case anybody asks. My policy has always had that feature."

"Sometimes it's amazing," he said, "how one resource gets you another. It's only the people who have none at all who are in real trouble."

"Where's that coming from, exactly?"

He shrugged. "One of many things I learned recently." He picked up the room phone and called a cab. Two hours later, they had a nice, anonymous-looking, two-year-old Toyota and a cell phone and were headed north and west.

"Now," he said. "Call your partner."

Chapter Forty-Two

Fallout

The next call they made was the next morning plus one. They made it from San Francisco, just so that if Black's people were listening, they would not realize their base location was compromised. Webb talked for ten minutes, grinning the whole time. When she disconnected, she said, "Your instinct is pure gold, Doug. We've not only got the mother ship, we've got all the escape pods. Sounds like there are only five people left."

"Including Black?"

"We'll soon find out, won't we? My people are going to mount an operation. They'll give me an hour or so lead-time to deal with Black, if I want it. After that, the sky is going to fall on the bar in Long Beach. We need to buy something I can send email with."

"What we need is something we can send howitzer shells with."

"The email one, we can get."

"Point taken. Let's go."

Doug walked into the Launch Pad bar in the early evening. The only other customer was a woman wearing dark glasses and a scarf. She sat at a table opposite the end of the bar and nursed a glass of white wine while she worked on a Mac Book computer.

Doug found that he was not all that surprised at the red hair and firm breasts behind the bar.

"Hi, Brenda. You look pretty good for a dead person."

"Yeah, well, I clean up good. I never expected to see you again, though. You don't seem to take any of the hints that should be obvious. Like that you should totally disappear? You want a gin and tonic?"

"Not this time, I think."

"On the house, for old times' sake."

"Screw the old times. Tell Mr. Black he has a visitor."

"What makes you think he's here?"

"Oh, he's here, all right. He just doesn't know I know that. Call him."

She produced a landline receiver from under the bar and spoke into it briefly. As she was hanging up, a door next to the end of the bar opened, and a familiar figure in a dark suit emerged. Doug turned on his stool to face his former captor, pulled the Glock out of his waistband and held it ready, his elbow resting easily on the bar.

"They always come back, you know. Even when they know it's for a beating, they all come home, like well-trained dogs." Black held a gun loosely at his side but did not raise it.

"Hello, Black. If you don't mind my saying so, you look like shit."

"I am quite probably dying of radiation poisoning. I assure you, though, I will live long enough to see you beg for your own death a long time before I grant it to you." He raised the gun that had been hanging limply at his side. "I'll take your weapon now, if you don't mind."

"I don't think so. Time for you to die now."

Behind the screen of her laptop, Webb chambered a round in her own Glock. Black visibly reacted to the sound but did not turn around.

"You think you're going to kill me? You can't do it, you know. All your instructors said so. And in any case, I am your father now. I gave you a reason to live and a way to do it. Listen to my voice and think about how much you want to come home. Why don't you just—"

Doug fired twice, once into Black's chest and then into his forehead. The big man dropped like a pole-axed steer. Even so, Webb walked over to him and felt his neck for a pulse. She left the gun in his hand but nudged the muzzle around with her foot, so it was pointing harmlessly across the room.

"You're wrong," Doug said to the corpse. "My father was an honorable man."

He looked up at Brenda and said, "If you ever really wanted to get out, now would be the time."

Brenda jerked her head in the direction of the door Black had come through and held up four fingers, pretending to be touching her face with them. Then she poured a shot of whiskey, downed it in one gulp, and headed for the back room.

Webb laid her service pistol on the bar, roughly pointing toward the door that Black had come through. The she took Doug's Glock from him and began to wipe it down with her scarf. "Since you don't exist anymore, it would not be good for your prints to show up on this gun."

"Are you sure it will work for yours to be?"

"You bet. I just took out the head of a rogue agency, single-handedly. This"—she held up the pistol—"is my ticket out of Kansas, Toto."

"What if they don't honor it?"

"That's another question for another day," she said. "Time you left. The FBI swat team is on the way, even now."

"Color me gone." At the door, he looked back and said, "Your father *is* proud, Abbs."

"I think he is, at that."

"Listen, if you ever decide to give up this life of gay abandon—"

"I'll find you."

"I'm not so easy to find."

"You're easier than you think. I know how your mind works now."

"Goodbye, then. It's been—"

"Will you please get out of here?"

He got.

Four days later, the regular tourist van stopped in the center of Acoma, the Sky City. There was a light rain falling, and only three people had been curious enough to ride the van to the high mesa in spite of it. One of them, a solidly built young Latino man, got out and walked to the church of San Esteban del Rey, away from the rest of the group. As he did every Monday, he made himself comfortable under the big archway of the main entry and waited. The driver of the van opened an umbrella and walked over to him.

"Is your name Sancho?"

"Maybe. Who wants to know, man?"

"Some guy named Doug."

"Hey, yeah? Is he all right?" He jumped to his feet.

"Are you Sancho or not?"

"Yeah, yeah. That's me. Is Doug hurt? Does he need help?"

"He's okay. He says he can't be seen in public for a while. He gave me something to give you. It's in the van."

"Hokay, let's see it."

They went back to the van. The driver didn't offer to share his umbrella, and Sancho didn't seem to care. Twenty yards away, the official tour guide stood under her own umbrella and told her two customers about the history of the adobe city. At the back of the vehicle, the driver opened the door with a key and took out an aluminum case, slightly bigger than a standard briefcase. Someone had printed Sancho's name on it with a felt-tip marker.

"He said I shouldn't watch while you open it."

"Then don't, man."

"Take it someplace, why don't you? It has a combination lock. He said you'd know how to open it."

Sancho took the case and went back to the church. He went inside this time. There were no pews in the cavernous structure and probably hadn't been for two or three hundred years. He put the case on the altar and dialed 547380 into the lock, thinking that was as close as he could come to spelling his name with numbers. It didn't work. So he took out his Swiss Army knife and popped the clasps. Either Doug had deliberately picked a really flimsy lock, or he had filed down the latch bars. They broke easily. The lock was just for show, for the people who believed what they saw. Like the driver. Sancho smiled. Then he gasped. Inside, the case was completely filled with money in varying denominations. On top of the bills was a note, probably written with the same felt-tip pen as Sancho's name. It simply said FOR THE LITTLE PEOPLE.

He took a couple of hundred-dollar bills off the stack and closed the case. On his way out, he dropped the bills in the collection box.

"I think maybe the spirits of the lost children finally gonna come home, Doug. And maybe yours, too."

He went back to the van and curled up in a rear seat to have a nap while he waited for the trip back.

In the months that followed, speculation was rampant about whether there could have been an atomic bomb in the middle of North Dakota, and if so, how. With no government explanation, people picked whatever theories took their fancy. The most popular one was that a bomb had indeed been built, by a couple of high school students from Minot who got the plans off the Internet and had died testing it.

A special Senate committee was convened to find out how such an incident could have occurred. For seven months, they heard witnesses and gathered evidence. Neither their proceedings nor their conclusions, if any, were made public. The reason cited for that was, of course, national security. Eventually the media lost interest in the whole topic.

In sites scattered across the continental United States, fifteen more nightmares from the Cold War sat in their silos and seethed with repressed chaos.

About the time the hearings were winding up, somewhere between Albuquerque and Gallup, New Mexico, an aging roadside diner was sold for cash. The new owners were a fiftyish man with a shaved head and a bushy moustache and his younger wife, a petite woman with dark hair. They both may have been Caucasian, but they had such dark tans that it was hard to tell. She had blue eyes. He wore a patch over one eye. They bought the place for the most seemingly trivial of reasons: they said they liked the name. It was "Atomic Cafe." The new owner put up a sign that declared the house specialty to be Indian fry-bread tacos. The specialty that he did not declare was helping illegal immigrants on their way to California. It gave him a lot of satisfaction.

Acknowledgments

As usual, huge thanks are due to my tireless critique circle, Rebecca Kanner and Sandy Steffenson, and to my trusted beta readers, Alex Kourvo and Peter Farley. Thanks also to my inspiring surveying professor, Jesse Fant, and my insightful editors, Chris Valen and Jenifer LeClair.

Many thanks to my wonderful wife, Caroline, for her love and support for, as of this writing, over 53 years.

Author's Notes

During the interval between the fall of the Berlin Wall and the tightening of security after 9-11, a great deal of new information was released about the conduct of the Cold War. Some of it makes one genuinely wonder how we ever survived the era. To the best of my knowledge, there has never been an entire ICBM site "lost," much less rediscovered by anarchists. But some of the real errors and accidents of the "nuclear umbrella" age make the idea of such an event a lot less far-fetched than they might have seemed when I first had the story idea many years ago.

The technical information about the mathematical discipline of geodesy and the early non-computer programmable calculators and the machines they drove is all accurate. I personally still own a Hewlett Packard 97, and I have done a lot of good engineering with it, with no help from any computer at all. The comments about the uncertainty of guidance on the early intercontinental missiles are assumptions on my part. Given the general state of technology in the '50s and '60s, I think it cannot have been otherwise. The onboard guidance system of an early Minuteman missile has been photographed and the photographs published, and it looks much as I have described it. But the box with the little odometer-like navigation settings is purely a figment of my imagination. I have no idea how the real system was set up, then or now.

Anyone past the age of, say, 40 has lived long enough to see the passing of not one but several entire eras. So it is easy to think of the Cold War as totally ensconced in very ancient history and of little pertinence to our lives today. But maybe just because I grew up in that era and vividly remember the extreme anxiety and even insanity of it all, I am hard-pressed to believe that those times will ever be completely dead. There are still a lot of holes out there with a lot of demons in them. And the idea that one of them will someday come out and bite us is at least worth chewing on. Hence this work of fiction.

Not Sure What to Read Next?
Try these authors from Conquill Press

Jenifer LeClair
The Windjammer Mystery Series
Rigged for Murder
Danger Sector
Cold Coast
Apparition Island
www.windjammermysteries.com

Chuck Logan
Fallen Angel
www.chucklogan.org

Brian Lutterman
The Pen Wilkinson Mystery Series
Downfall
Windfall
www.brianlutterman.com

Steve Thayer
Ithaca Falls
www.stevethayer.com

Christopher Valen
The John Santana Mystery Series
White Tombs
The Black Minute
Bad Weed Never Die
Bone Shadows
Death's Way
The Darkness Hunter
www.christophervalen.com

Coming Soon
Broker by Chuck Logan
Dead Astern by Jenifer LeClair

For more information on all these titles go to:
www.conquillpress.com

CPSIA information can be obtained at www.ICGtesting.com
Printed in the USA
LVOW07s0721210916

505328LV00004B/4/P